Toecap and
the Fiddler

Thank you
for support

[signature]

Toecap and the Fiddler

Sid Wright

To order additional copies of this book, contact:
Xlibris
800-056-3182
www.Xlibrispublishing.co.uk
Orders@Xlibrispublishing.co.uk
746298

Just a quick word before we start. Please do not be fooled by the childish front cover. This book is for adults. Your sproggletts will not thank you for making this purchase, and you, the loving parents, will face many awkward conversations if you allow them to read on.

I think you'll agree that you've had fair warning.

At the time of starting this book I'm close to turning twenty-five. For some reason, twenty-five seems a good age to take stock. Twenty-five is a good number, a solid, sturdy number. I have been led to believe that wild turkeys can run at up to twenty-five miles per hour. How about that? Did you know that the number twenty five is the sum of the first five odd numbers? Incredible. It's fair to say I've squandered a few years acquiring useless information, but twenty-five does feel like a good number and therefore a good age. Long gone are the shackles of childhood; I'm firmly an adult. I can now hire a car abroad or become a volunteer for the United Nations. I can even back a lorry driver into a space without him telling me to get my dad or simply to piss off.

I never worry about getting older. I've become more comfortable within myself the older I get, which is how it's supposed to work. Plus, I'm bald so I actually enjoy getting older as I'm slowly reaching the age I look. I'm a bald man with a beard, so I look considerably older than I actually am. I'm allowed to grow a beard because I'm single, so it's well within my rights to let myself go a bit. I enjoy being single. I've come to learn that being alone doesn't have to be a bad thing. I don't want to be alone forever and there was a time when I thought I'd found someone I wanted to grow old with, but it wasn't to be. I don't want to die single but, certainly for now, I embrace it like a hot water bottle in winter. During the turbulent teenage years love is something you had to go out and get, quickly, along with everyone else, so you weren't deemed odd. Adults are more cautious by nature and my door is still open to love, it's just that now I ask it to take its shoes off before it comes in. Few get to twenty-five without learning exactly how their heart fits together.

Anyway, I'm proud of the goals I've achieved. I'm an artist and for me art is all about the progress. Progress, not perfection. Some people might say I'm not progressing with my writing but I'd have to call them liars. This is my sixth attempt at some form of book and I've come to learn exactly when my readers are going to call me up and say, 'That is too offensive'.

That's progress.

I don't know what the future holds, but that's what's infinitely exciting about the future. All I can say is that I've made it through the first twenty-five years and I'm still standing. I've lost friends, people I've loved and - most importantly - I've lost my hair, but I'm still kicking about. It's good to take stock now and then. I make enough money to get by, I'm single, I'm bald, I don't drive and I'm not yet on the property ladder but...

... Christ, what a dreadful exercise. I feel awful now.
Let's get on with it.

1

"One man can make a difference" - Daredevil

A team of heavily armed officers progress through an old, abandoned building in the middle of nowhere, deep inside the gloomy lands of northwest England. Covered in tactical gear from head to toe, they glide over worn-out floorboards that creak under forgotten weight and years of accumulated dust stirs from its slumber and wafts gently up into the rooms they pass through swiftly. Doors lead to more doors, passing covered table after covered table like a scene from *Scooby-Doo* as they pad out an episode (or an opening paragraph in a book). Flower pot, lamp, chair. Flower pot, lamp, chair. On and on, one after the other, breach and clear, breach and clear. This is an experienced group of hardened professionals. The beams emanating from small lights perched atop semi-automatic machine guns snap from side to side, guiding the team through an unknown location with the perfected familiarity of routine. Hands do all the talking in short swift orders, clear and precise. Power to the building has been cut and the only noise that can be heard is the night rain sulking outside. It taps against the windows like small children trying to get their parents' attention. Of course it's raining. This is England.

* * *

There are things in life that you can't trust. Things like junkies, politicians and, occasionally, the odd fart. But friends should trust friends, patients should trust doctors and employers should be able to trust their employees. I was here tonight because of the man who worked for me. I was in the middle of nowhere, hunted by the very people I had sworn to protect. I was in over my head, endless forward rolls in a sports day for a school I didn't attend. I sat frozen with fear, a dead body in my lap for company. I was too late to save her, way too late. I had been outplayed by The Fiddler.

The glazed-over eyes of the innocent female stared up at me with disappointment. I held her in my arms as I knelt on the floor. I was getting cramp. The faint, fast-paced thudding of footsteps bounced through the old hallways and I glanced around the room upon hearing them, trying to pinpoint their direction. Close to where I knelt was a chair, recently in use. The room was thick with betrayal. A headache was retrieving its key at reception, having booked a long weekend in the hotel of my mind. When you die you can only hope it's quick, but I know The Fiddler would have dragged out this lady's suffering. She would have been in this room for hours, poison that shut her down one cell at a time and I couldn't save her. Anger brewed within and to be honest I could have cried - you know when you just get one of those days? You wake up and everything is downhill (or uphill, depending how you look at things). I lay her on the floor gingerly and stood up; the cramp was too much.

Think, Toecap, think.

The SWAT team was getting closer and any moment the wooden double doors to this room would burst open and it would be game over. I couldn't let the Fiddler win like this. The double doors were the only way in. Behind me the rain vied for my attention by slapping against the window panes. The windows would take me outside, but I was on the first floor. I unlocked the hatch on the nearest window to me and opened it as far as it would go. Refreshing cold air rushed in. It's good, clean air up north, that and damned fine drinking water. In fact, I've yet to taste better, and perhaps I'm biased because I'm from here but it really is good. I imbibed the night air and my mind began to refocus. My headache had checked out early, unhappy with the service. It was pitch black outside and looking down proved useless; I could barely see a thing but I *could* hear more police arriving and setting up a perimeter. I had to act fast. I was gearing myself up to move outside and carefully scale down the building to avoid giving away my position, but I'd left it too late. The SWAT team had reached me.

A team effort brought the door off its hinges and armed soldiers flooded the room, breach and clear. The lady on the floor was approached. Small lights scanned over her and found the name Toby Malloy in permanent marker on her head, shoulders, knees and toes, knees and toes. That's me, by the way. I'm Toby.

Luckily for me, my plan of slipping on the wet window ledge and plummeting to the ground in a big ball of flailing limbs had worked brilliantly. With minor injuries and leaving a distinctly distorted-looking bush quivering in surprise behind me, I limped away from the scene and got as far away from there as possible.

2

Molly Cooper was in a relationship when I came to know of her. She was in my year at school and, unknown to her, we shared some classes. But she was dating a boy called Jacob Pike, forcing me to love her from afar. Come to think of it, the last few people I've found attractive turned out to be in relationships. I'll be a bit annoyed if that's my type - I like films, nights in and home-wrecking.

I've never liked anyone the way I did Molly; it was all brand new with her. Molly and I were Facebook friends, which meant I could legally stalk her, an activity that occupied a lot of free time. Time that should have been spent doing homework, or masturbating (I'm a teenager - it's important). Molly was great. I had picked out names for our children and yet we've never held a conversation. I kept that to myself for obvious reasons. I kept lots of things to myself. Things like my inexplicable crush on Jo Brand or, to be more precise, my love of her voice. She talks how I imagine a drunk bee to sound and it does something strange to me. That seems a minor secret compared to other thoughts I hide from society.

I have a gift.

A talent.

A power.

I'm a superhero.

Although, to be fair, that's a bit of an exaggeration, for I have not used my power for anything as yet, primarily because I have no control over it. It's a violent mixture somewhere between the mists of rage and strength. I've always felt its presence, lurking under the surface, slowly rising to boiling point. It's only since I became a teenager that it's become worse. The shift in hormonal balance and the chemical warfare that currently plagues my body has exacerbated my idiosyncratic behaviour. My power isn't as cool as having my bones coated in Adamantium like Wolverine, or even having been exposed to a mental amount of gamma radiation, like the Hulk. It's nothing that epic.

It's my toes.

It's a problem because it's triggered when I least expect it. Whenever I stub my toe I'm consumed by rage and for a short window of time I have god-like strength. I become a different person, so full of anger that I have no control over my immediate responses. It's extremely unpredictable and nothing short of a nuisance. It's a shame really because, apart from my curse, my life was pretty good, or as good as it can be for a teenager. It would be a lot better once Jacob Pike sods off.

I live in the county of Cumbria. A country lad born and bred (strong in the arm, thick in the head). If the shoe was on the other foot and I was a villain (I'm not saying I'm a hero *yet*), I'd still want to live in the country. Heroes like Spiderman and Batman would be almost useless in the country, for we have no tall buildings out here. I don't want to be the bad guy though; it's too much hard work. I want to harness my power and put it to good use and although I don't have Bruce Wayne's wealth or Peter Parker's genetic modifications, I do have the advantage over them of being real.

I live with my mum and dad, who are happily married. My mum is called Jenny and she is tall for a woman, with dark brown hair that sits neatly on her shoulders. I have been told I have her eyes. She is kind and loving. Then there is my dad. He was my first hero. I call him Sam, the same way everyone else does. He's also tall and built like a brick shit-house. He's the sort of man you feel safe around. He has hair the same colour as my mum and he's always halfway towards having a beard. When I was a baby he would pick me up in one hand and hold me above his head.

My mum is an artist and spends most of her time at home working on commissions. She paints landscapes, as most artists do in the northwest, surrounded by the beauty that is the Lake District. She's talented and gives classes to enthusiastic retired folk filling in their remaining years. It had taken a long time for her art to become her only source of income, but nothing worth having comes easy. Art is a wonderful lifestyle but a hard living. I used to watch her paint when I was a child. When she was finished she would attack me with her brushes and I'd come out of her studio looking like I'd been murdering Smurfs.

My dad, on the other hand, is a dry stone waller. Plenty of work in the county for him. His massive hands are perfect for his job and the sheer size of him allows him to endure most weather. Dry stone walling is the art of construction without mortar. Structural integrity arises from compressional forces and the interlocking of the stones. Considerable skill is required in this line of work. With the introduction of modern wire fencing, fields can be fenced with less expense and time, and so wallers are few in number. But with the increasing recognition of the value of heritage, they remain in demand, which means a roof remains above us.

I grew up wanting to be just like my dad. He made everything exciting. He used to tell me bedtime stories of how his walls kept out terrible, evil beasts such as the Vikings, dinosaurs and the Scottish. He would work on walls thirty feet high to ensure no harm would come to us. Armies a thousand men strong would turn up at our borders and not a single one would ever get over his walls.

So you can understand how upset I was when I learned the truth about his employment. The disappointment I felt when, in reality a thousand strong army was a rogue sheep that had wandered too far. Parents lie. It's part of the job. They bend the truth to protect us and to keep us excited. The world is wondrous when you're young, everything is shiny and new. We hear incredible stories of incredible people who in time whittle down to being nothing more than unpaid babysitters, people like Jesus, working seasonal shifts. Jesus had a belter of a story. The great comedian Jimmy Carr once said, 'If we're all God's children, what's so special about Jesus?' Well, let me educate you...

A very long time ago there was a man. A Jewish man by the name of Jesus. Like all men, Jesus died. But Jesus came back to life, so technically he was a zombie. He is the only recorded zombie in the history of man, with a very poor kill count of zero. Don't have a go though, because Jesus was a humble carpenter whose talents lay elsewhere and which didn't necessarily include eating the living. Sorry, I should also add that Jesus could live forever. But (there's always a but) he could only live forever if you, by the amazing force of telepathy, accept him as your master. Then, and only then, can he rid your mortal soul of evil forces that are only present in humanity because a woman, made from a man's rib, was convinced by a talking snake to eat from a magical tree.

Pretty good, right? On the face of it, putting everything else aside (primarily logic and sense), that could make a great summer blockbuster. It needs bringing up to date a little, but we could get a professional to do that. On a serious note, the Bible has sold well enough that the author never needed to write another book, which is a missed opportunity because sequels and prequels are really in at the moment. AC/DC could provide the soundtrack to the film and the opening sequence could be Jesus riding down from heaven on his Yamaha. What an intro that would be. Or it could even work as a TV show, as a sitcom with a live studio audience, perhaps? It could be the right platform for an up and coming actor, a breakthrough role. Fair play though. Quit while you're ahead; I get it.

I can't remember what I was talking about. Ah yes, my parents. They had known each other for some time before they had 'hooked up'. A friend of a friend type thing. My dad was an old romantic and persistently asked her out, chipping away at her until she caved in. As far as I know, they still have a healthy relationship. They laugh a lot and make the effort each week to go out somewhere new, be it a highly recommended restaurant or a late night showing of a new film. I looked forward to the day they saw my name on the credits of special effects epic *To Hell and Back*, a two-hour thrill ride of Jesus H Christ breaking necks and cashing cheques.

I could only hope that one day I'd find the same love my parents had. My parents knew nothing of my secret. Incidents would come and go that I couldn't explain but I blamed it on being a teenager; so maybe I could explain it. I am their only child and so I guess they accepted it as some form of normality - hormones an ever-present scapegoat. The incidents were pretty rare anyway and I paid for any damages out of my own pocket.

I worked weekends as a waiter at our local watering hole. I lived at 15 St Helen's Street in the town of Cockermouth and I worked at The Old Grey Goat Inn, a mere ten feet from my front door, which made pulling sickies really hard work, perhaps harder work than working hard. The money was ok but in a job like this it's the tips that make it worthwhile. It was my first taste of independence and it made me feel grown up, a useful part of the world order. When the apocalypse finally comes I like to think that while NASA picks out the best doctors and scientists to send into space, searching for a planet to rebuild our race on, I'll also be given a seat because of my impeccable customer service and passion for delivering the best possible eating-out experience. They will need someone to set the table on the spaceship and while I don't know how many waiters there are in the world, I do feel confident about my abilities.

We come back to Molly because it was while working here that I first met her properly. Molly lived a short walk away, somewhere on Kirkgate. She had started not long after I had and we learned the ropes together. She vaguely knew of me from school, whereas I knew exactly which famous landmarks she had visited while holidaying in Greece last year, thanks to the wonders of social networking. I became her friend and she became almost everything I wanted from my time here on earth. It wasn't long before she found she could confide in me and after the basics of discovering similar tastes in music, film and her passion for political propaganda techniques in South East Asia (I winged that one, let me tell you - a masterclass in bullshit), she eventually spoke to me about Jacob. Most things I'd known before she told me, but I entertained her relationship rather than tell her how I spent my evenings going through her various internet profiles. I'm not a proper stalker and if anything came up in court let's just remember that I was already an employee here before she started. Stick to the facts, your honour. We grew close but I was forever aware of the 'friend zone'. Men don't have a friend zone. We can attach ourselves to a woman, grow close in friendship and laugh our way around all the stalls and attractions of a busy, joint social life but regardless of time spent and promised, if a woman offers it up we're the first to say 'get your knickers off' with no thought to the aftermath. With women though, unless you act quickly, before you know it she's burdening you with all her problems and you haven't so much as seen her elbows. Molly would ask me about other girls and I'd reply nonchalantly or I'd throw a curveball into the conversation. I'd pretty much do anything so I didn't have to tell her that my nob was like an unused piano - free to a good home.

3

"You can't live in fear" – Ghost Rider

Randall White is my best friend. He is an idiot, but he is *my* idiot.
In primary school we were given the task of growing a sunflower. I
think the idea was to get us to understand how flowers grow but also
to teach us that things take time and care, and how to be responsible
for something other than ourselves. Randall was my sunflower. I
had helped him grow, I watered him each day and I'd worry if he
didn't get enough sunlight. We knew everything about each other. I
hadn't told him about my power though. It might be safe to divulge
information like this to a certified moron as no one would believe
him, but I thought it best to keep it to myself just in case. It's not really
that exciting anyway. If I could fly or turn invisible we might discuss it
and put it to some sort of use but as it stands, my toes just aren't that
interesting. It's typical that I get a power but it's something as lame as
sensitive feet - that's just my kind of luck. I'm surprised I got off that
lightly. Knowing me, I'm amazed I wasn't bitten by a butterfly and
transformed into one, only to find out my natural enemy is a closed
window. I'd look pretty though.

Not many people like feet, I'm not sure why. Some time ago,
I read about a watchmaker who lost his hands (somehow), so he
learned to fix watches with his feet. Isn't that incredible? His will and

determination must have been outstanding, because if it was me I'd just hire an assistant. I don't think I could be bothered with all the hassle (I'm not shaping up to be a hero anytime soon). I hoped my apathy was due to being a teenager and that one day I'd snap out of it. I'd grow out of it even sooner if I could be bothered.

Randall and I had travelled through time together, a double act much like Mitchell and Webb, Gervais and Merchant or, more fittingly, Dumb and Dumber. He lived on the same street as me, he always had. I had put a good word in for him at The Old Grey Goat and, after some persuasion, an audience with the managers was granted and an interview for the position of waiter was allowed. Getting straight down to business, they asked him why he would be suited to the job – what made him a good waiter? He replied by saying that he was always waiting on something; once he had missed his train back to Cumbria and he had had to wait almost two hours for the next one. He didn't get the job.

As my teenage years progress I might have to find someone I can talk to about my power. It was only recently that I had had more than one 'incident' in the space of a month. The first followed very swiftly after I had begun getting trouble from a kid at school who had taken a liking to calling me names. It was in French, and I mean the lesson, not the name calling. If the name calling had been in French I don't think it would have bothered me so much. I'd almost admire the effort the bully had put in to slander my good name; we weren't taught those sorts of things in French lessons, so he would have had to work on that in his own time. Mr Price had the downright privilege of taking us for French. He was one of those teachers that just couldn't control a class and you could tell it was all heading towards a mental breakdown or an early grave. His eyes were once full of love and dreams but now they scowled and did a lot of rolling. He was a nice enough bloke, just a crap teacher. You can't let your pupils see they're getting to you. In year eight, on the very first day of the new school year, we had a supply teacher taking us for History. He was doing his absolute best to excite the class, but we wound him up so much that he cried. A few of the boys (it's always boys) would hum. Simple but very effective. Not too loud, but loud enough, and they would take it in turns so the noise would circulate the room. What can the teacher do? A standard lesson is fifty minutes long and within half an hour he had cracked. His year, and very possibly his career, was over. There is no coming back from that. A teacher's death.

Anyway, Mr Price was useless but pleaded through the lesson in a desperate attempt to be taken seriously. I sat near the back on a table with a boy called Luke Cook. A really interesting kid actually, but I don't want to go into that; this story is about me, not him. You can forget about him. Sat behind Luke and me was a boy named Neville. What makes me laugh is Neville had bright ginger hair. There is nothing wrong with ginger hair or being a 'ginger' - I'm sure they all have souls - I'm just saying that it's rare that you get a ginger and a bully that are the same person. Although aren't most bullies bullies because they have been bullied? So it could make sense. Neville was easily irritated and since I was in his direct line of vision, I became his target of amusement. Maybe he was irritated because he hated French or maybe it was the risk of turning to stone in broad daylight. No more ginger jokes, I promise (I can't promise that).

Maybe he just didn't like me because I was good at French. He began by kicking my chair, which I ignored. Then he would rip up tiny bits of paper from the back of the text book, roll them into balls and try to land them in my hair, which I ignored. This only spurred him on. Luke had noticed what Neville was doing but had decided to ignore me ignoring him. Cheers, Luke, nice one, mate - there's your chance gone for any sort of back story and character development.

The bell rang and we stood to leave. I pushed my chair under and turned. Neville was stood in front of me, blocking my path. With one foot already on the ground I went to steady myself with the other. I put it to the floor and made contact with the back leg of the chair I had been sitting on.

Everything went quiet. Everything slowed down. It felt like a four-inch nail had been lined up with the tip of my big toe and Thor's hammer itself had buried it into my foot. An explosion of pain, heat and blind rage coursed through my body, reaching every joint, muscle and limb in a nanosecond. My vision turned a deep shade of red. My lungs stopped, along with my heart and brain, all energy being redirected to the fist of my right hand. I was no longer in control, a program overridden, unable to abort. My clenched fist burned with desire and my fingernails dug into my palm. My arm outstretched in a heavy jolt and disappeared into Neville's face. His mouth let out a burst of white confetti and his nose hosted an expensive red fireworks display. His head pinged backwards and, among a cloud of exercise books and chewed pens, he vanished over a table, taking three people with him. I could breathe again. I refocused and looked around the room. Everyone was staring at me. I stood frozen, my arm still outstretched. Everyone looked scared and I didn't know what to do. Neville lay motionless in a heap on the floor. People closest to him leaned over and checked he was still alive. One girl shook him a little and gave a nod to the rest of the room, signalling he was ok. Mr Price asked two pupils to take Neville to the school nurse and I was ordered to follow him to the headmaster.

Regaining control of my thoughts and actions, I sank like a deflated balloon. I walked past my peers, hunched over like a dog that's peed in the house, fully aware punishment wasn't far away. Outside the room normality continued and my attack wasn't yet news, but gossip spreads like bacteria in schools and by lunch I'd be famous. I followed Mr Price down the hall, round corners and through doors. I followed him so closely that when he stopped outside the headmaster's office I walked right into the back of him. His opinion of me wasn't improving. I apologised, but it was a waste of time. He knocked once and stepped inside, gesturing for me to wait. The door handle clicked shut and I turned to lean on the wall. I sighed and wondered what my punishment might be. Down the hall, Neville was waddling into the nurse's room and Randall came into view through an open door just a little further on. He spotted me and came over.

'All right, mate,' I said.

'What you doing here?'

'You know that ginger kid Neville from my French class?'

'Yeah.'

'I punched him in the face.'

'Ha ha! No way!'

'What are *you* doing here?'

'I was heading to the nurse. I've cut myself.'

'Aw, do you need a plaster?'

'Yeah, but I might ask for some thyme as well.'

'What?'

'T-h-y-m-e,' he said, slower and clearer as if talking to a foreigner.

'What do you need time for?'

'I heard it's a good healer. Must be a paste or something.'

'No, you're thinking of *time*.'

'Yeah, thyme' he said, getting irritated.

'No, you're getting confused. You're thinking of the flower thyme, but that's not the right kind of time that heals. The saying "time is a healer" means that over time pain is lessened. As far as I know the flower thyme has no healing powers to speak of.'

'Right... ok.'

'You don't understand, do you?'

'I'm confused.'

'Which bit is confusing you?'

'Well, how am I supposed to get more time?'

'You've outdone yourself.'

'My finger hurts.'

'How did you cut it?'

'Johnny said he'd stuffed my lunch box up a drainpipe, so I tried to get it out and I cut my finger.' I gave him a moment to think logistics. Nothing.

'You're a waste of my time,' I said.

'Have you got some?'

'Shut up, Randall,' I sighed.

The headmaster's office door opened and once he had shooed Randall away, Mr Price asked me to step inside.

Sometime later, I was released. It was better than I had been expecting. Nothing really happened with the headmaster. I've never really been in trouble so they were surprised more than anything. I explained what had happened and I asked if Neville was going to be ok, which I thought was a nice touch. It was decided that my form tutor would be made aware of what had taken place and Mr Price would ask my teachers to keep an eye on me. He also added that at some point I'd need to make an apology to Neville. I agreed. They told me to let teachers know if I was getting hassle from other pupils and not to take the law (they actually used the word law) into my own hands. I couldn't believe my luck, really. I had punched a child over a table and I didn't get so much as a detention. I could handle forcing out a stiff 'sorry' to Neville and so I went about my day. I'm also pleased to announce that Neville's grades in French have since improved. You're welcome.

The other incident was just a couple of weeks later during the living hell that is Physical Education. Our teacher, if you can call him that, was a man named Ian Brown. Mr Brown's wife had recently left him, which was just awful. Everything suffered, including his appearance, his ability to keep time and, at the top of the list, deserving of its own league, his pupils. Teachers don't care when I need a piss or when I've lost my pen but Mr Brown has his life partner - someone who swore in front of all the people they love in the world that she would be with him until death - leave him, and he expects us to sit and openly care. Relationships are give and take, Mr Brown. Give and take.

P.E. had descended into madness. Mr Brown would take us out to the field and throw a football at us as if it was his heart, shouting, 'Get on with it!' before falling to his knees and rolling about in the mud. The beautiful game. We picked our own teams and got underway without adult supervision. I always played defence, or rather I was always put in defence. This is so I had no chance of scoring and subsequently receiving praise and admiration, but also so that if the opponents scored I could be blamed first and foremost. My main opponent was a boy called Chris Peck.

He was an aggressive player and took the game very seriously. He had fouled me twice but with sir throwing up into a bin and crying, Chris's fouls went unnoticed. There wouldn't be a third (but if there was, then there wouldn't be a fourth). From their goal-kick the ball was hoofed up-field, landing just inside our half. It was a midfielder of ours who retrieved it and, because he'd spotted a winger bearing down on him, he passed back to a central defender. However, the pass was blocked by Chris Peck and he began his run. I moved across our back line to make up for the missing defender and I stood firm, waiting for Chris's contact. I placed my left foot in front of the ball and stopped any further advance from it. Chris went to kick the ball and found rather bluntly that it wouldn't move. With his momentum he came over the ball, colliding with my top half and taking us both out. I got up and passed the ball. Chris rolled around in agony, screaming for a free kick. I laughed at his blatant performance and he marched over (proving that he wasn't injured).

'Fuck off, you gaylord,' he told me.

I laughed again at hearing the use of 'gaylord', a word I haven't heard since 2004. Who still called people gaylord? After a quick glance around he took me by the shoulders and stamped on my foot. His studs embedded into my boot and I succumbed to the other me like the flicking of a light switch.

That was the first time I had hospitalised someone. Needless to say, another trip to the headmaster's office was in order and this time it was more than just a talk. The control I had over myself was slipping rather than getting better and my sentencing was swift. I was banned from participating in P.E. for several weeks. Not really a punishment, but I pretended to be devastated, pleading and fisting the air. As a self-conscious teenager I was more than fine with not having to get changed in a room full of people and then head into the cold and have angry, hormonal young men, high on testosterone, swinging boots at me as hard as they could as if that were a game in itself. My punishment reminded me of when God punished the snake in the Garden of Eden by condemning him to crawl on his belly for all his days. I bet the snake, who normally FLIES AROUND couldn't believe his luck. I was concerned, however, about a phone call made to my parents, for they would now know about Neville and Chris and a grown-up conversation would be inevitable.

My dad had finished work early that day and both he and my mum were waiting for me when I got in. I couldn't explain my outbursts of violence; I couldn't tell them the truth for fear of their reaction. Because of the small amount of time in between helping Neville lie down and booking a night away from home for Chris, my parents decided I needed to be grounded as punishment. They thought long and hard and decided that obviously I would still attend school (that was too important to miss) and that working my shifts at the pub was ok (I couldn't let my employers down), but other than that I'd have to stay at home. I looked at them in disbelief. I bowed down to them as if they were gods as they treated me like a snake.

4

There are some things I worry that I'll never understand, like maths, or why Donald Duck spends all day with no pants on and yet when we see him coming out the shower he has a towel wrapped around his waist. Also, that Goofy is a dog that can talk but he has a pet dog that can't talk. What's up with that? So many questions in life go unanswered. I could go on.

What, you don't believe me? Fine.

I don't get why, when people are looking for something they've lost, they say, 'It will be in the last place I look'. Of course it will, you don't keep looking for it after you've found it. What about the way that in every depiction of Adam and Eve they have belly buttons. I'll give you a minute to think that one through.

These are pressing issues that are all equally important to me but grinding up nice and tight against my frontal lobe was something a little closer to home. Why did I have this power? Out of everyone in the whole wide world, why me? Because, let's be honest, I'm not an ideal candidate for human redemption. I'm a teenager; I consider it an achievement if I wake up before lunch. I shouldn't be saving people. I didn't ask for this. I don't know where it came from. Maybe I was given it. But there is no history of super powers running in the family, as far as I know, and I think someone would have mentioned something by now. My mum and dad are just normal people. Unless they have powers and they have learnt to control them or, better yet, hide them. But even then they would have said something to me by now, surely. My behaviour at school would have prompted a family meeting. Although I actively avoid those after the last one, when my dad tried telling me about the birds and the bees with a series of crude drawings that, for a time, scared me into celibacy. Maybe I had a freak accident as a baby that my parents don't think I'm old enough to know about yet. I could research on the internet the year I was born and try to look through local news but, then again, I would surely know about it by now if that was the case.

The only good point I've made recently is that if my parents have powers they must have them under control, which is something I really need to sort out for myself.

The evening meal on the historic day I was pointlessly grounded was quiet. Grounded is an aviation term from the military: if a pilot had misbehaved they would be grounded, so they couldn't fly. If I ever get my power under control I could join the military; I could be of use with my power. I don't like the idea of people shooting at me though. Maybe if they promised to just shoot near me, just until I got used to it, then I might be interested. But how would they know I'm me? I'd be wearing the same getup as everyone else. Do you know what? I'm not joining the military – it's too much hassle.

Both parents had expressed deep feelings of disappointment and I was remorseful that I had dragged the Malloy name through the dirt. I was repeatedly asked why I did it, but I could only explain so much and a boy putting paper in my hair apparently didn't justify me punching him off his feet. All I could do was keep apologising and they weren't impressed. I did feel bad for my actions. Neville and Chris hadn't deserved free tickets to the 'gun show', but I can't control myself. Jenny and Sam kept reinforcing the point of how serious this was and that I should learn from my punishment. I didn't argue with them. My sentencing was merciless. Three weeks. The courtroom gasped in horror. Three weeks at home unless I had school, work, or a long-term commitment to a family event or something like the dentist. So, pretty much unless I had something booked, planned or socially expected of me, I'd stay at home. Well, it's a good job I'm a tough cookie or I might very well crack under the brutality. And this is England so I'll only have to serve a week and a half (brilliant rule, that is).

Unfortunately for me my diary wasn't even exciting enough to have a dentist appointment somewhere within the next three weeks so once I got in from school and had completed my homework I would need something to fill in my time before lights out. I decided to use my evenings to try to control my power. But how? Within seconds of that decision I had the pleasure of the conception and birth of the answer. I would learn how other superheroes gained control over their abilities.

It all came to me while I was watching television on day one of house arrest. I was scanning the channels in the forlorn hope of finding something worth watching, a task I failed. There is never anything on. Year after year more channels are added, but what's featured on them stays the same. If you like cooking you'll be very happy and you could easily lose three to four days watching non-stop celebrities eating as much as they want and never gaining a pound. If you like things that have already happened, or if you like sharks, you'll be over the moon with the history and discovery channels. But it's come to the point where one on its own isn't enough any more. Our attention spans are getting shorter and shorter and I fear that in the coming years the only way both channels will keep me as a loyal viewer is if they start discovering sharks that are Nazis. Even that idea didn't excite me for long and so I pressed on, my right hand getting a small workout for the charity wank-a-thon I'd soon be creating and entering if nothing could steal my imagination.

And then came my bright idea. I turned off the television and I shifted my attention onto something else that is winning the war on intelligence - the internet. The worldwide web has taught me a hell of a lot. Mainly that people have far too much free time and also that if something is written down, no matter how ridiculous and implausible, people will believe it. Once online, I found an entertainment shop and began searching for superhero films. By the time this book is published many reading this might not know how online shopping works. There are different ways of doing it but I used the tried and tested, albeit ancient, technique of transferring funds with a payment transaction from my bank to the shop. This is called 'paying for stuff'. It's quite simple and all above board. I register with the shop and that gives me an account with said business. While browsing I have a virtual basket that I can put products in. Once I've finished searching and selecting, I then pay for the things I want and they are delivered to an address of my choosing. It's just like a real shop but it takes a few extra days for what you've bought to arrive. Another way of getting music and films also involves using the internet, but without the drawback of paying for what you want. It costs nothing, as already mentioned, and requires fewer morals and principles. There is, however, a risk of being caught and having to pay a big fine and/or even having to serve time in a prison, but that risk is low. The other downside is that you are directly having a negative effect on the entertainment industries, but shamelessly thick people who have grown up trapped inside their own bubbles of self-entitlement don't really care as long as they are getting something for free. And it's not to do with money, it's a question of principle and by continuing the practice of illegally downloading art forms, more than anything, you're saying that stealing is ok. We can beat around the bush with terminology and statistics, but you can't escape the fact that it is stealing and I really feel for the artists of the world because no one seems that bothered about it. Art is a luxury and should be protected. What separates us from animals is that we gave ourselves a code to live by. We made clear distinctions between right and wrong and I choose to pay for art because I learned before the age of five that taking something that isn't mine is wrong. People who commit crimes will always find a way to justify it – if only to themselves - and one of the hardest things in life is trying to argue with a complete idiot. Rant over.

My virtual basket was overflowing. I had been earning money for some time and I'd had absolutely nothing to spend it on, so there it sat in my account, the figure getting bigger and bigger, with me just waiting for the day when the bank would ring and say they'd lost it. I didn't go mental online though; I bought most of my research second-hand, averaging out at maybe two pounds each, even less for older titles. The list was impressive. I had searched for superhero films and it had given me a lot to get started with. I was grounded for three weeks. Five days of the week were spent at school. That left me with seven evenings and two full days at the weekend. Minus shifts at work and I was left with five evenings and two days a week. The average film these days is maybe one hour and forty minutes, so I worked out I could watch at least two an evening and four in a full day, but I'd have to take into account the three to five days it would take for them to be delivered. After three weeks I wanted to be ready for the next stage, whatever that would be. My aim for the next few weeks was to consume, like a greedy fat kid in a pantry of food rapidly going out of date.

My email inbox beeped merrily at me and my order was confirmed. Being grounded was going to be easy. Soon the world would be ready to marvel at me as I have marvelled at Marvel. I've said 'marvel' too much.

Marvel started in 1939 as Timely Productions and by the early 1950s it was commonly known as Atlas Comics. Marvel has had many talented people working for the company, but most famous is probably Stan Lee. Stan Lee (Stanley Martin Lieber) was born on the 28th of December 1922. He is an American comic book writer, editor, publisher, media producer, television host, actor, voice actor and former president and chairman of Marvel Comics. He collaborated with several artists, most notably with Jack Kirby and Steve Ditko and co-created characters such as Spider-Man, the Hulk, the Fantastic Four, Iron Man and Thor. A talented chap I think you'll agree.

The only real competition for Marvel is DC Comics. DC is responsible for such fictional beacons of hope as Superman, Batman, Wonder Woman, Green Lantern and Aquaman. DC comes from the company's popular series Detective Comics, which featured Batman's debut and subsequently became part of the company's name.

From now on I'd watch two films a night. Not the hardest challenge undertaken by man but Neil Armstrong never had to sit through *Ghost Rider*.

Are you impressed that I was being so positive about my incarceration? Please stop me if I start coming across as too much of a nerd. I'm not sure how you'll stop me. Perhaps I could put NERD at the beginning of certain sentences so you know to skip them if you're not interested. We'll see how it goes. My phone rang.

'Hello, mate,' I said breezily.

'You coming out to play?'

'Randall, I don't think I've "come out to play" since I was about ten.'

'Well, are you coming round to mine?'

'I can't. I'm grounded for hitting Neville and Chris.'

'Oh my god, was that you?'

'Randall, I saw you outside the headmaster's office. I told you it was me'.

'Oh yeah.'

'Yeah, so grounded for three weeks.'

'Are you making an appeal?'

'What are you talking about?'

'When people get arrested they make an appeal.'

'I haven't been arrested. I'm just not allowed to leave the house.'

'Three weeks is too much. Two is more than enough.'

'Well, my parents disagree.'

'Shall I have a word?'

'No thanks.'

'Three weeks is too much.'

'So you have said, but you don't have an equal stake in raising me. Two parents are more than enough. Please don't enforce your parental wisdom on my mother and father. You shouldn't enforce your ideas on anyone; this has nothing to do with you, like it or lump it. If you were at a party and you weren't enjoying it, it is better to leave than to put your own music on.'

'What if it was *your* party?'

'Why wouldn't I be enjoying my own party?'

'What if someone you didn't get on with was there?'

'Why would I invite someone I didn't get on with?'

'To make up the numbers.'

'If I was in a situation where I had so few friends that in order to have sufficient numbers to constitute a party I had to invite people that had specific reasons for not liking me, then I probably wouldn't have a party.'

'Probably best.'

'You're supposed to be my mate! You'll be there!'

'When is it?'

'What?'

'The party.'

'There isn't going to be one.'

'Do you want to talk about it?'

'Goodbye, Randall'

Click.

If we were wild animals there is no way Randall would have survived his first winter.

5

"With no power comes no responsibility.
Except that wasn't true" – Kick Ass

I had school the next day and it was only when I started getting dressed that I felt nervous about going. The last time I had felt a similar quantity of butterflies fluttering up a stomach storm was on my very first day of secondary school. I looked up to everyone – physically, if not on particular moral or reputational grounds - and they seemed at least four times my size and acted as if they had been bred with specific instructions to make my life difficult. I spent the whole day waiting to be knocked out and then wake up wearing an expensive neck brace that would blow up if I left the immediate area; a rapier would be thrust into my unwilling hand and then spectators would wish me luck as I participated in a hearty game of Battle Royale.

I didn't mind that by now every attending pupil would know what I had done. What troubled me was the possibility that it might happen again. My parents had told me I needed to control my actions and I had to sit there and nod while inside I was screaming blue murder that I *had* no control, *that* was the problem. My power could be triggered at any moment and then I'd be in deep trouble. I took the only precautions I could think of. I wore two pairs of socks. Aside from that I tried to tap into man's natural gift of spatial awareness. It's thought that the male sex hormone testosterone plays a big role in spatial ability. One finding that supports this states that women with above average levels of testosterone in their body perform better at spatial awareness tasks. It's not a definitive conclusion but suggests our brains have evolved to meet the demands of differing needs between genders. So, dare I say that due to high levels of testosterone which make us better with spatial awareness, that might... possibly... sometimes... on a good day... make men better at parking a car?

Silence.

But women are great at lots of other things. I could name loads of things women are better than men at, things like... You know what, I could name tons of things but we're already getting off topic, and this new topic seems fraught with peril that my superpower doesn't equip me to deal with.

I walked with Randall to school, which was an education in itself. I'd walk to his house because his mum didn't like him crossing roads on his own.

CHILDREN!

That's something women are better at than men. That comes naturally to almost all of you. Although... I could give examples to argue that statement, but far be it from me to decide on who should and shouldn't be allowed to have children. There is a pregnant girl at school and she has decided to keep it. Fair play to her, and that's her decision; all I will say is that I let her borrow a pen once and I never saw that pen again. Maybe they should have some sort of test to see if you will cope with being a parent. I remember a school project where we teamed up in pairs and had to look after an egg for a week. The test could be something similar. If the egg survives, sure, you can have a baby. If the egg breaks, take the test again down the line. If the egg ends up in an omelette then maybe a private word at a secure location is needed. Either that or, instead of a child, just get a chicken.

'Morning!' Randall chirped cheerfully.

'Hi, mate.'

'It's good to see you. Feels like I haven't seen you in ages.'

'I saw you yesterday.'

'Are you ok? Are they feeding you?'

'What exactly do you think has happened to me?'

'Sorry for worrying.'

'I'm grounded; it's not Guantanamo Bay.'

'You look different.'

'Are you fucking mental? I saw you *quick calculation* seventeen hours ago.'

'Are you allowed visitations?'

'Shut up.'

'I could write?'

'Please shut up.'

'I could sneak a file in through a hollowed-out book. You could break out and come to school with me!'

I stopped walking, lifted my arms out to shoulder height, palms facing the sky, and gestured to the world around me that at this very moment, I *was* walking to school with him.

'Of course,' Randall slapped his forehead playfully, 'stupid thing to say. You're right.'

'Thank you,' I said. He had realised.

'... Your mum works from home; she'd notice you're not there. Hmm, there must be another way of getting you out of that house.' He continued to ponder this non-existent dilemma. We hadn't even reached school yet and I was getting odd looks from all directions. Randall was the only one who wasn't making me feel awkward, aside from every time he spoke. As outrageously dumb as he is, he is a good friend, although sometimes I wonder if he's not the idiot but that I am. Why wasn't I friends with clever people? Or cool people? Why is it that the only being that will talk to me, that is roughly the same age and currently attending the same educational facility as me, is a complete plonker? It must say a lot about me, but I've changed my mind, I don't want to know. He is a faithful sidekick.

School came into view, an ever-growing edifice that held within it all our hopes and ambitions. Patrolling the corridors were guardians of young dreams, protectors of future minds, and stressed out middle-aged hacks. All my teachers had been informed to keep a close eye on me, which I found unnerving initially. Once at school, Randall went his separate way as he and I didn't share a form together. A school year is divided up into forms; they're like classes, but you only meet once in the morning and once in the afternoon, mainly to make sure no one has run away from school during the day. Sometimes announcements

are read out or you have to endure periods of personal development
or sex education where you can watch your teacher put a condom on
a cucumber with his mouth.

I always felt sorry for the cucumber. You start off in the lovely
moist ground, surrounded by everything you need in life. The
conditions are perfect and you're left to grow, watching all around
you your cucumber friends grow and be sent off to supermarkets,
and from there onwards to a home. You'd hear tales of cucumbers
you've known contributing to succulent sandwiches and scrumptious
salads. You dream of cucumber heaven, knowing you've gone there
after satisfying, and providing a healthy option, to your master. Your
big day comes and you're picked and shipped off. And then, before
you know it, you're in a classroom with thirty spotty teenagers staring
at you while an inexperienced teacher puts the equivalent of a plastic
bag over your head. Gutted. When my mind wanders like this, as
it frequently does, I have to remind myself that cucumbers aren't
people.

I was sitting in my form now, waiting for sir to turn up, as other
students indiscreetly talk about me and how mental I am. I kept
my head down; I didn't like this kind of attention. Sir barged in
with papers flapping everywhere and apologised for being late. He
took a quick register, in the form of a very brief, and inaccurate,
headcount, and then made an announcement that there weren't
any announcements today. The bell rang and sir was silenced by the
sounds of chairs, bags and persistent gossip. I had barely reached the
door when sir called out to have a word with me. Great.

By lunchtime I was living on the edge. I have never had to
concentrate so hard on something before. I was weary with every
step I took, from the sheer concentration it took to make sure no one
bumped into me and that I didn't trip over something I hadn't seen.
Lessons weren't as bad, as I was seated for the duration, but moving
to and from proved exhausting; navigating corridors through a sea
of hurrying limbs. During morning registration I was informed that
within the coming days Chris' parents would be coming into school
to see the headmaster and complain about me; just a little something
to look forward to. I had to keep my head low for a while. I couldn't
afford any more slip-ups. But guess what.

I always had lunch with Randall, but today he was running late. I paced the small area of ground I had given myself to wait in and on a return walk to the point from which I'd begun, I very nearly knocked Randall to the floor.

'Hungry?'

'Starving,' I shot back, and we joined the queue.

There is usually some sort of order for eating. Each year has slightly different times when they're allowed to go into the canteen, so as to keep people moving through. The hall in which everyone ate wasn't big enough for the entire school to be seated at one time, so dinner ladies (although you can't call them that these days, I think the proper term is midday supervisor (very posh)) circled the room like prison guards and once you had finished your meal you were expected to free your seat. There was no chance of post-meal small talk or an After Eight mint. In and out was the system, very much like cattle. You didn't want to take long to eat anyway; heaven forbid your food actually gets warm, which was another problem if it was your year's turn to eat last. That and the fact that the remaining food would have been fingered multiple times by unimaginably dirty hands. The worst part of this whole ordeal came directly after paying for your lobster and champagne: finding somewhere to sit. We know other people, it wasn't just Randall and me against the world, but trying to find someone you know in a crowd of people who are all wearing exactly the same thing, at a time in our lives when we're trying to look exactly the same as everybody else our age, is a daunting task. In the far corner of the hall a large group stood up, being ushered away by a dinner - whoops - midday supervisor. A small window of opportunity had just opened and the space caught the attention of everyone wanting a seat, all sharing the same lunchtime dilemma. There were five of us waiting for a table. A table that seated ten, but that wasn't the point. Whoever gets to the table first is governor of all ten thrones. There was a moment while we eyed each other up. They were goody-two-shoes from the first year who were having lunch late, probably because they had just attended a chess club or had been wiping down cucumbers. They had the advantage of size, as they were tiny, very possibly a different species, which made them agile and light - good movers. But we had experience on our side, we had run this gauntlet many times before, we've lost good friends on this battlefield, and here we stand again. Even Randall is ready and appreciating the scale of the situation. A careless cretin walks behind us and bumps into Randall. The sudden movement frightens the first-years into a premature start. They dart off and Randall and I are slow to follow. The first-years are hard to keep track of due to their size, but every now and then they jump into sight like a dolphin popping up for air. Randall and I take big strides and simply step over school bags and wandering legs. We dodge, duck and jump, all the while trying to maintain a level tray. People are shooting across us and darting in between like busy traffic. It was human traffic, but not the nasty illegal kind that upsets parents. I took a couple of knocks, but shifted in front of Randall, who was displaying impressive footwork. The first-years were moving in for the kill, spread out in formation like velociraptors in long grass, when suddenly one of them fell. They lost their footing and tumbled over someone's bag as gruel sprayed into the air. Another of the first-years turned to help their fallen comrade. Just one of the little shits left, and we were gaining on him. He had lost speed as he'd turned to see what the commotion was about. All pupils in the room started to stamp their feet and cheer. Not sure why they do this, I think it's just to make whoever has fallen feel embarrassed - because face-planting a bowl of cold shit in front of three hundred people isn't embarrassing enough. The noise grew impressively quick and spread like wildfire until every wall of the great hall was shaking. The remaining first-year was startled, not knowing what was going on. The noise is scary if falling on new ears. This was where our experience counted most. We knew it was coming; we had stamped our own feet many times. During the confusion visibly on show from the first-year, we gained some important ground. The first-year managed to compose himself and adapted quickly. He whizzed past a table of fellow first-years (even they were stamping away, happy to finally feel a useful cog in the big machine). They knew him. My momentum was too great. I couldn't slow down. I looked up at the first-year, who had stopped just short of the free table. He smiled at me and then I collided with a purposefully placed leg. Down I went, after first having gone up.

On my descent I caught a glimpse of Molly. She was at a table with friends, eating an apple. I've known some unlucky cucumbers but that is the world's luckiest apple. Just before I disappeared from sight our eyes met. Even before my tray crash-lands, the room stamped with renewed passion. Thankfully, I wasn't that embarrassed because the room was already making a lot of noise, much to the distress of all the teachers and dinner – whoops – midday supervisors. I landed on my chest and squeaked a little. My head clipped off the wooden floor and I winced at the pain. The feeling of napalm coated my left foot, a phenomenal gas leak in my big toe that paired up with a spark as contact with the floor was made. Rage overrode every instinct and I was instantly up on my feet and glaring at the perpetrator. Teachers were desperately trying to quell the noise and get people back to eating their dog food. I had a new target. The kid that tripped me up was laughing with his friends. Until he turned to face me.

I had no control over what I was doing. I wasn't even sure what it was that I was going to do. Mr Price was heading right for me, a general of the battlefield. Objects and pupils just moved out of his way like the parting of the Red Sea. I reached out for the child; I wanted to punch his nose out through the back of his head.

'Toby!' Mr Price shouted.

'Are you ok?' I heard and the faint smell of apple wafted into the cloud of air I was huffing and puffing about in.

There was a crunch as Molly took another bite and smiled at me. I let go of the horrible little squirt that had nearly cost me a lot more than bruises (he runs off) and, just like that, I was fine. I say fine - I was still red-faced, had a room full of eyes watching me and was for some reason struggling to form words, but other than that, yeah, I was fine. How did she do that? My power had switched off as easily as it had on and it was Molly who had done it.

'Yeah, you're ok,' she smiled, before walking off with her friends just as Mr Price shuffled in close. He gave me a very detailed look and pointed a finger without saying anything out loud. I knew what he meant though: close call. I was baffled and unsure about what had just happened. I looked up and saw a dinner – whoops - midday supervisor tidying my lunch off the floor and then I saw Randall and the first-year seated at the free table, sharing a bag of crisps and becoming firm friends.

6

For the next few days I disappeared into the background, escaping all forms of interaction that could lead to another incident, especially at lunchtimes, when I'd eat outside or in a toilet cubicle. Molly had saved me at school. Who knows what trouble I'd be in now if she hadn't?

I had a shift at work with her that night and I was looking forward to getting out of the house. I never really left home all that much previously, but now that I wasn't allowed to I felt like a big lion trapped in a small zoo. I wanted to see Molly because I fancied the pants off her but also because I wanted to know how she had stopped me killing a first-year in front of a rather large number of witnesses. The pub in which I worked might only have been next door, but after a few days of solitary confinement (between the hours of 4pm and 8am the following morning - I don't like to exaggerate), going to work seemed as liberating a prospect as a two-week holiday in the sun. I even got there early and received something better than a pay rise, or even the added responsibility of restocking AND maintaining the cupboard where the sachets of sauces are kept.

Molly and Jacob were over.

There weren't too many details given and understandably Molly didn't really want to talk about it at the time so I'd have to wait until the news at ten −this was surely important enough a development to be featured. She wanted work to take her mind off her personal problems. Needless to say, I was bloody chuffed and had a hard time concealing it. She had cried though, which worried me as she must have actually had some feelings towards him. How long would they last? Sometimes I think people cry at these moments purely because it's expected of them and they don't want to look too much like a machine - which is a shame because if Molly was a machine I could just program her to love me forever instead of going through the really annoying and lengthy process of having to earn it.

When the time came to welcome in our patrons for the evening, Molly wore, very convincingly, the fake smile and caring manner adopted in unison by every other member of staff. Apart from me, as I actually was extremely happy. Hours flew by as I bent over backwards while you, the customer, abused your position of power, while in my head every time you looked at me I pictured you being mugged by a bear. I've yet to win employee of the month but I must be getting close.

Customers came and went and I think most were happy; it's hard to tell with the English. I don't think I've ever enjoyed a shift so much. Molly was holding things together well and I tested the water now and then with a hilarious joke or anecdote about being a waiter. She didn't laugh. She didn't even pretend to but I think she liked someone trying to cheer her up, so it was worth looking like a prat. I felt different around her, not like anything was possible but more like everything seeming a little less *im*possible. As the evening died down I managed to snatch a few words with her and I used the opportunity to thank her for stopping me from doing something foolish at school. As I showed my appreciation I could remember the smell of the apple she was chewing that day.

'It was nothing,' she said.

'Well, I owe you one,' I replied, because that's what people say, isn't it?

'I'll bear that in mind,' she said in the way that meant she would never take me up on it.

'Yeah, so, you know,' I carried on, not knowing when to stop, 'if you need help studying, or I could walk you home or pay for your school dinners for a year? You know, just whatever.'

She extended her insouciant smile and was summoned to a nearby table. What am I doing? I asked myself. She had just split up with her boyfriend. I needed to learn not to rush these things. Trouble at school was dying down, I had a plan for my power, Molly was single and Chris Peck was starting to walk without crutches. Everyone was coming on in leaps and bounds. Molly was heading back over but before she reached me I was distracted by a man wanting to pay his bill. While I printed it off I read the name Simon Webb on his card. I asked if everything was ok with his evening, to which he replied, 'Yes, it was perfect' and then tipped me forty-three pence. That was the first time that night I was showcasing a fake smile. Forty-three pence? What an extremely random and pointless sum of money, and that's what he tips for a 'perfect' evening?! Who even carries around forty-three pence? I watched him leave with a wife and child and thought to myself that she was one lucky lady.

It was almost forty-three minutes later when we locked the doors for the night and tidied up for the morning. Everyone was quiet out of respect for Molly but it was starting to annoy me. She had split up from her short-lived school romance, she wasn't fucking dying. I couldn't help myself and I kept trying to talk to her. Way earlier in the night I had been warmly received in trying to cheer her up but now I looked like an owl stalking a mouse and everyone else was acting like a BBC camera crew, happy to watch the carnage unfold to boost the ratings. Her fake smile had long gone, melted away the instant the door had been locked and I saw no hope in any kind of resurrection. I gave up. Tables had been wiped, mats and cutlery put away and the bar had been restocked and cleaned and, if I may say so myself, the sachets had been beautifully restocked. The kitchen staff had gone and one by one waiters and bar staff said their goodbyes. Molly had also gone. Tips were divided up and dealt out like a pack of cards to the last few employees that weren't in a hurry to get home. They were then put in small brown envelopes that made me think of sleeping bags for mice. A package for Molly lay close to mine and I snatched it from the table and shouted, 'Bye', heading for the door.

I ran through the night to catch up with Molly, knowing full well that the tips I held so tightly in my hands would be put towards a restraining order. The cold air was quick to remind me that I only had a shirt on. I never took a coat to work as I lived next door.

'Molly!' I shouted down the street. I couldn't see her, I was just shouting to give her warning, in case she wanted to run - a sporting head-start. I turned a corner, dodging a few bins and a cat. Another corner and I could just see her slip out of view. I picked up the pace.

'Molly,' I mustered in between deep breaths and while nursing a stitch.

'What are you doing?' I'd finally caught up with her and we stopped and stood outside a little house with the lights on.

'You forgot your tips', I answered, holding out a small brown package. If a sweaty man chasing you in the dark with loose change doesn't reek of romance then I don't know what does. She took the bag without saying anything.

'So,' I tried, 'you ok walking home?'

'You can walk me home if you like,' she said. I couldn't believe it. I really did try my best not to expose my excitement but my excitement exposed me.

'Yes please.'

'Well then, thank you,' and with that she turned towards the house with the lights on and opened the garden gate.

'Right, yes, of course.' She was already home. She stopped before the door and turned back to face me. She could see I was cold and disappointed. She unzipped her coat and brought it to me.

'You'll freeze,' she said. Her coat was clearly a girl's coat, no chance of any ambiguity. It was a little tight on me and too short. Its sleeves didn't reach anywhere near my wrists and it was a dark shade of purple. Don't get me wrong; it looked great on her, but the same couldn't be said for me. But who cares? I was wearing her coat! It smelled of her and as she zipped me up we were in close proximity. I was still catching my breath and panting like a wounded moose but I didn't care about that either; she was inches away from my face.

She put her hand into her coat pocket and my mind started going crazy. What was she doing? Was I supposed to do something back? What sort of lovemaking ritual was this? I wasn't prepared. What was going on? She pulled out her small envelope of tips.

'Get home, Toby, before you catch your death,' and before I could say anything she was closing her front door.

I wasn't sure what had just happened or whether it was good or bad. I was wearing her coat though; that's a good sign, right? She wouldn't have given me her coat if she didn't care about me being cold. I decided it was a good sign. She wouldn't entrust her coat to just anyone. I would proudly wear it home. I left her (nice to finally know exactly where she lives – information I couldn't learn online) and marched home with my head held high like a soldier proudly returning home from overseas. This coat was tight, mind you, and I feared any major movements would cause it damage. I grew quite fond of it in the short space of time I was its owner. An unorthodox rebel, the only laws I broke were fashion-based. I was on the run from the fashion police. There were wanted signs up all over town offering a huge reward for any information on me and my gang of cutting-edge mould-breaking hooligans. I looked like an alien I was so far out. Paparazzi would snap pictures of me at parties with my best mates Andy Warhol and David Bowie. Yeah, I was rocking this look; girls wanted to be with me and guys wanted to be me. All this nonsense rather gloriously evaporated when, deep in reverie, I had failed to notice a bench of real-life hooligans just up the road from me. A road I had to walk down to get home. They hadn't been there before. Any other route would take too long and I should have been home some time ago - I am grounded, after all. The hooligans had spotted me as well, so I couldn't turn back now. I was committed. It doesn't take much from the outside world to burst your bubble and remind you that you're not a 70s trend setter but a teenager wearing a small woman's coat.

Shitting hell I was getting nervous. They wouldn't do anything would they? This was Cockermouth. You heard about beatings and what-not around the country but this was a small tourist town in the middle of a national park. It gave the world poets and scientists, not criminals and statistics. Play it cool, Toby, play it cool.

'Evening gents,' I threw at them with a casual and swift wave that looked like a weak salute. No immediate response. Safe.

'What the fuck are you wearing?' one said, while the others got up off the bench.

'What, this old thing? Just a coat, mate.' I was being far too casual and why on earth did I refer to one of them as my mate?

'I'm not your fucking mate,' he spat with intense, unresolved childhood issues that deep down, if he was being honest, had nothing to do with me. A man wearing a woman's coat cannot inspire anger of that tone, even in Cumbria.

'What's the hurry?' another said, quickening his pace to keep up with me.

'No reason.' All the confidence had gone from my voice and I was beginning to stutter. There were six of them altogether and me and my power were nowhere near ready for this. It was light years from being under control, so I just kept moving. One of them put his hand on my shoulder and I spun round. It was Jacob.

'Don't I know you?' he said, his eyes fixated on the coat.

'Nope, don't think so.'

'That's that Toby kid,' one of his cronies informed him.

'You're the mental kid that put Peck in hospital!' He took a step back.

'I'm not that mental,' I said to deaf ears.

'Well you do spend your nights walking around town wearing women's clothing!' They all laughed at this.

'He is mental!' one of them shouted. Another one started to do an impression of me. It was woefully inaccurate but I took the opportunity and ran. I ran as fast as a coat that would barely fit a badger would allow me to. I wasn't far from home and neither Jacob nor his friends were in sight when I finally flew through the front door to my house.

Close call.

I had my back to the front door and as I laughed a sigh of relief I flicked a light on. My parents had been sitting in the dark waiting for me.

'You're supposed to be grounded, Toby. This isn't on,' Jenny said with the seriousness of a judge. My dad looked at the coat, then at me and then back to the coat. He looked mortified.

'What is happening to you?' he said.

7

"All that homophobic shit makes you sound super gay" - Hitgirl

The trouble with trouble is that it attracts trouble. For my insubordination I was punished and, much like my first bout with justice, I came away feeling quite pleased with my performance. My parents had decided to ban me from using my phone when inside the house; I had to surrender it on entry. I could still use it when lost out there in the big bad world, in case an emergency arose, but at home it was now off limits. It's like they weren't even trying to punish me as I had access to the internet at home and didn't need my phone unless I was on the move, which, by their own ruling, was when I was allowed to use it. I made a beautiful fuss though and if people could have overheard the kerfuffle they might have thought my left leg was being confiscated. I'm tempted to go without a phone anyway; it's ridiculous how much time I catch myself spending on it. I swear to baby Jesus it's stripping me of intelligence rather than allowing me easier access to a digital world of it. Without a phone I could tell people if they want to reach me they can write a letter and if it's urgent they should use a pigeon.

I was becoming all too familiar with trouble and I didn't like it. I was, after all, attempting to be a hero. I wasn't doing a very good job of it so far. I wasn't used to being in trouble either; I'm usually too afraid of feeling guilty to attempt anything incriminating. I used to be riddled with guilt when I had missed the acceptable window of opportunity to say 'bless you' after someone had sneezed. Unless you say it immediately after someone has sprayed snot all over their hand, then forget it, it's game over. People often follow up a sneeze with, that's right, another sneeze but if I missed saying 'bless you' the first time I feel I can't say it for the second nasal explosion because I worry they will want to know 'what was wrong with my first sneeze?' If I say 'bless you' after the first sneeze and then they sneeze again I have to say 'bless you' to every after-sneeze so that all sneezes are treated equally. It's a difficult situation to find yourself in and I wouldn't wish it upon my worst enemy.

Anyway.

It was worth losing phone access to walk Molly home because, as you know, I was now in possession of her coat. I had her property and aside from being able to smell her as and when I please it also gave me reason to see her again. Sadly, I would most likely give her back her coat on our next shift together but it was a free conversation-starter and I was grateful for the crumbs. It had a sweet smell that teased the senses and thankfully overpowered the residual smell of fear that I had leached into the material after wearing it home. Thinking about it, I could have taken her coat off straight away and just run home, which would have kept me warm. A part of me didn't want to take it off though. It belonged to Molly and having it made me a part of her life, if only superficially and if only for a short while. I would say it was almost like I was wearing her but that makes me sound absolutely mental - that even sounds mental just in my own head, so lord knows what you're now thinking of me.

I saw Molly the next day at school, from a distance. She didn't notice me. She was stood talking to friends, just getting on with things. Her life wasn't rapidly slipping downhill on sensitive toes, interspersed only with brief moments of cross-dressing. She was single and yet seemed more unattainable than ever. As with every other area of my life I was utterly clueless as how to take control of the situation. Why had she and Jacob split up? Did she like someone else? She was talking to female friends, so maybe she now liked women. Maybe she liked both. I'm not sure I could date a bisexual; I always feel they are twice as likely to cheat. But if Molly was cheating on me that would at least have to mean we were going out and I had more chance of convincing Big Foot to apply for a loan than I had dating her. I could swear she was giving me signals now and then, like when she helped me out in the canteen, because she didn't have to, or even the bloody coat, that wasn't necessary. I didn't know what to make of it. Women are hard to work out. I had to think smart. I had her coat, which is more than most can say. I had my foot in the door. Jacob and his friends walked past me and laughed. He wouldn't be laughing if he knew whose coat it was. I would be the last person to tell him though, as I like having a face.

Oh Molly. If only you knew. If I had a girl like Molly I'd never cheat on her. I've never cheated on anyone before. Not really had any chance whatsoever to do so but that's not the point.

Suddenly Randall appeared, as if by magic.

'Hiya mate,' he said.

'Where have you been?'

'Been helping fix some lad's bicycle.'

'Why?'

'It's nice to be nice.'

'And?'

'He's doing my English assignment.'

'There we go. Hang on, what do you know about bicycles?'

'I know some things. I'm a Randall of all trades.'

'You mean Jack of all trades.'

'No, I'm Randall.'

'But Randall of all trades isn't a saying; the saying is Jack of all trades. The term 'Jack' was used originally to denote an ordinary man, it comes from Middle English. Do you know anything? The phrase Jack of all trades is a person who can do many different types of work but who is not necessarily very competent at any of them. Look, it doesn't matter, what 'things' do you know about bicycles?'

'Nothing.'

'Well good luck with that.'

'It will be fine.'

'I wish I had your optimism.'

'You don't, my mum keeps telling me off for scratching it.' There is no experience quite like that of an idiot looking at you as if you're an idiot.

'If I never see you again, I wish you all the best.'

'Aw, thanks mate,' he smiled.

My walk home was uneventful. I scurried out of school along with everyone else, an ant's nest under attack from a full kettle. I was careful where I put my feet within the crowd and so I made it out alive. More importantly, so did everyone else. As I was grounded I headed straight home, and quickly at that; I had disappointed my parents enough in the last month.

There was post waiting for me when I got in. It's rare for someone my age to get anything in the post. It feels quite grown up getting post, knowing that someone out there in the world has spent some time in a previous day to send something addressed specifically to me, for my eyes only, so to speak. Good things come to those who wait and today I had a mountain of packages all smiling at me.

'What is all this?' my mum asked suspiciously.

'Research,' I said plainly, which wasn't untrue.

'For what?'

'School,' I said. This was a lie but I can't be honest all the time, it's exhausting always having to explain yourself. There is a saying that goes: 'Never explain yourself. Your friends don't need it and your enemies won't believe it.' But if you get drunk and try it on with your mate's girlfriend, he will probably want an explanation.

'School, you say. Ok then.' And she began walking away, dripping paint on the floor with every step. 'Oh, can I have your phone please?' she asked without really asking.

'Oh mum, please don't.'

'Toby. Phone. Now.' She was holding out her hand.

'Fine!' And I slapped the phone into her hand for added effect.

'Go and do your homework,' she said with her back to me as she set off again. I smiled and went upstairs to open my presents.

Not all the films had arrived yet but I had more than enough to get started on. My research would begin tonight. I hoped the help I needed was on these fragile discs of fiction. I wanted to be good at this. I don't like doing things if I'm not good at them. In fact I don't do most things unless I know I'll be good at them. I won't go bowling because I know I'm not very good at it but bowling on a games console I'll give a go because I'm a confident gamer. What a terrible way to live a life, trapped within the confines of an inaccurate measurement of skill as an avatar celebrates imaginary success for me. I really needed my research to go well.

8

When watching a film I expect the same courtesies as when I'm on
the toilet or copulating with a fair maiden. I hate being disturbed,
truly hate it. Disturbing a film breaks the entire illusion the art form
is trying to create and you can only watch a film for the first time
once. It's in your best interests not to interrupt me when I'm enjoying
a film on first showing. If I have already seen the film then talk away,
segment the script, proportion the plot and analyse the actors to your
heart's content, but if I'm watching it for the first time then either
shut up or fuck off. There are exceptions to most rules though and
if it's something extremely important that has a direct impact on
my time left on this earth then feel free to brave a conversation. But
before you take that as a catch-all, even if it is a terrorist attack I'd
want to know how bad it is, whether they're on my street and if it is me
they're after. Did I really need to know? Or if a relative has died, sure
it's sad, but if they are dead it really doesn't make much difference
when I'm told about it. It can keep for a couple of hours, is what I'm
saying - they're not going anywhere.

Films are a hobby of mine but one that I clearly take seriously.
Books are up there as well. People talk to me all day long when I'm
not reading, and never ask if I've enjoyed any literary delights of late,
but as soon as I have a book in hand they're struck by some apparently

irresistible desire to know my reading needs. Well, they can keep that desire contained. I don't know why people think it's acceptable to talk to someone while they're reading. It's not.

Speaking of monstrous behaviour, and I'm really venting now, here is something else that really gets on my tits.

I could be on a night out (not drinking, obviously, as I'm underage; let's say it's a work's night out), having a good time with friends and mixing with the ladies in the pub, when I find myself needing the loo. I break from the group and enter the gents. I shuffle over to a free urinal and relax into a very satisfying pastime. Suddenly the man next to me starts talking. What's going on? The man in question has been standing with me at the bar all night without sharing so much as a smile and now he's asking if I'm 'having a good night?' What the hell does he think he's doing? He doesn't even start with a hello, he's *that* confident, and because we're now within the safety of the toilets, holding our nobs (each our own, to clarify; it would be less odd to be asking about the evening's enjoyment score if we were already swapping todger control duties), it's suddenly a relaxed enough environment for him to comfortably collect my thoughts on my evening away from home. If I was in a cubicle he wouldn't slip a note under the door asking if I'm having a good time. I hate urinal etiquette where it's expected of me to make sure the man to my left is all right - we're not in the trenches. The fact that we're both pissing into urinals isn't enough in common to make us friends, the foundations aren't strong enough. Out of all the friends I have, when people ask how we met, I've never said, 'we were pissing in the same pub one night and the rest is history.'

Grrr.

So, yeah, films. It's nice to add some more to my collection. My personal hoard wasn't at all impressive but films are a hobby of mine. The etymology of the word hobby originates in the 13th century. The term 'hobyn' had the meaning of a small horse or pony. A hobbyhorse, originally called a tourney horse, was made of wood, in a basic frame, with a tail and a head. They were designed to mimic real horses (obviously - I doubt many farmers were fooled) and a hobbyhorse would be used for religious activities and civic occasions. Eventually, over centuries, 'hobby' was introduced into

English vocabulary and it came to mean 'recreational' or 'leisurely' pursuit. There you go, always learning.

Among this first arrival of films were such blockbusters as *The Punisher, Catwoman, The Green Lantern,* all three *Iron Man* films, *Superman Returns,* the first three *X-Men* movies and *Daredevil.* I had done my homework and we had all eaten the evening meal together. My dad had asked how school had gone and then, as if I wasn't in the room, asked my mum what time I got home. The grounded facade continued. I had rushed my meal and asked if I could be excused, to which my parents unanimously agreed.

There is no time like the present, although the past and future are pretty close, and so I unwrapped one of the DVD boxes and opened it to retrieve a disc. It was squeaky clean and I carefully placed it into my player. So here I was, bright-eyed and bushy-tailed, lying on my bed with a fresh notepad and pen. With the remote in hand I pressed play and let the teaching commence, a night class in the nocturnal. *Daredevil* began.

One hour and thirty-nine minutes later and my notepad and pen hadn't touched each other. I wasn't sure what to make of the film and even less sure what I could take away from it and apply to my own life. The only real thing to learn from it is that care really must be taken at all times when handling dangerous chemicals. You can never be 100% safe and accidents will happen if people aren't paying attention. In the film Matthew had taken a shortcut home and witnessed his dad in the company of some unsavoury characters and, as he tried to run away, he was blinded in a chemical accident. Because of this his other senses were heightened. Later on he saw his dad die at the hands of Wilson Fisk (aka The Kingpin) and an ensuing tail of revenge unfolds as Matthew, a successful lawyer helping those others wouldn't, fights crime not just during working hours but also at night, chasing down criminals in a tight red get-up, particularly criminals who have beaten the system. He must have been exhausted; there is no way he was getting enough sleep. He looked a mess and was more often than not a bit grumpy.

It seems most of these films have strong themes of revenge running through them. Bruce Wayne became Batman because his parents were murdered and he could see Gotham City going to the dogs. Frank Castle became The Punisher and sought revenge because his entire family were murdered at the hands of Howard Saint and Spider-Man only began fighting crime after his uncle Ben had been fatally shot. But I couldn't be driven by revenge as my life was... well, it was fine, wasn't it? Unfortunately for me my parents haven't been murdered. The selfish bastards sat downstairs effervescently navigating a crossword. They were never in harm's way, unless you count living with me, but despite my iffy reaction to toe-stubs I was no threat to *them*.

So what was my motivation? What was driving me to do good? Do you need an incentive to do good? Surely just wanting to do good is good enough reason to do good. What makes someone good? What makes someone bad? I suppose bad people are bad people because bad people do bad things when they know they're bad and it's in knowing something's bad that makes bad people doing something bad bad people.

That's obvious.

I don't know why I was doing any of this - no one was asking me to - but then again, everyone needs a purpose in life and as I have a power, my purpose must be to use it for something. I would harness my power and put it to use simply because I could. I didn't need my parents to die for me to make a difference, no matter how hard I prayed. They were going to live for ages and there was nothing I can do about it. I would do good because it was the right thing to do, a moral obligation, a civic duty. I would be just and sensible with the gift that had been bestowed upon me. I would learn to use my power to help, to aid, and to pull women. And if that failed I'd take a back-alley loan out in my dad's name and see what happens.

From that moment on I soaked in all the films, one after the other, learning what I could about this new world. Days disappeared as I watched the Fantastic Four save the world, Tony Stark escape imprisonment and I even stopped by to see Steve Rogers apparently defeat the Nazis singlehandedly.

Captain America (Steve Rogers) is known as the first Avenger. There is some debate on this but I'm nowhere near nerdy enough to even want to get involved. He is called the first Avenger, let's leave it at that. Steve Rogers was from Brooklyn and when World War II kicked off he wanted nothing more than the chance to fight for his country. He wasn't motivated by revenge; he just wanted someone to give him a chance. A chance he was repeatedly denied due to his small physique and a rather bad bout of asthma. He tried and tried, a great example for young viewers not to give up in life (although if we are following this example through to the end then the lesson being taught is actually try and try again and if that still doesn't work then turn to drugs).

Eventually Steve was accepted as a test subject for a secret project designed to make the world's first super-soldier, helped by Howard Stark (Tony Stark's dad (Tony Stark is Iron Man - small world)). Well, what can I say? It worked a dream but Rogers wasn't put to the battlefield. He stayed at home and was used as propaganda to raise money by selling war bonds. In time he wanted to prove himself and so ran off to beat up some bad guys. One man wearing the American flag taking on huge amounts of Nazi scum almost singlehandedly? A bit cocky really, and what about the Brits? We might not have had as many troops as the Americans but we had a population five times smaller, and the Americans didn't even join the war until 1941. We'd been pushing on through for two years before they turned up, but whatever. Most nations love themselves. From personal experience I've found, from the Americans I've met, they love their own country. I, as an Englishman, don't feel too proud to be English. I think a big difference is Americans are brought up to believe they could become the next President whereas in England we're brought up being told 'it won't happen to you so don't bother'. It's more realistic but not as inspiring. We've had our moments in the sun though, such as the British Empire, that's a good example, or the bloke that made the anti-bandit bag. I'm taking the piss with that one because the anti-bandit bag was a ridiculous invention consisting of a bag, which, if someone tried to rob you of it, had a chain which could be pulled so that all the contents of your bag would fall out of the bottom and scatter all over the floor, forcing the robber to give up. There is a very good reason why you've probably never heard of this invention.

Being English is certainly not something I brag about, but that in itself, I feel, is a very British trait. Nothing really excites us; we're always expecting the worst. Handy in a war though, I will say that. Millions of men gave their lives in the war so we wouldn't be speaking German today and yet I spend several hours a week at school learning how to say, 'I have blonde hair and blue eyes' in German. Funny how life turns out sometimes.

My next couple of weeks were set out for me. I had work to do. I would emerge from my incarceration a nerd, a dork, a dweeb, a nimrod and a geek. I'd resurface fully equipped to take on a world of heroism. I had at hand the tools to transform myself into a crime-fighting legend. I'd be taking down mob bosses and drug cartels before you could say, 'I'll never get those two hours watching *Punisher: War Zone* back'. I needed to do this. I wanted to do this. I was focusing all my attention on just this. Imagine a training montage set to sounds from the 80s of me working day and night. There would be no running along the beach or me at the gym because I was grounded, but there would be shot after shot of me ripping open post, loading the DVD tray and taking toilet breaks in between each feature. The montage would look great, don't worry about it.

Even Molly was pushed to the back of my mind. I was trying a new tack. The old 'treat them mean, keep them keen' motif. I was ignoring her essentially, to see if she would come to me. As long as I could avoid another incident, within a few weeks everything should be right on track.

9

"Freedom is power" – Catwoman

On average there are 35 pages and 124 illustrations in a comic book. A single issue ranges in price from a dollar to $140,000 and 172,000 comics are sold in the U.S. every day, which is over 62,780,000 each year.

I don't know if these statistics are true because I haven't checked, but they appear at the very beginning of the film *Unbreakable* starring Bruce Willis as superhero David Dunn. It's a great film, a delightful entry into the genre. It tells the story of a man who is the sole survivor of a train crash. 131 confirmed deaths and yet he comes out of the wreckage without so much as a scratch. The film takes off from there and slowly but surely he discovers he has superhuman attributes. It is one of the better films I have seen recently. I'm not having a go, but how some of those scripts got commissioned I'll never know. In one particular vampire romp someone used the insult 'cock-juggling thunder cunt'.

Some of you will read the last word in that sentence and you'll be disappointed. You'll be all like...

'The 'c' word? Oh no, not the 'c' word. What a shame. Sharon?'

'I'm busy! What is it?!'
'He's only gone and used the 'c' word!'
'Get your coat, I've got the receipt!'

Well, firstly what I will say is get over yourself. It's just a word. It's an awful word but it is just a word. Secondly, I'm quoting it to make a point so just take a deep breath and carry on, all right?

A 'cock-juggling thunder cunt'. Yeah, I know. I thought the same thing. I had to press pause and give myself a moment for that to sink in. Then I rewound the disc and made sure I hadn't made a mistake. A cock-juggling thunder cunt? Really? How upset do you have to be for that combination of words to come tumbling out? The film was already on an uphill struggle to win me over because it was depicting a story focusing on vampires. Of all the fictional creatures humankind has fabricated, including things such as zombies, mermaids and god, vampires have to be, by far, the lamest. Suspicion of real-life vampires arose in the early 18th century after the term vampire became popular in Western Europe. In 1897, when Bram Stoker's novel *Dracula* was published, people went vampire mad, they couldn't get enough of them. *Dracula* is widely known as the quintessential vampire novel and provides the basis for all modern vampire legends. For those that care, vampire was originally spelt vampyre because, like most words, we nicked it from the French. Having said all that (I'm bored even writing about them) the notion of vampirism has existed for millennia. However, despite the occurrence of these vampire-type thingamajigs, the vampires most women, thanks to the *Twilight* series, have come to know and love originate almost exclusively from the 18th century.

It's worth noting that in 2006 a physics professor at the University of Central Florida wrote a paper arguing that it is mathematically impossible for vampires to exist. According to the paper, if the first vampire had appeared on the 1st of January 1600, and it fed once a month (which is less often than is always portrayed in films) and every victim turned into a vampire, then within two and a half years the entire human population of the time would have become vampires. Although I fear this professor's good brain was being wasted accommodating tripe such as this, I think his paper should have been used to nip all this vampire nonsense in the bud. But you can't change human nature and regrettably our nature is to do stupid things. For example, two years before the professor's paper was published a family in Romania were moronic enough to believe a dead family member had turned into a vampire and so they dug up his corpse, tore out his heart, burned it, and mixed the ashes with water.

Which they then drank.

True story.

We fear things we don't understand and we don't like, so we speculate and boy does the human race know how to speculate. Even today, maybe even right now, someone in the world is drinking someone else's blood and treating it as a harmless hobby. I've mentioned hobbies before and this really isn't what I meant. Read a book or take up knitting. If you're thinking about other people's blood at all, just getting some fresh air will do you good.

Anyway, where was I? That's right, a cock-juggling thunder cunt. It's something you'd hear in a school playground being said by some kid who didn't know what half those words mean. Whoever wrote that line, I hope you're still managing to find work. If my boss came to me and said, 'Ok, we have a scene coming up and we need a really good insult for it, something snappy and fresh. What have you got?' and if I came out with 'cock-juggling thunder cunt' I'd expect to be cleaning out my desk while the rest of the office watched on in silence. If they were trying to be funny with the line then, trust me, the film was laughable enough on its own, it didn't need this on top.

I realise I have used the word cunt a lot now. I was going to write it as c*** but what's the point? That doesn't change what I mean. I hate people who use this technique as if it somehow makes it less offensive. Everyone reading it knows exactly what you're saying. It's almost like people who, when describing someone who's a bit odd, twirl a finger that's pointed to their ear - you're better off just saying it because by performing the mime all you're really doing is letting foreigners and deaf people understand you as well. Either use a word or don't. It's just a word. We can agree, unequivocally, that it's not a very pleasant word and even its sound alone will never be easy on the ears, but it is just a word. Having said that, let's not see it again.

So here I was. A couple of weeks had passed and I had been released. I stepped out the house a free man. My period of incarceration had changed me, for the better, and I could now empathise with people like Nelson Mandela.

I had become a fully-fledged nerd, I had earned my stripes. I now had so much pointless information about a specific topic it was unreal. I had watched over thirty films on superheroes and crammed my skull with information that I'd never need in the real world; it was like I'd done an intensive course on another language.

It felt strange being a bit nerdy on something. If I started talking about tesseracts and The Bureau of Paranormal Research and Defence only fellow nerds would know what's going on. One thing at least that had come out of this was that I felt sure I could now pull a nerd; I had the right tools for the job. I wouldn't want to though, because I only cared for Molly, but maybe someone should let Molly know and she might pull her finger out. Over the last couple of weeks I had seen her here and there, and at work of course. If you're wondering about the coat, then I'm sad to say that it had been and gone. My nose was bereft of her feminine scent. I was hoping she'd have to trade it back for her heart, or a limb or something, but she just politely asked for it back and so what could I do? I didn't know what to make of us anymore and the longer it went on the more defeated I felt about the situation. If only it was socially acceptable for me to point blank ask her whether I should be continuing this pursuit or bag myself a nerd and try to lose my virginity while listening to the *Iron Man* sound track. Not that I'm chasing Molly just to lose my virginity. Time is ticking on though and I have a lot to get through; I have a personal statement to write soon and a cross-country run to train for.

I had been trying to play it cool with Molly but cool is somewhat alien to me. I kept my distance and whenever we did happen to speak I could never find the right balance between casual and rude. Maybe it was to be a nerd's life for me, but I kept telling myself Molly might be a secret nerd. I didn't know I was nerd material until I was locked away in solitude and forced to reflect. She could be a secret anything to me at this rate; I'd never be able to confirm anything substantial about her.

I had been concentrating on becoming a better superhero so maybe I should continue to focus on that. If only I could give Molly what she wanted. But then again, everyone wants a hero, don't they? The world needs heroes. We need them because it gives us someone to model ourselves on; they set good examples for all of us. We are inherently selfish creatures and possessed by an indelible need to protect our own before others and we only care about problems when they begin to affect us personally. Heroes remind us we should look out for everyone, and these worthy role models just as equally include a fictional hero such as Batman, a soldier who throws himself on a grenade to save those around him or someone willing to eat the Bounty bars from a tin of Celebrations so others can enjoy a Snickers or Mars. Heroes put themselves in danger to ensure the safety of others. A society without superheroes is a society without hope. We all have role models, people we cling to when facing hardships or decisions. They lead and we should follow. Without superheroes we're lost.

Molly was just lost, that's all. She needed a hero. She needed me.

I'd hate for you to think I'd just been watching films every night. I've been doing some serious work. I had given a lot of thought to my outfit, for instance. I'd wear black; it actually didn't take that long to sort that out. A black hoody, black sweat pants and black shoes. Done.

Ok, so dress code was fine. I should point out that my shoes were basically plimsols. They were for easy movement and comfort, and thin enough around the toe area that my power might be triggered more readily. We'll come back to my power later.

I had also figured out a basic route around Cockermouth, incorporating all those areas with a high potential for crime - the pubs. My route went a little like this. I'd set off from home and head left, walking along St Helen's Street and into Market Place, moving past popular pubs 1761 and The Castle Bar. At this end of Market Place you can take a left that leads to Main Street or a right that starts with a short, steep climb onto the long Castlegate Drive that leads up to Cockermouth Secondary School and on out of town. I would take another left and, once over a small bridge above the river Cocker, I was on Main Street. Most of the pubs in Cockermouth are on Main Street and all on the same side, bar The Kingfisher. From the direction I was facing the pubs lined up on the left. I couldn't go into the pubs because I was still a minor and because, frankly, it would give the game away, so I'd stick to the right-hand side and make my way along. I would pass The Black Bull, The Globe, The Brown Cow, Hunters, Wordsworth's, The Bush and Fletcher Christian. Eventually you'll come to William Wordsworth's house.

Look him up if you want to know who he is, I'm sick of inadvertently promoting him.

It's here that I would turn up the road instead of continuing along to places such as New Street and Derwent Street. A little way along I would take yet another left and find myself on South Street. I'd follow this street all the way along, passing The Cock and Bull and Tithe Barn as I go, until I come to a smaller bridge back over the river Cocker. Another steep hill leads onto Cocker Lane and once I'd passed the church on my left I'd turn left, down Kirkgate. The Bitter End pub can be found there, ever welcoming with its bright lights and the sound of happy customers drifting outside into the night air. Still I'd keep walking. The Kirkgate Centre is the last big landmark and at the bottom of the road, when presented with a choice, I finally make a right and before I knew it I'd be home. Not a bad route really, it's a nice walk.

So I had my power, my outfit and my route. It was all coming together. I needed a name though. I was struggling with that. It would have to be something relevant to my toes, like other heroes.

There is an old story that tells us the moon is lonely because she used to have a lover. The lover was called Kuekuatsheu and they lived in the spirit world. Every night they would wander the skies together, but one of the other spirits was jealous. Trickster wanted the moon for himself, so he told Kuekuatsheu that the moon had asked for flowers. He told him to come to our world and pick her some wild roses, but Kuekuatsheu didn't know that once you leave the spirit world, you can never go back. Every night he looks up in the sky and sees the moon and howls her name. But he can never touch her again. Kuekuatsheu means "the wolverine". This is where X-Man Logan got his superhero name from, after his missus had tricked him in *X-Men Origins: Wolverine*. If Kuekuatsheu was a wolverine, where on earth did he and the moon meet? Friend of a friend? What sort of party can you attend where a moon and a dog are in the same place? Sad story though and Logan was betrayed time and time again, which makes all his sarcastic comments understandable. He's a proper cool character. He has the ability to heal extremely fast and his bones are coated in a metal called Adamantium, which makes him almost impossible to kill. It can be done though, you just have to remove his head. Good luck with that. For myself I couldn't think of anything as cool as Wolverine or The Punisher. I had sat with pen and paper to write ideas down but so far I'd only managed to come up with Athlete's Foot and I didn't think that gave out the right message.

Putting that to one side, I had also created a weekly plan for when I could watch over this glorious town. Monday is a horrible day for countless reasons, so I didn't fancy keeping watch then. Friday and Saturday I worked, so that's no good and Sunday was bath night and when *Heartbeat* was on, so forget it. That left midweek but I couldn't do too much otherwise school, work and my life in general would suffer.

So Tuesdays and Thursdays it was, giving me Wednesdays to recover. I know what you're thinking: I've picked two quiet nights of the week but a) police are out at the weekends so if I was a criminal a midweek heist must be more appealing, and b) I'm new to all this and I don't want to dive in at the deep end. I'm only a beginner.

10

It was raining when I woke up. For a country that should expect rain on a daily basis we don't half act surprised when we get a lot of it. Would I have to fight crime in bad weather? I hadn't thought of that. You know what, I don't think I've seen any of my fictional friends serving up justice in wet and windy weather. I bet Spider-Man looks nothing short of a fool trying to swing between skyscrapers in strong winds, or Batman having a conversation with Two-Face about moisturisers with his cape flapping all over the place. I was starting to think the films I'd been watching aren't that realistic. In a perfect world I'd only have to fight crime in good weather, but that just wasn't going to happen, was it? I'd have to find a way of using it to my advantage. Strong winds are noisy, that could come in handy, and I supposed rain would make me wet so I'd be slippery and harder to grab? I was clutching at straws here. I'd take each day as it comes. Today was brand new, reloaded with potential after yesterday's shoot-out.

I set off to meet Randall before heading to school. He wasn't a fan of the rain.

'If rain was warm it wouldn't be so bad,' he said.

'Well, hmm maybe, I suppose.'

'Then when places get flooded they wouldn't mind so much.'

'I don't think the major concern with flooding is the temperature of the water. I think volume is the big worry.'

'Hmm.' He wasn't convinced. 'How are you, anyway?'

'I'm good, thanks. I'm feeling very inspired at the moment. I've been watching a lot of films for something I'm working on.'

'It's powerful stuff. I was watching that cop show called *Justified* and it really makes me want to buy a cowboy hat.'

'Nice, but I was thinking of something a bit bigger than head attire.'

'You mean like how *Sons of Anarchy* makes you want to buy a motorcycle?'

'No, that's not what I mean.'

'Or how *Dexter* makes you want to kill people?'

'Yeah. No, sorry. What?'

'Come on, we've all thought about it.'

'Who is "we"? And I haven't!'

'I have. I make lists of people at school I wish I could kill.'

'What do you do with the lists?'

'Oh nothing. It backfired once though. Close to my birthday my mum found a list in my room and assumed it was the list of guests I wanted to invite to the party. It was awkward.'

I laughed. 'I remember that. I wondered why they were there. Hang on a minute, it was your mum that rang and invited me.'

'Did she? I don't recall.'

'It was barely four months ago.'

'We're friends now.'

'I can't believe there was a time, and recently at that, when you wanted me dead!'

'The lists change all the time.'

'What had I done?'

'What?'

'Well, I must have done something pretty outrageous for the only course of action you could take to be adding my name to a list of people that you wanted dead.'

'Aw mate, who knows?' he said, far too casually for a conversation like this.

'Well *you* fucking should! I'm worried now!'

'Calm down.'

'You calm down. Stop making lists. And stop watching *Dexter*.'

'No, I like...' Randall went all quiet as we passed Mrs Tuck, a lady who lived on our street.

'What was that about?' I asked once Mrs Tuck was some distance away.

'Nothing,' he said.

'Do you still fancy Mrs Tuck?'

'So?'

'Ha ha.'

'What's so funny?'

'She's old enough to be your mum.'

'I happen to know she likes younger men.'

'How on earth do you figure that?'

'I always see her out with teenagers.'

'They're her kids, you idiot.'

'Really?'

'Ha ha ha!'

'Shut up!'

'How would you pull her anyway?'

'I'd be confident and charming; women like that'

'Well, it's easy to say that but, yeah, right, I'll pretend to be Mrs Tuck and you try to woo me.'

'I'm going to nail this,' he said.

'Have you started?'

'Hi Mrs Tuck...'

'Do you not know her first name?'

'I've just always known her as Mrs Tuck. Hello Mrs Tuck,' he said pointlessly as he must have known I was going to sabotage this.

'Hello, are you looking for something?' I replied coquettishly.

'I was looking for you.'

'For me? Why?'

'To tell you I'd like to make love to you all night long.'

'Well, that is a very kind offer. Is tonight ok? We can do it in my bed.'

'Yeah. That's great.'

'I do share the bed with my husband though, so he will be there, that ok?'

'Oh. Does he have to be there?'

'Well it's his house, not just mine, and he helped pay for the bed so I'd feel rude asking him to sleep downstairs. It's quite a small bed as well and he has to be up early for work so we'll have to be quiet. Oh and he sleeps naked.'

'Right. Can we do it another night maybe?'

'No, this is the only night I'm free so it's either tonight, with my naked husband in the same bed, or never.'

'Hmm. I'm just not that keen on your husband being there, I think it might put me off.'

'Well, it's up to you.'

'Ok, I'll do it.'

'Ugh! You'd actually do it? With her naked husband lying a foot away from you?'

'Yeah, I can put a line of pillows down the middle of the bed.'

'Oh yeah, why didn't I think of that? It won't be awkward at all now,' I said, a rich heritage of English sarcasm on tap.

'But I'd get to tell people I'd slept with her.'

'Anyone who hears that story will think you've helped a struggling marriage spice things up.'

'It would be worth it just to see her naked.'

'You're right, go for it.'

'I can't, I'm busy tonight.'

'Her loss.'

'Shut up. Why don't you go for it?'

'I'm more than happy with Molly, thank you very much.'

'Well, maybe I'm more than happy being single.'

'Randall, governments the world over are happy you're single.'

We walked in silence for the rest of the way to school as we both let certain revelations about each other sink in. I used my thinking time to wonder what I could have done to warrant a death sentence from my best friend but nothing came to mind. It had really come out of the blue that Randall, who I'd known since forever, had at one point in time wished death upon me. I took a quick glance at him while he wasn't looking. I wondered what went on in that head of his but all I could picture was a light bulb and a moth bouncing off it repeatedly. Moths only come out at night but they love the light. I really want to catch one and tell it that if he just stays up a bit later than usual it will blow his mind. No one really knows why moths like light but somebody with way too much free time came up with a hypothesis to do with the moon, visual fields and something called transverse orientation. I could go into more detail as I have the information at hand but it's really not going to better your life. I should just be grateful that the light in Randall's head is switched on. School came into view.

I had a dreadful day set out for me. I had French at some point in the morning and P.E. after lunch. That meant seeing both Neville and Chris within the next five hours and both teachers for these subjects, since the incidents, had treated me like an armed bomb wanting to explode. I was almost annoyed that my P.E. teacher hadn't come to me at some point and asked if he could train me to become the next world heavyweight champion or, at the very least, ask me to join the school rugby team. He was probably annoyed that I had hospitalised one of the best all-round athletes the school has ever had, so it was doubtful he'd want to spend much time with me working on a knock-about comedy of an underdog rising from rags to riches. Neither Neville nor Chris were punished for what they had done to me because what I had seen fit as retribution was interpreted by everyone else as overkill, so their sins were forgotten.

I hadn't had another incident since Chris Peck, but that's because I had exhausted myself avoiding one. I needed a better solution than living on tenterhooks. I wanted to get on with life; I wanted control over whatever it was I had. I couldn't lock myself away each night and spend my days avoiding everyone. And I still needed a superhero name. A man isn't strong enough; as a man I can be broken down and destroyed, stripped of everything. With a name I could become more than a man. I could become a symbol, a beacon. I had a route planned for after my next shift at work, and if I didn't have a name by then I'd just have to go with Athlete's Foot and hope that criminal activity would cease because people were either scared of my strength as an athlete, or because they were worried about catching a fungal infection in a mild form of ringworm.

Ah, French. There are lots of stereotypes surrounding the French. One is that they are short. This probably comes from Napoleon but did you know that in Napoleon's time a French inch was a slightly longer unit of measure than an English inch? So the stereotype shouldn't be that they are short but more that they are thick for not understanding unit conversions. People always associate the French with eating frogs but they are widely consumed in China, Spain and even the United States. They are also eternally mocked for letting the Nazis just stroll in during World War II, but have a heart, people; they had been devastated by World War I. So the stereotype shouldn't be that they surrender easily, it should be that they are crap at fighting. Lastly I'll mention another popular stereotype about the French which is that all women go topless on the beaches. A lot of beaches in France are top optional but it's actually becoming less and less popular with the ladies. Bit annoying really, just as technology is allowing almost every mobile phone to have a small camera built in. Oh and they are also frauds because French fries were invented in Belgium.

I can't leave it there. I'm going to have to say something nice about the French to strike a balance. Here we go: more than 350 kinds of cheese are made in France. That's impressive (no wonder they smell). And how could I forget that France has its very own superheroes. In 1961 the world was introduced to a very formidable Gaul by the name of Asterix. Along with his best friend Obelix, they defended a small Gaul village from Roman occupation in 50BC, with the help of a magic potion that gave the recipient temporary superhuman strength. The potion was brewed by local druid Getafix. The chief of the village was called Vitalstatistix and Obelix's dog was called Dogmatix. They all have such wonderful names and it is a wonderful cartoon. So, no matter how small the French are, no matter what they eat and no matter how many times they let other countries occupy them, they gave us Asterix and (if popular stereotypes are to be believed) a lot of tanned boobs. Cartoons and breasts, is life for anything else?

That is my knowledge of France exhausted, I'm afraid. Don't ask me about the language. I have been finding myself in this classroom week after week looking at the same words over and over again but nothing seems to sink in.

I sat down in my usual seat and Luke slumped down next to me. He was a quiet chap, nice to sit next to really and he gave off a remarkable amount of heat. I'd never known anything like it. I won't go into detail because this story isn't about him, he's very much expendable. I'm only mentioning him because he happens to sit next to me and because of his thermal output. As dull as French lessons were, I could never complain I was cold.

Time ticked on, minute after minute. The heat from Luke was deliciously soporific combined with the monotonous hum coming from the front of the class. My body swayed as the heat relaxed me into submission. My mind was telling me I'd never need any French. My eyes were joining in and wanting to shut up shop early, a mutiny coursed through my body like a wave upon a shore. I had no plans to even visit France; they are places in Cockermouth I haven't been to yet. My breathing slowed and my head became difficult to hold up. I tried to concentrate on the lesson but that made things worse. I felt like I had been drugged, there was no fighting it. I slumped a little and my pen rolled off the table. Luke looked at me and then faced forward again. That was the last thing I saw. I watched a daydream gladly accept a promotion but then I heard a loud, shrill noise snatch it back. The bell had rung and I was snapped back into the very real world of hungry teenagers, carrying their rumbling bellies off to lunch.

'Thought I had lost you there,' Luke joked. It was a rare occasion when he spoke and he always sounded different to how I remembered.

'Yeah,' I replied.

'It reminds me of the time...' he said.

'Luke, please, this story really isn't about you,' I interjected as politely as I could. He shrugged this off, obviously hurt.

Smells of the canteen wafted through the hallways as I collected my lunch from my locker. That's right; I was now on packed lunches. It was a decision I had made myself so as to avoid any further embarrassment in the school hall while trying to race year sevens to free tables. I now ate in my form room with Randall. He had been a good friend and switched onto packed lunches so I would have some company. Not my first choice, but beggars can't be fussy. He had also switched to a homemade meal because I had told him that school dinners contained a drug to make us comply more with teacher's demands. He was gobsmacked. So while the school gathered in the hall for fine dining I sat in a room with Randall and we scratched the surface of some of life's important topics. We'd talk in great depth about politics or human rights or famous people we'd like to see

naked. We had even started playing cards to pass the time; it was all
very sophisticated. Women always think men only talk about trivial
things. This is something we let them believe - men have their mind
games as well. Women think we are only interested in sport, machines
and female mammary glands. This is so unfair but we have learned to
live with it and even take advantage of it. If they want to think we are
that shallow then so be it. I took a bite out of my sandwich as Randall
got the ball going.

'Did you watch the news last night?'

'Of course, of course.'

'It's terrible, since the war broke out its something like three
thousand dead already.'

'I know.'

'The presenter has such amazing breasts.'

'I know! War has never looked so perky.'

'I wish I could invade her capital.'

'Well played, sir.' You have to give credit where credit is due.

'Speaking of breasts, I saw a woman breastfeeding in public the
other day.' Randall's face morphed as a mix of emotions all fought
for facial dominance.

'Ok,' I said, not sure what response he was hoping for.

'I always find it a bit weird.'

'Randall, breastfeeding isn't weird, it's totally natural.'

'So is masturbating, but I don't do it in front of people.'

'Yes, which is something we're eternally grateful for, but you're
not seriously comparing a mother feeding her young to you having
a Tommy-Tank, are you?'

'I just find it weird. How are you supposed to know where to look?'

'What do you mean? If you're talking to her then look her in the
eye. She's not getting her breast out to confuse you.'

'And why do we start off in life drinking our mothers' milk and
then, before we know it, we're drinking milk from a completely
different species altogether?'

'You mean cows?'

'Yeah.'

'I can't answer that. What have you got against cows?'

'I just don't get why it has to be cows.'

'Well I don't know, what would you rather – cats?'

'There are just so many things I don't know about.'

'Ignorance is bliss.'

'What does that mean?'

'Exactly.'

I dealt another hand and waited for Randall to organise his cards. The room was quiet but we weren't alone. A few nerds were sitting here and there, hiding from people that didn't understand them. The form room was a safe haven for outcasts like us. People at the upper levels of the school hierarchy would never find us here. This was a room full of equals and for an hour a day we could relax and breathe. I had nothing to worry about. The form room door opened and Molly and a couple of friends came in.

I started to worry.

I began heating up. That prickly kind of heat you get all over when you're embarrassed. I was suddenly conscious of every move I made. She spotted me - a packed lunch, playing cards with Randall, surrounded by nerds in a form room at lunch. This was social suicide.

What am I talking about? I wasn't anywhere near cool enough to commit social suicide. This was pretty standard for me. Think positively. Cards are cool. James Bond plays cards and you can't get much cooler than him; poker is very sophisticated. Molly was heading over.

'Hello Toby.'

'All right,' I said without looking at her, pretending I was focusing on the cards I was holding.

'Playing cards?' she wondered.

'Yeah, just a flutter,'

'Cool. What's it called?' she asked.

'Shithead,' Randall said without a second thought and I sort of coughed and snorted at the same time. I had been so fixated on how I could mess this opportunity up that I had almost forgotten that Randall could do that with minimal effort.

'What?' Molly said.

'The game. It's called Shithead,' Randall repeated, in a tone that suggested he was amazed not everyone in the world knew about it. It is a superb card game, it just has an odd name, although it is also known as Palace, Shed or Karma. Rules vary depending on region but the object of the game is to lose all of your cards, with the last player to do so being the eponymous 'shithead'. With a standard, shuffled deck of fifty-two cards, each player is dealt three cards in a row, face down. Players are not allowed to see or change these cards. On top of these three cards, three further cards are placed face up and then the remaining cards in the deck are dealt out (just three each, the rest acting as a stack to pick up from - you have to have three cards in hand at all times until this stack has gone), which the players hold. After the cards have been dealt, players lay cards in turn, starting with anyone who has a three. If nobody has a three, then the holder of a four must lay and so on. Play will continue in a clockwise direction until the cards dictate otherwise. You can lay more than one card at a time as long as it's the same number, equal to or higher in value than the one at the top of the pick-up pile. If you can't play a card then you have to take the pick-up pile. Collecting the pick-up pile can put that player at a great disadvantage, although it is still possible to quickly recover from this. Once you've played your hand you then play the three face-up cards and then the three face down cards (which are also known as blind cards). The first to do so has won the game. Playing four of a kind will burn the pick-up pile and start it again. The player who clears the pick-up pile may then play another card to start a new pile. The two, five and ten are known as wildcards with special attributes. The two means the next player can lay any card they like, the five means the order of play is reversed and the ten burns the pile in the same way four of a kind does. I should have talked about it in enough detail for you to have a game (I've probably missed a couple of things). Don't do it now though because you're reading. I've rambled on, but it really is a great game.

Regardless of how good a game Shithead is it's not something I'd want a girl to know I was playing. As much as skill was considered when the game was conceived, I can't help but feel that maturity was sidelined when naming the poor thing. With a better name it could really catch on, but as things stood Molly was looking at me as if I had picked my nose and was waiting to see whether I'd eat it or not. Randall could have said Texas Hold 'Em, Gin Rummy or even Snap for all I care, but Molly had asked a question he knew the answer to and in his mind it required no more thought beyond that. I had the urge to voice justification, to express just how much skill was involved, that a good memory was key and that planning four or five turns in advance was essential to victory, but no matter how you look at it I was playing a game called Shithead.

'...or we normal people call it Karma,' I said after a year had gone by. Good save, Toby.

'Oh right,' she said. I finally had the nerve to meet her eye. It was only then that I noticed she was wearing her coat, the same coat that had temporarily found its way into my possession. I missed that coat, I missed the smell and the ephemeral hope of it symbolising something more than an odd clothing loan.

'Are you well?' I began, but her friends were calling for her attention. She turned to them and then back to me.

'Oh, you know,' she smiled.

'Molly?'

'Yes?'

I froze. I knew what I wanted to say, I knew how to say it, I could hear the words in my head right that second but nothing came out. Her friends called for her again.

'I've got to go.' She smiled and then she walked away. Even Randall looked disappointed in me. He played his last remaining card.

'Shithead,' he said bluntly and it was hard to believe he was talking about the game.

I stood up.

'Molly?' I shouted over the noise of the room. A shout was over the top; it was a quiet collection of people – my outburst even made a few of them jump. Molly had opened the form door but she turned to me. Her friends surrounded her. Everyone was watching me with anticipation.

I walked over to her, shuffling and bumping into things on my way.

'Can I walk you home after work this weekend?'

'Yes,' she said. All her friends erupted into fits of giggles and then they poured out into the corridor, dragging Molly away from me. I watched them go and glanced the other way to see Jacob staring at me. He looked at Molly as she headed away down the hallway, clearly noticing the coat, and then back to me. I smiled a very weak smile and slipped back into the form room, pulling the door behind me. It clicked closed and I let the potential happiness wash over me. I pretty much minced back to Randall and reclaimed my seat.

'Who is the shithead now?' I said.

'Yes, yes, well done. Very brave.'

'It *was* brave, which can be more than said about you and Mrs Tuck.'

'Brave? I'll tell you what bravery is.'

'Go on then.'

'Ever heard of a panic wank?'

I took a moment to study his face but he was being serious.

Sigh.

'Go on...'

'It's where you're "pleasing yourself" and then you call for your mum and you have to try and finish before she reaches you. It's terrifying. That's bravery.'

'That is the stupidest thing I've ever heard of.'

'Is it though?'

'Yes. What do you mean it's terrifying? Oh god, Randall, no?' He nodded his head.

'Why? Did the Jones brothers put you up to this?'

'Yeah, they dared me to.'

'If they told you to jump off a bridge would you do it?'

'I did, remember? I got all wet.'

'So you did. What did you expect to find under a bridge?'

'I dunno. I wasn't thinking.'

'Christ, Randall, I can't watch you all the time. Dare I ask what happened with the other thing?'

'Well, it started ok, but I thought my mum was downstairs. She was just across the landing. I didn't have time.'

'Your poor mother.'

'I know. They were disgusted.'

'They?!'

'She was showing some friends round.'

'How have you not died of shame?'

'I'm a teenager, I'm embarrassed about seventy per cent of the time.'

'What's the other thirty?'

'Sleep.'

'And this is all coming from the man that thinks this kind of behaviour is as natural as breastfeeding.' He had no response to this.

'Any time you call for your mum she is just going to ignore you. It's like a pervert's version of the boy who cried wolf.'

I was on a high when lunch ended, regardless of Randall's efforts to bring me down to his level, and I left my form room with renewed vigour for the afternoon ahead. Randall and all his worldly wisdom had scuttled on down the road. Variety is the spice of life and I'm all for trying new things but I thought that meant things like visiting new places or trying a different kind of curry every once in a while. I don't think when that quote first entered common usage anyone at the time was hoping it incorporated "panic wanks". Who invents these things?! I wanted to ring Mrs White and check she was ok. She might not have been that shocked; I think both she and her husband had figured out early on that Randall wasn't going to be a lawyer or a doctor. What was to become of my little sunflower? I had wanted so much for him. I wanted him to stand tall among roses and tulips not be stuck behind a shed with the thistles and weeds. The Jones brothers have a lot to answer for.

My afternoon was set to be one of utter boredom and mind numbing nothingness. I was still banned from P.E. I was glad really, what with the ever-present threat of someone else bringing out my worst. It's supposed to be physical education, but I knew all the rules of football and I knew how to put one leg in front of the other, so there really wasn't much more I could learn about it. It's not like by being banned I was missing something important for an exam later in the year. I'd go as far to say that I knew everything physically educational about football. Let's be honest, I could do sir's job. As long as you blow your whistle every now and then and don't shower with your pupils you'll be fine as a P.E. teacher.

Sir and Chris Peck sat together and I sat a short distance away. They must be pretty close by now. Mr Brown would be telling Chris all about his failed marriage, pouring out his heart like lumpy custard. I was really starting to sympathise with his wife; he doesn't half go on about things, dragging everyone down. I was quite prepared to freeze for the next forty minutes on my own but today I had company. A boy named Evan sat next to me and gave me a little tilt of his head skywards, the universal gesture of "I'm not a mental case". He slipped his arms out of his crutches and sat down.

'What happened?' I asked.

'Bad tackle a week or so ago.'

'It wasn't me, was it?'

'No,' he laughed, 'not one of yours.' I guess I was famous. 'It looks worse than it is. I'm bandaged up pretty tight and I have a toecap on for protection'.

'A what?'

'A toecap.'

'What's a toecap?'

'It's a piece of steel, or you could have leather, fitted over the front part of a shoe as protection or reinforcement. That or you can buy actual toecaps that fit right onto whichever toe needs it. It's like a cast really. Is it true what happened with Neville?'

I blocked him out, my mind was working overtime. A toecap. Could this be the answer I was looking for? Could I at least suppress my power for now? I could move freely around the school, I could play P.E. and I could eat lunch in the hall like normal people. My power would never take me by surprise again. A toecap could at least hide it until I knew more. Then another thought came to me. I could just wear a toecap all the time and not have to bother with any of this hero business. No one need know. I don't owe anyone anything. That wouldn't really solve the problem though, would it? I'd always be left wondering what could have been. There must be a reason why I had been given this power, there must be something I needed it for. My life would always be hindered somewhat if I couldn't fully understand this part of me. I owed it to myself to find out more. It was settled, then. From this day forward I would be known as Toecap.

11

"As a symbol I can be incorruptible" - Batman

Some moments in time are imprinted on our minds forever. Some actions, regardless of location, have such an impact on us as a species that we can never forget them. We can remember exactly what we were doing when they happened. They are detailed memories in which we vividly recall sights, sounds and smells, because of the sheer gravity of the event unfolding at the time. They are events that have shocked the world for eternity, events like 9/11 or when Kerry Katona won Mum of the Year. I would forever remember the day I became Toecap, sitting in the cold, slowly freezing to death.

I don't mind admitting that Toecap isn't the sexiest of names for a superhero. But Toecap is just a name - it's what the name *stands for* that counts. Hopefully, in time, Toecap will come to mean a great deal to the people of this small town. Maybe I'll get my own ale named after me down at the local Jennings brewery. Although people might not want to be reminded of feet when sipping on a refreshing pint. Having said that, in Dawson City, in Canada, more than 65,000 people have consumed a cocktail with a human toe in it. This is absolutely true. It's on the internet, so there's no chance it's made up.

Dawson does indeed have a famous drink, which is called the Sour Toe Cocktail and it contains an actual alcohol-preserved human toe in it. You can have this cocktail for just \$5 and if you drink it you even get a certificate. It all started in 1973 and it's said to be the amputated toe of a miner (the toe had been amputated in the 1920s). To get the certificate the rule is: 'You can drink it fast, you can drink it slow - but the lips have got to touch the toe'.

Do I have ugly feet? I really don't know, having not seen enough feet to build an argument on. You've probably seen better, you've probably seen worse. I'm certainly proud of the strength within mine.

The more I ponder over Toecap the more I like it. It's not as cool as Batman or Wolverine but it's surely more desirable than Mr Fantastic or The Thing. Mr Fantastic is a terrible name. It's the sort of name I imagine hearing at a party when a gay man is introducing his partner. And The Thing just feels lazy; I think they were really up against the clock that day. Could have called him Rocky or Meteor or Ten-Ton, something like that.

Toecap is my alter ego and also an integral part of my costume, much like Superman's cape; he'd feel daft without it. Every now and then in Superman comics, films etc, you see him running off down a side street or alleyway opening his shirt and revealing his costume, but where does he keep his cape? It's not on him all day, how could he hide that under his shirt and tie? He must just keep it scrunched up in a big pocket. A very big pocket. The other thing I don't get is why the homeless people of Metropolis aren't better dressed, given how many suits Clark Kent leaves lying around. It is possible I have spent too long thinking about this.

A couple of days later, a small, square package arrived at the door. Today was hyped up to be a milestone in my life. I opened the delivery and was pleased to find that the Toecap fitted perfectly around my big toe. I would be walking Molly home tonight, which I was very much looking forward to, especially as she had approved it, but tonight would be my first night as Toecap. I'd walk her home first, but then I'd follow my route, in character and keeping the peace. I wouldn't normally take part in my destiny on a Saturday night but this was a trial run as it were, getting the feel of things, the lay of the land. If I got good enough at this maybe I wouldn't have to go to school anymore. I could leave all that behind and do something useful with my life. I wondered what deep underground criminal activity was at work in this old market town. Who would be my first target?

A Chinese drug lord?

A German arms dealer?

A northern pie thief?

The excitement was palpable, but heavily outweighed with nerves. I could run into a Chinese drug lord who would cut off my fingers one by one and send them to my parents or I could piss off a German arms dealer who would rig my home with explosives. Worst of all, Molly might never let me walk her home again. I had to get the walk home with her right. But before that I had a shift to do. Waiting on people was easy. I spent most of my shift checking the time and trying to get Molly's attention. What if she had forgotten? What if she was joking? Was she joking? All her friends laughed when I had asked her. She was joking. Of course she was joking. Why would she let me walk her home? We barely speak. I'm annoyed at myself that it took this long for logic and reasoning to put their hands up in the auditorium of my mind. My cruel mind that so often seats those two near the back. Well, that was that then. After work I would take my frustration to the streets and hope someone smaller and weaker than me would give me reason to vent. Now I was hoping for the rest of the evening to drag; at least at work I could be near Molly.

Food eventually stopped leaving the kitchen and the last mouthfuls of conversations, reunions and romantic gatherings were chewed and swallowed. Women are like meals to me: they turn to shit overnight.

The pub closed its doors and we relaxed a little as we followed the nightly routine of cleaning up and preparing for the next onslaught of hungry diners tomorrow. Eventually Molly grabbed her coat, said her goodbyes and left. My heart sank a little. I don't get it. Maybe she was just being polite and thinking of my feelings by saying yes at school in front of people. Saying no might have been worse but it wouldn't have let me build my hopes up. I mumbled goodbye to everyone, pulled the heavy pub door open and set off into town to begin my new life.

'You ready?' Molly said. She had been waiting outside for me.

'Yes.'

'Well, you know how people can talk,' she explained.

'I thought you had forgotten, or that you were joking.'

'No of course not. Why would you think that?'

'I don't know. Seemed a little too good to be true, maybe.'

'It was sweet of you to ask,' she said. I didn't know what to say and I continued to let her do all the work. 'Are you still in trouble at school?'

'Not really. I'm banned from P.E. but I can think of worse things.'

'You don't enjoy sport?'

'It's ok but it's just an excuse for some of the boys to muck about and try and hurt the others.'

'Like hospitalising someone?' She had a point there.

'That was a one-off. That's not what I'm usually like.'

'What happened?'

'He started it, I promise. Chris Peck is a shitbag and I don't even feel that bad about it.'

'So what about Neville?' Had she been hired by the headmaster to get a confession from me?

'Neville is a dick that can give it but can't take it. He also started it, by the way.'

'A shitbag and a dick, nice.'

'Sorry.'

'Don't be.' We took a turn down another street. Come on Toby, think of something to say, but she beat me to it again.

'They won't bother you again, quick and simple. Must be nice.'

'Is someone giving you trouble?'

'Hmm,' she groaned. We stopped walking.

'Is Jacob still bothering you?'

'He's doing his best.'

'He will tire in time,' I said.

'I'm not so sure.'

I looked at her lips. I had imagined a thousand times what kissing Molly would be like. A thousand is a bit over the top, it wasn't a thousand, but I'd say definitely more than thirty. I imagine kissing her would be much the same as when I practise on my arm, but hopefully with less hair. I could try to steal a quick kiss now and hope she just went with it. It was quite a nice moment though and I didn't want to risk ruining it.

I struggled to think of something to say as we began walking again and the silence was mocking me. In time, her house appeared and I felt utterly useless.

'Thank you for walking me home,' and with that she kissed me on the cheek. 'I'll see you at school.' She was gone. I was dazed. Had that really happened? What was going on in the world? I stood there trying to take it all in. Either Molly Cooper liked me or she was really committed to the joke. Did she have a friend in the bushes filming us? Would the footage be played the next time my year has an assembly. We had kissed, kind of. Shut up, a kiss is a kiss. She had willingly put her lips onto my face. If her friend *had* been filming I would really like a copy. She must like me, at least a little bit. The shock was being replaced with unadulterated joy. I thought today was going to be special because I had become Toecap but Molly dwarfed my superhero status. I felt good about myself, like I could do anything. I was ready for anything. Molly liked me; what could go wrong? I flicked my black hood up and embarked on my first outing as Toecap, smiling all the way.

Town was busy as always at the weekend. Saturday night was well under way. The town had hosted the Friday Fun and now it was time for the Saturday Shag. It's common knowledge that primarily young people paint the town red on Friday nights whereas Saturday sees the more mature come out the woodwork and try to paint the town red with the little paint they have left. It's funny but if you see a young woman pissed and making a fool of herself you just think 'What a nutter!' but if you see a woman in her forties pissed on a Saturday night acting like a right ruddy tit, I feel sorry for her somehow. I want to buy her a mug of soup and tell her everything will be ok. I don't know why that is. Men, regardless of age, are all perverts. There is no cure for it.

I wandered onto Main Street and made my way along. The Fletcher Christian is the last pub I pass this way and I was just coming up to William Wordsworth's house when I heard a noise. I stopped where I was and looked around. It sounded like a scuffle. It was coming from Bridge Street. I peered down and in the darkness I could just make out two bodies. I had never been so excited in all my life. This was only supposed to be a trial run and yet just a matter of feet away from me was an actual crime taking place. I slipped into the darkness and edged my way closer to them. I thought of Molly and her lips upon my cheek. She gave me strength, strength I would use now. One man was holding someone else to the floor and repeatedly thumping them. Short, sharp moans came from the victim.

It was now or never - in at the deep end.

I stepped out into the light and stood with my arms akimbo. I coughed once. My heart was racing. Adrenaline was flooding my body. I was shaking all over but I hoped in the low light it wasn't noticeable. The attacker punched the body on the ground once more before looking up at me.

'Who the fuck are you?!' he hissed, aware that occupied houses surrounded him.

'Step away,' I said. I hadn't practised a hero voice yet and my first warrior words of warning came out as more of a squeak.

'Fuck off!' he reiterated and resumed his mugging. I watched for a little while, not moving.

'I must insist you leave,' I said, louder than before but no more confident. The attacker pulled a wallet from the heap on the ground and headed towards me. He had seemed a lot smaller from a distance. I was regretting this. What the hell was I doing? My power. I needed my power more than ever. I bent my right leg upwards and kicked the ground. Nothing happened.

Shit. I've just remembered.

I'm still wearing my toecap. With the excitement of Molly I had forgotten all about it. I knew it wouldn't work but I kicked the ground again and again. I had to think. I pulled out a pen I had been using at work and took the top off. The attacker laughed and kept heading in my direction. I was shaking violently, barely able to keep a grip of the biro. I could stab him with it and hope the ink would act instantaneously as a debilitating poison. Hopeful. There wasn't much ink left in it though and I didn't know how much was needed to take down a fully grown human. It was a small weapon but a weapon nonetheless. I pulled my arm back ready to strike. The attacker was closing in and the only thing I could think to do was close my eyes. I heard him laugh again. Everything went black.

Nothing.

With my eyes closed my hearing ruled my senses. The first thing I could clearly hear was my heartbeat. It was like a bouncy ball in my ribs. A loud, dull thudding. Aside from that I could hear distant moaning from the man who had been mugged and, oddly enough, that was all. Shouldn't I be in agony by now? What was the attacker waiting for? Did he want me to watch? Had the pen scared him at close proximity? I opened my eyes ever so slightly. Then a bit more. And a bit more.

He was gone.

I turned around and saw him in no rush walking to the end of Bridge Street and then he turned onto Main Street. Well, that was that. No matter what you think, my intentions were good. It was a promising first attempt and I'll have nothing on the contrary said about it. Although something inside of me wonders if absolutely any part of what had just happened would have been any different if I hadn't been here. Someone was mugged and the mugger got away with it. I couldn't even go to the police after the event because when the attacker was close enough for me to see him I had closed my eyes. I wasn't sure what to do now.

The victim was starting to clamber to his feet.

So I ran away. I ran all the way home and sat in my room thinking about what had happened. Ok, so that didn't go as planned. I had hoped I was braver than that. Today was only supposed to be a trial; I wasn't expecting to fight anyone tonight. Although crime wasn't going to wait until I was ready, was it? I needed to always be prepared. This whole foot nonsense was frustrating. I couldn't go into battle hoping it will turn on. I couldn't start every fight by taking my shoes and socks off. I needed to have control. All I'd learned so far was how to stop it; I needed to know how to start it. I needed to switch in and out from that part of me. I had failed, I had let someone down. I had stood by and watched when I should have done more. Right, from then on, I would never just stand by again.

Although, as bad as I felt about the whole thing, I had been kissed by a girl, so, you know - every cloud and all that.

12

On Monday I saw two boys fighting and I just watched. I know I said I wouldn't do this again but this was neither a crime nor that serious. And if I got into any more trouble at school I didn't know what would happen to me. So instead I watched, I mean really watched. Both boys were angry, both stood tall and both had clearly done this before. They were good at it; it was almost a shame when a teacher finally broke it up. When my power was active I didn't have to think about what to do; something took over and I became a single-purpose machine. Everything came back to my power. I had to unlock it. Maybe it just needed more practice. I may have shamed myself by doing absolutely nothing to stop the mugging but it had spurred me on to get straight back out there and try again. Say what you like but I was new to all this and I was doing my best; it's not like there is a guidebook on how to be a hero. I was desperate to show the criminal world that I was only just getting started. If I had used my power last night it would have had a very different outcome. Screw the timetable I had so lovingly prepared and laminated; I would head back out tonight, but I had to get school over with first and that meant conversing with Randall.

'Morning,' I said.

'Good morning,' he replied.

'It is good, isn't it?'

'What is going on?' He could see my eyes twinkling.

'I walked Molly home the other night.'

'That's why you're so happy?'

'She kissed me on the cheek.'

'I kiss my grandma on the cheek every time I see her. So what?' Randall mocked.

'Yes, but presumably you don't fancy your grandma?'

'Er, no way. She's old enough to be my grandma. So what now?'

'I don't know, that's the agony of it.'

'Are you going to ask her out?'

'I really don't know. If Molly and I were together we could double date with you and Mrs Tuck.'

'Why is it that your love is real and mine is a joke?'

'Because I don't crave the affections of a married woman with children.'

'It isn't a problem for me that she has children, I could be a good father to them.'

'One of them is older than you.'

'You have an answer for everything.'

'Smart people do.'

'You will be eating your words when Mrs Tuck and I are together. She is my soulmate.'

'That's hard to believe, especially as you still don't know her first name.'

I'm not sure I believe in soulmates. It's a nice idea but highly unlikely that out of seven billion people on the planet, the one human who is a perfect match for you in every way usually turns out to be living in the same area code. You never hear anyone say, 'I've found my soulmate but annoyingly they live in utter poverty in a third world country and we can't even write because they don't have basic education.' People who claim to be soulmates have always met at a party, met at work or had mutual friends. I think people can be more suited to others but soulmates statistically just doesn't seem likely. Molly wasn't my soulmate, she was all set to be my first love though. And you know what people say about your first love - it's like having the flu, the quicker it's out your system the better for everyone.

But before I knew her, I needed to know myself. I needed to get back on the street and as soon as possible. I needed a win. I needed to take down a two-bit crook or a drug dealer. And surely a druggy would be easy to take down; they are often really skinny and too spaced out to know what's going on, you can just fling them about. You rarely see an overweight drug addict. And what's strange is that with the rest of the west getting fatter and fatter, eventually drug addicts will look better than everyone else. Imagine that reality. All their hard work will have paid off.

A progressively loud beep stole the attention of my ears. They twitched, almost recognising the lifeless robotic melody as it swarmed the air. I had heard it before, years ago, I could swear it. A firm vibration was pulsing from my left leg like a blocked artery. My vision shifted to where these abnormalities were coming from. It was my phone! I had long believed that even my network had decided I was no longer in existence but someone, somewhere in the world had just sent me a text. Oh my god. One of my parents was dead. That was it, I knew it. No one ever texted me, ever. Someone had died. Actually, if one of my parents had died then there was still hope for a revenge story. Someone couldn't have died. Who would text news like that?

I reached into my pocket and pulled out my phone, destroying a handful of cobwebs in the process. One new message. It was from a number I didn't recognise. The plot thickened. Even if someone had the wrong number I could still reply with 'wrong number' and see where it went from there.

The text was from Molly. This was stranger still but she explained in her message that she got my number from work. We kept a list of staff contact numbers on a sheet of A4 paper under one of the tills. How very cheeky of her to take it without permission. I could use that in court if need be. Why hadn't I thought of that?

She thanked me again for walking her home and even asked if she could repay the gesture today. My first thought was that this wasn't Molly texting me. Someone was playing tricks on me. I was starting to doubt that it was even Molly I'd walked home with the other night. It's an elaborate trick for someone to pull off, sure, but it seemed more likely than the girl I liked liking me back. Things like this didn't happen to me, I usually had awful luck and yet I was on a roll at the moment. Who was I to question any of this? Of course

I'd let Molly walk me home. Even if this was a joke, let them joke. Long may this joke continue. I'd smile right up to the punch line. It could end up in the world records for the longest running joke but I wouldn't care. Molly had already kissed my cheek and that was more than I deserved; I might even laugh along when the joke is ultimately revealed. I'd really be dying on the inside but I'd laugh along on the outside.

Hearts are like lifting weights. You have to build up to the big ones. You don't go straight into love because your heart can't handle the lifespan. You build up with crushes, lusts, holiday romances, flings and one-night stands you only talk about with your doctor. By then you're ready to challenge love and the fall isn't so severe. It's like death. That's why children have pets. You build up to the pain and understanding of death. It goes something like goldfish - cat – your nan. You can't jump straight to your nan because it's too much to understand and take in, you're not emotionally ready.

I hadn't really had that many relationships so I was setting myself up for a fall, but once your heart sees something it wants, even your mind finds it hard to resist. You're sucked in and fooled, robbed and stretched out, laughing all the way to the pawn shop selling sentiments of worth for as much as you can get. Molly and I arranged a place to meet and I put my phone back into my pocket so the spiders could regroup and rebuild.

Molly and I hung back a little after school in the hope that not many would see us together (paparazzi can be awfully intrusive, I find). I waved across the locker room and she glared back, a warning to get me to stop and so I pretended to be busy in my locker.

'What is taking so long?' Randall asked, appearing from nowhere.

'Randall! I'm walking home with Molly.'

'I know, what is taking so long?'

'You're not coming! It's just me and Molly.'

'Well how am I supposed to get home?'

'On your own and I'm not drawing you a map again, it takes too long.'

'Oh, charming that is! A girl you know nothing about shows the slightest bit of interest and I'm cast aside like a used tissue.'

'Exactly. I've waited years to replace you and I finally have a shot at it.'

Right, that's it!' And he jerked his bag from his back, unzipped the main pocket and tore out a scrap of paper from the back of one of his exercise books.

'What are you doing?' I asked.

'Oh nothing, just making a list.'

'A list? You are joking. You want me dead because just for one day I won't walk home with you?'

'Yes and that's twice you've appeared on my lists. You don't want there to be a third time!'

'Humour me, what happens after three?'

There will be severe assessments as to whether this friendship will continue.'

'All because I want to walk home with Molly?'

'Bros before hoes. I don't make the rules.'

Molly was walking over. My voice quietened and I was as serious as I could be at this restricted volume.

'Here are my rules. One, you walk behind us, never in line with Molly and me. Two, be respectful, only talk when spoken to. And three, no matter what, don't say a single word. Got it?'

'Fine.'

'Hello,' Molly said.

'Hello,' I replied, leading the three of us out of the school. With Randall walking with us I felt very uneasy. He had me on edge, although to be fair he was following my rules, walking behind us, keeping quiet.

'I didn't think I'd be seeing you again so soon,' I said to Molly.

'Even though we attend the same school and have the same job?'

'I meant, alone, in our own time. Not in an environment where you had to be there. By choice, is what I'm trying to say.'

'You were kind enough to walk me home; it would be rude to not repay'

'So it isn't really by choice, not if you feel you have to.'

'Look, I wanted to walk with you,' she laughed.

We must have been late coming out of school as the streets were all but empty of blue uniforms.

Molly leaned in close and whispered to me, 'Does your friend not talk very much?'

I threw a quick look at Randall, who hadn't heard.

'He's a deep thinker,' I whispered back.

'Oh right, is he clever?'

'Define clever,' I joked, but as she didn't know Randall she didn't understand. I felt a bit mean and the seed of guilt had blossomed into a forest within seconds.

'You ok, Randall?' I asked, cutting the metaphorical trees down, stockpiling for the winter. He looked at me, asking with his eyes if it was really ok to speak. I stretched my smile and he looked as happy as a dog with a bone.

'I'm great, thank you. Just thinking.'

Molly raised her eyebrows as if impressed, whereas my forehead adopted some very advanced wrinkles, years beyond my age.

'What are you thinking about?' she asked him. My wrinkles cemented their position and alerted the brain to the situation unfolding.

'I was just thinking how good you two look together and how in an increasingly cynical world it's empowering to see young hearts resist and find pleasure in something as simple as a short walk together.'

'Aww,' said Molly, as if Randall was a lost puppy (that's two dog similes, no more).

'Fucking hell,' I said without thinking. Damn it, I had broken one of my own rules. Rules specifically designed for Randall.

'Toby!' Molly snapped, disgusted at how I had spoiled the sentiment.

'Sorry,' I said, dumbfounded at Randall's effort. Where had that come from? By doing something nice for me but by doing it unexpectedly it had still managed to blow up in my face. He was shining in comparison.

After everyone had a moment to appreciate Randall's thought, which deep down I'm happy he'd shared, Molly continued digging for more gold.

Are you single, Randall?'

The hell was this?! I had shown her two of the three steps to being the world's greatest waiter, walked her home and, let's not forget, taken immaculate care of her coat. Randall had spouted one line and suddenly Molly wanted to know if he was available, so much so that she hadn't beaten around the bush at all and had come right out and asked. I was gobsmacked. If Molly and Randall got together I might have to make my own list.

'Yes, I'm single,' Randall sighed as if he was a failed connoisseur in the art of love. He was repeatedly breaking rule number three and he didn't care who knew it. I should have drawn him a map and sent him on his way. I don't know why he didn't just push me out into the road.

'I have a friend who would be perfect for you,' she explained.

I'm back in the game.

'Really?' said Randall.

'Yeah, give me your number and I'll pass it onto her'

'Great,' I said, realising I hadn't spoken for a while.

'What is her name?' said Randall.

'Willow,' Molly offered.

'I like trees!' Randall said. Then he squealed, 'Ah!' and clutched his chest.

'What's wrong?' Molly and I said in unison.

'I'm in love,' Randall replied.

When it finally came time to bid Randall goodbye I didn't drag it out. He had done enough for one day. My planned walk with Molly, alone, had whittled down to a mere thirty yards of asphalt. At a pace of several yards a second I had an impossible amount of time to think of something sweet, funny and thoughtful, all in equal parts and delivered in one. So I just came right out and asked her.

'Would you like to come in?'

'Ok.'

As we approached the front door I warned Molly that my mum would be in, but with a bit of luck she would be tucked away in her studio, painting the Lake District with the radio on. I took hold of the handle and turned it slowly. I pushed the door open and silently signalled for Molly to follow. Once inside I took the lead and headed upstairs to my room. My door was closed and my memory began to fail me. I couldn't remember what state I had left my bedroom in. I was quite a tidy person, certainly for a teenager. I haven't seen Molly's room; that could be a right tip. I opened the door and had a quick scan before I let her in. There were some clothes on the floor and my bed wasn't made but apart from that it was ok. She came in and I closed the door. We were safe. Molly instantly began patrolling the room, looking for anything that might have an interesting story behind it.

'Toby?' my mum shouted from downstairs. 'Is that you?'

'Yeah,' I shouted back. There was nothing after that. Molly touched the odd thing and laughed now and then. It seemed just yesterday I was stalking her over the internet. Within weeks I had her in my room and laughing at my belongings. I had a girl in my room. Not the first but certainly the first that I really wanted here. You have to kiss a few toads and with Molly in my room all other previous relationships were automatically reduced to practice. Harsh, but what are you gonna do? Love is merciless. Everything that had come before had merely been leading to this moment in time. I think I have kissing pretty much in the bag and I knew basic pulling procedure, like build-up to touching, don't just start kissing and then give her boobs a honk. It's not a sprint. What am I saying? It's nothing but a sprint at this age. It's a 'do as much as you can before an adult catches you' age.

I was getting ahead of myself. With each object Molly touched she questioned its history and I made them as interesting as my limited imagination could. Eventually she sat down on my bed, soaking it all in. She smiled at me. I think that was her approval. I sat down next to her and asked how she had been. She asked if I had heard why she and Jacob had split up, and I didn't know the answer. Then she asked if I knew why she'd got a job at the Old Grey Goat Inn, and I didn't know the answer.

Then she kissed me.

It was sudden and full throttle. Procedures were abandoned from both parties and hands roamed with V.I.P. passes, encapsulated in pure excitement and wonder. Our teeth made contact twice and every now and then we'd catch each other with our eyes open. It was over as quickly as it had begun. We were breathless and our hands receded. We fell onto our backs and took a moment to collect ourselves.

The front door opened and very quickly footsteps were heard coming up the stairs. I knew that rhythm. It was my dad. We jolted upright and checked we were both decent. Molly stood and fixed her hair by touch. I stood up and looked towards the door. There was a knock.

'Yes?' I called out. After a pause the door opened and my dad stood there looking at Molly.

'Oh, hello,' he said.

'Hello,' Molly replied.

'Dad, this is Molly. Molly, this is my dad, Sam.'

'How do you do, Molly?'

'I'm very well, thank you,' Molly answered, both of them reading from a very predictable script.

'Did you want something?' I asked.

'Yes,' he said, still looking at Molly, weighing her up.

'Which was...?'

'We are having to eat early as your mother and I are out tonight. Will you be joining us, Molly?'

She had been put on the spot but she took it in her stride. 'If you'll have me.'

I didn't know whether she was just being polite but if she didn't want to eat here she could have made an excuse. My dad left, closing the door behind him. I had never had a girl stay for a meal before and Molly was about to embark upon conversation with my parents and we're not even a couple. I should be more relaxed but it felt like Molly and I should be together, so having a meal with the parents was a big deal, it was important. After what had just happened I would have thought we were more than friends. I wanted to be in a relationship with her; I've pursued her for some time. I don't go around kissing just anyone like that and I hoped she was the same. We hadn't had the chance to talk about it though because my oaf of a father had barged in. It hadn't been that long since she was with Jacob. Maybe she was just wanting some fun. Do people do that after a relationship? If they do they should really make that clear to all interested parties. They should wear a badge or something. Molly must know I like her. Women know that sort of thing. And I certainly got the impression she liked me. Why can't we just come out and say it. But I don't want to say something if it's not so. I don't want to ruin whatever this is. Does everything need a label? Molly was at my house and we had just had a mini romp on the bed. I should be pleased but the idea of her romping on other beds made me feel sick. I *did* want a label for this. I wanted her to wear a big fat label hanging from her neck saying 'SOLD' or, failing that, a cow bell, informing everyone that she was mine.

Was that wrong? I wanted her to romp only with me. I had kissed my toads but what if I was a toad to her? It was painful thinking that one day Molly might think of me as 'practice'. So many things to think about. Molly really didn't seem the type to be romping (I keep using that word and I don't even like it) around. We had been growing close, very close indeed if the last twenty minutes are anything to go by. Everything was much simpler before today. Before today I had wanted to kiss her, that was my goal. Now I wanted more. I wanted everything. She had soft lips, like marshmallows, with dimples either side. What if I never kissed her again? What if that had been my only kiss with her? What if I was rationed to just one? She could leave my room and never speak a word of this to anyone; it would be her word against mine. I could have just made it up. How did I know it was even real?

'Toby?' she said. 'It's going to be fine.'

'Are you sure you want to do this?'

She walked over to me and we kissed again. Then we went downstairs and I was tortured for an hour and fifty-two minutes. I counted.

I put on my black hoody while Molly thanked my parents for a lovely meal. I smiled sarcastically at them and said I wouldn't be long. I opened the front door and the cold came in. Molly had her things and after a final goodbye we left. As soon as we were outside I apologised profusely for every single word exchanged during the course of the meal. Molly laughed loudly and told me not to be silly.

'Your parents are great.'

'They're not usually like that.'

'And your mum! She's so talented with her art.'

'Yeah, she's not bad reall-'

'And your dad is hilarious,' she interrupted and started laughing again.

'He's really not. He's so embarrassing.'

'He's you're dad, he's supposed to be like that. I look forward to embarrassing my kids - it's one of the joys of being a parent, don't you think?'

'Yeah, I suppose it is.'

'Do you think you'll have children?'

'I haven't really thought about it. Seems a long way off.'

Was she just asking because it had come up in conversation or was this one of those tests that women do? We'd kissed, so was she now trying to weigh up what sort of man I was going to be? Trying to find compatibilities? Whether we wanted the same things from life? I had never had to think about children before. I was just a kid myself. I had spent so much time thinking about my power that I didn't know what I was going to do after I had finished school.

In that moment I realised something. Superheroes don't have children. The life of a hero doesn't allow it because it's too dangerous. Children become a means of getting to the hero and you can't put people in danger like that. Although I wasn't a superhero. I hadn't done anything heroic yet. I had tried to stand up for someone and I had proved useless. I had tonight to change things around though. Possibility lingered in the air, ready for the taking. We walked in silence for some time.

'You've been quiet. Have I done something wrong? Was it about what happened in your room?' said Molly.

'Wrong? God no. Nothing's wrong.'

'Are you sure?'

'What happened in my room was great. It was more than great. I didn't want it to stop.' This was more convincing. Molly blushed.

'So I'll see you soon?'

'Of course,' I smiled. Her front door opened and there stood her parents. I suddenly felt very aware I was being watched. Her dad stood with his arms crossed, making sure I knew who the alpha male was in this scenario. Her mum waved and she thanked me for having her daughter. I smiled and Molly giggled.

I had a power. I had a superhero name. I had a costume and a goal. But then there was Molly. Could I have both? Could I be a superhero and get the girl? I was wearing my toecap now, my power was restrained. I could still taste Molly on my lips. Our quick fumble on the bed was exciting. I thought about it now and tried to remember the details. She was a great kisser. She was firm but somehow soft at the same time. Listen to me blabbering on as if I know what I'm talking about. I liked kissing Molly. I liked Molly. Who says I have to choose? I could have both if I wanted and I did want both. I wanted to know how far my power could go and I wanted to be with Molly. I was on my designated route tonight. Take two. My first outing hadn't gone so well, so I wasn't sure about tonight, but there was a time when I could only dream about kissing Molly and look what had happened with that. I had an ability to surprise myself and it was rare for me to be caught off guard.

Jacob and his friends leaked out of the darkness and made themselves aware.

They had caught me off guard.

'Who are you trying to be?' said Jacob. I stayed quiet. Jacob was such a dick, hanging around Molly's house most nights, spying on her. It wasn't healthy, for him or me.

'Who are you? And what are you doing around here?'

If he found out it was me he might have just enough brain cells to add to the equation that I was seen here not so long ago, and wearing a woman's coat at that. Even he could put this together and work out what was going on. I couldn't let him find out it was me. His friends spread out and tried to lock me in.

The story goes that every generation has a Ghost Rider. Some damned soul, cursed to ride the earth collecting on the Devil's deals. Many years ago, a Ghost Rider was sent to the village of San Venganza to fetch a contract worth one thousand evil souls. But that contract was so powerful he knew he could never let the Devil get his hands on it. So he did what no Rider has ever done before. He outran the Devil himself.

I was no Ghost Rider but Jacob was certainly the Devil. I eyed up his friends and picked the smallest. I charged at him, taking the offensive to them. He panicked and I knocked him down. I picked up my pace and tried my best to outrun them. They were delayed in giving chase. I didn't dare look behind me. I ran as fast as I could. I cut through gardens and slipped down alleyways to try to throw them off course. I couldn't hear them but it was hard to hear anything with this hood on. I turned a corner and decided to have a quick look behind me. SMACK! I was airborne and coming down to crash land. Someone had shot straight into me. I fell onto my bum and rolled backwards over myself. Whoever had hit me had also come down. It was a man with a handbag. I quickly got to my feet and stood over the transvestite. His head came up for air and I instinctively stamped on

the back of his knee, crushed between the concrete and my shoe. He
yelped like a dog. He wasn't going to stand up for some time. I pulled
my hood up over my head and picked up the handbag. A woman
came crying into view and a man came running over from the other
side of the street to see what was going on.

'Thank you, thank you, thank you!' she said. She reached out for
her handbag and I let her take it. After a quick check to make sure
nothing had been removed she went back to thanking me.

'Are you ok miss?' someone new asked, while giving me a funny
look. Neither could see my face and I just stood still, looking behind
me now and then to see if Jacob and his mates had caught up. The
man on the floor was rocking back and forth cradling his knee.

'I'm fine, thanks to this young man.' She smiled through her tears
and hugged her handbag.

'What's your name, lad?' the man asked. I didn't say anything.

'I'm Toby,' I said in my head but no sound came out. A part of me
had enjoyed this. I had done something good for no personal gain;
this was exactly the sort of result I wanted. It had been accidental
but no one knew that. To all intents and purposes I had gone out of
my way to stop a crime. I was her hero. She had needed help from
someone and it was me that had answered the call. I had stepped up
and I didn't have a scratch on me. The man on the floor must have
been twice my age at least and he lay defeated on the ground from
one serendipitous hit. I still hadn't answered the question.

'Lad, what's your name?' he asked again. From under my hood
my mouth opened, my throat cleared and I said 'Toecap' for the first
time.

'Toecap?' The man grimaced. 'Really? That's what you're
going for?'

'Yes, shut up, its Toecap,' And then I disappeared into the night.
I didn't look back. I ran and ran. By the time I got home I was out
of breath. Back in my room I could still smell Molly's presence. I
looked at my bed where she and I had been only hours ago. And
then I thought about what had just happened. It had been a vast
improvement from my first encounter with the enemy, however
unplanned it had been. I'm at a 50 per cent success rate now. But
I had only won tonight by accident. We had run into each other. If
he had come around the corner and picked a fight with me rather

than fall into one, who's to say what could have happened? I could be injured right now or possibly worse. I'd had a loss and a win. 1-1. I'd let fate decide. I'd go out once more and see what happens. If I won, I'd continue and if I lost then I'd bow out and devote my life to Molly Cooper. That's fair. Best out of three.

There was a knock at my door.

'Can I come in?' my mum said softly though the wood. I gave a quick scan around the room just to check everything was ok and then I opened the door.

'What's up, mum?'

'Just wanted to have a chat, make sure you're ok.'

'Make sure I'm ok?'

'You know what I mean. Did Molly get home ok?'

'No, she didn't make it, I'm just about to call the police.'

'She's nice. Your father and I like her.'

'Good. I like her too'.

'Do you think we'll be seeing more of her?'

'I don't know.'

'We're pleased for you. Well, just take your time, slow and steady is the key.' I didn't know if this was my mum giving away the trade secrets of a happy marriage or her way of telling me she doesn't want me bringing girls home when no one was in. I went for the former.

'I will.' My replies were getting short; I wanted her out the room and for this little 'chat' to be over. It's weird talking about these things with my mum and dad. I yawned in an over-the-top manner and she wished me goodnight. Once alone I got ready for bed and before I knew it I had drifted off.

13

"I've done terrible things too" - Spiderman

I slept well that night but days had passed since. Only you and I know that what happened was a fluke, but maybe I could make a career out of that. There must be some people in the world that enjoy successful lives founded on dumb luck. Individuals that bask in consistently poor but somehow profitable choices. You often hear about people who were just in the right place at the right time. I was one of those people but I'd never admit that. If anyone asked, which they wouldn't because I was masked as Toecap and no one knows who that is, I would be adamant that I had stalked my prey and taken action at the opportune moment. I don't think even the mugger knew it was an accident. I almost bounced back up whereas he had, fortunately, taken a nasty fall. I hadn't even had to use my power. I had been a hero without it. I think we should stop talking about it being an accident. It was, yes, but that's not what's important. I had stopped a crime. It doesn't matter how or whether it was intentional. I had been integral in a positive outcome, that's all anyone needed to know. I had even got my name out there. I had spoken to the public as a hero. Damn, I wish I had a catchphrase. I had run off having told someone to shut up - that won't do. Something else to think about. As a hero I was at a fifty per cent success rate. Not bad, the same odds as flipping a coin, supposedly.

Persi Diaconis is a professor of mathematics and statistics at Stanford University. It might also be worth mentioning that he was formerly a professional magician – that must have got him laid a lot, seriously. He and his fellow researchers discovered that in most games of chance involving coins, the odds aren't as even as you think. They found that even the coin toss isn't really 50/50. It's closer to 51/49 biased towards whichever side was facing upwards when the coin was thrown in the air. Don't get shirty if you disagree, this is just something I've read.

If you take a standard American penny, with the Lincoln Memorial on the back, and spin it, the penny will land tails side up roughly 80% of the time. The reason for this is that the side with Lincoln's head on it is a bit heavier than the flip side, causing the coin's centre of mass to lie slightly toward heads. So if you're an itinerant conman in America there is a career for you.

Fifty per cent - wiggle room for improvement. I was even more excited about getting back out in the field. I had had a bad first take and a lucky second. My third run out was going to be the one. It was going to cement my new life and quell the doubts that formed in my mind every time I was in danger. I had helped someone without even meaning to, I was clearly born to be a hero.

I would get out again tonight. My schedule had been laid off, crime can't be scheduled. I would shine under the moonlight, brighter than the stars. Right now though, I was just lying in bed, staring at the ceiling. Sunday is a beautiful day, meant for reading the paper, roast dinners and open fires. Light seeped in and explored my room through cracks in the curtains. My bed was warm and left me uninterested in the world outside of it. Are there any jobs where you can work from your bed? Besides a hooker I mean. I couldn't do that kind of work; night shifts are very unsociable. Prostitution is a very old business and still going strong as far as I know. Probably one of the few jobs where office romances don't occur. Maybe they do, far be it from me to make assumptions (or is it presumptions? I'm not sure I know the difference) on the inner workings of an industry I'm not involved in. Maybe they do find love. Maybe they find love, take bank holidays off and have Christmas staff parties - I really don't know. I could always befriend a hooker and find out, but they work nights and I'm at school during the day, see what I mean? The hours aren't good for me. I wonder if I could love a hooker. I know they are people just like you and me but it's hard to picture leaving the house in the morning and calling over my shoulder, 'Have a good day at work, dear.' Sex might be odd as well; if she's had a stressful day at work the last thing she is going to want to come home to is candlelight and the very best of Celine Dion. I could maybe date a part-time hooker. A 'three-day-week' kind of lady. But I don't know if you get part-time and full-time prostitutes. Look, I don't want to date a hooker; I'm going to leave it at that.

I don't think we get many hookers in Cockermouth and if we do I'm just going to avoid that crime. I'm not taking on any pimps, it's too much hassle.

My phone beeped and I knew it would be Molly. She had no plans (we have so much in common) and she wondered if Randall and I wanted to go out. This was great, but why did she want Randall there? Did she consider them friends already? I texted back saying I'd have to find out what Randall was doing, even though I knew fine well he would have nothing in the diary. She replied saying he needed to be there as she would be bringing Willow. A double date - nice. I texted Randall and jumped out of bed, releasing all the heat and dreams that had seen me through the night. Once on my feet I looked down at them and smiled. 'One day we won't need these,' I said out loud, picking up two toecaps and heading for the shower.

I was getting used to wearing my toecaps. They were uncomfortable to start with but we all have to put up with our hardships. I was glad to have them. After showering I put on dark clothes just in case we stayed out longer than expected and I could do my route without having to go home for a pit stop first.

It was a coldish day but birds were tweeting and now and then the sun stopped hiding behind the clouds. Randall was waiting outside and wondering what I wanted from him as I had chosen not to explain in my message. I wanted to surprise him.

'Just follow me,' I said. 'I have a surprise.'

'A surprise? I'm not sure I like surprises.'

'Do you like women?'

'Yes.'

'Then you'll like this surprise.'

'Is it a bike?'

'Where did you get that from?'

'So it's not a bike?'

'If you're lucky it might be a kind of bike.' I winked.

'I'm confused,' he said. Somehow I wasn't surprised.

'Just follow me.'

We headed for Harris Park, where Molly and Willow were already waiting.

'Glad you could make it,' Molly said to Randall after smiling at me. Randall was still confused. He looked at Willow and then at me.

'She doesn't look anything like a bike,' he said. I was mortified. Molly frowned and Willow didn't understand what was being suggested.

'Ha ha, what is he like?' I laughed it off. 'Are you both well?' There was a moment more of agonising silence.

'Riigghht,' Molly said.

'Fine thanks,' said Willow. 'Is this Randall?' she asked and he nodded.

'Come on then!' she squeaked and took him by the hand, leading him deeper into the park. Molly looked at me.

'A bike?'

'Who knows what goes through his mind?' She didn't believe me but she didn't pursue it. We linked arms and began walking in their direction. Randall and Willow were sitting on the swings and looking over at the tennis courts as a father drilled into his boys the perfect serving technique that he had been shouting at the TV for years. They were all smiles when we finally caught up with them. Willow slumped off her swing and giggled over to Molly, snatching her away from me. I took her seat and clasped the chains with both hands.

'What are you both smiling about?'

'I asked her out,' said Randall.

'That explains why she's laughing.'

'She said yes.'

'You're going out?!'

'Yeah.'

'How long did it take Molly and I to walk over here?!'

'Pretty good eh?'

'Do you not think it's a bit sudden?'

'She's nice. What else do I need to know?'

'So you just asked her out?'

'She might not be a bike but I like her.'

'That's not how these things work. They take time, you have to give them time.'

'What do I know of time? I don't even know how much time I have. I can't plan my life around a measurement I can't quantify.'

'So if you see something you want you just go for it?'

But Randall had stopped listening. I was looking at Molly and Willow laughing. I wanted to bottle her laugh and pickle my ears in it. Randall was one of the thickest people I have ever met and yet, annoyingly, every now and then he left me feeling like I had misunderstood a fundamental of life which required no thought from him to process. He saw something he wanted and went for it. A beautiful mantra stitched into the very fabric of his being. He failed every school test and yet in the life exam I was having to copy his work, peering over his shoulder, hoping no one could see me struggling. He was an enigma. Willow didn't know his second name and she had agreed to pursue a deeper connection. Would Molly say yes if I asked her out? Willow came back to Randall and they began kissing. I jumped off the swing and headed for Molly.

'Aw, how sweet!' she said when I was close enough.

I panicked.

'Yeah, it's good. Can I ask you something?'

'Of course,' she replied, but as she did a yellow fuzzy blur whizzed past and we both jumped. A tennis ball had landed near us. I looked over to the courts and a middle-aged man shouted for help. I had only wanted to ask her out, now I was going to have to display some sort of physical strength in front of her. I bent over and picked the ball up. I gently squeezed it and looked back at the dickhead who had thrust his balls into my life. I eyed up my target and took aim. Even Randall and Willow had stopped snogging to join Molly in spectating.

It's just throwing a ball.

It's just throwing a ball.

I snapped my arm back and released. The ball landed roughly half way between me and the world's greatest tennis coach. He looked at me like I'd run naked onto the court and pissed on his kids' shoes.

Randall and Willow started kissing again and Molly politely said nothing. The father was still marching over to get the ball when I sat down opposite Molly again, only this time my face was a cracking shade of crimson - hot enough to fry an egg on.

'What was it you were going to ask me?'

I couldn't ask her now; if my face turned any hotter the fire service would be called out. But asking a question you might not like the answer to might be better to ask if already embarrassed. The damage has been done. Randall could do it, he just had. I never thought my inspiration to do something would come from Randall White. Come on, Toby, take a leap.

'Will you go out with me?'

'About bloody time. Yes I will.' And then we kissed. When that ended I wondered, what happens now? I looked at Randall and Willow, who were somehow still kissing. Molly and I had done that bit; I was looking to him for the next stage.

'We need a song,' she said.

'What?'

'We're a couple now, we need a song!' she said as if I was stupid and should know about these things. Randall and Willow probably had a song. 'I'm going to get my iPod out and the first song that plays on random will be our song.' I was suddenly excited to be embarking on this new experience together and at the possibilities of what it might be. She fumbled for a moment and then pressed play. Lights flashed and "Club Foot" by Kasabian began. She expressed her love for this song and I smiled at the almost apt name. We had our song. That was pretty easy. We had picked a song together and now I felt a bit better about getting a house and raising a family. I loved "Club Foot". We let the song play through to the end (apparently another rule) and then she turned off her iPod.

The rest of the day melted away. We stayed in the park for a little while and then headed into town to get a bite to eat. We drifted in and out of every shop the town could offer. Hours disappeared as the four of us rediscovered Cockermouth with new eyes. In time Willow and Randall headed for home and Molly asked me to walk her back. On this occasion we stopped round the corner from her parents' house so we could eat each other's faces off. She tasted different now we were going out. Not bad different, just different different. We were getting good at kissing. Once we had swapped enough saliva Molly hid any evidence her face had been visited and we finally reached her house. Her parents were there again, waiting on the doorstep as she walked up the drive. Her dad waved at me this time and Molly blew me a kiss.

Her dad stopped waving.

The door shut, she was gone, and I was in agony. Time in between her was of no use to me. Then I remembered what that time was for. I put my game face on. I felt invincible these days. Love is more powerful than most things. I wanted to find danger tonight; I was on a roll. Molly made me want to do good.

I walked the streets, checked the alleyways and even returned to Bridge Street where I had had my first encounter. Nothing. The evening was settled and the night sky faded in above me as I continued down Bridge Street and crossed the water that lead to Memorial Gardens. I took a right after the bridge and followed the path alongside the river and round. No one was about except a dog walker who had lost his dog - I'm assuming it was a dog he was looking for in the bushes. Across the river opposite from me I could make out Cockermouth Castle. I found a nearby bench and seated myself to admire the view. A dog could be heard barking for its owner and the slight sloshing of the river running by me sounded strong between its banks. I waited for some time with my hood up. Molly and I texted, I sorted my emails out and got a new high score on a game designed to make you forget you have real friends. Finally I decided to ehad home. I retraced my steps and came back to Bridge Street. Déjà vu. A man was held against a wall by another man, who was demanding his wallet. He smacked the victim's head against the wall.

'Step away,' I said, remembering that that's what I had said last time. Why couldn't I think of something better than that? Two thumps to the stomach and the victim lay winded on the floor. The attacker turned to me and said something I wasn't expecting.

'Back again, kid?' It was the same man I had done nothing to stop last time, in the same place and, for all I knew, attacking the same person. I had no idea what to say. The attacker put the wallet into his pocket and walked over to me. My heart rate sky-rocketed and adrenaline did its thing. I pictured Molly and this time I wasn't shaking. Adrenaline was present but under control and my heart rate kept me focused. Closer and closer he came. I just needed to trigger my power. I had taken my toecap off while admiring the castle. I lifted my foot and kicked the ground to transform myself. Nothing happened. Shit. A bear of a man stood over me and laughed in my face.

'Quite the little hero, aren't you?' he mocked, eyeing me up and down. 'Tell you what, I'll let you throw the first punch,' and with that he lowered his face and placed his arms behind his back. I looked at him for a moment, trying to gauge his seriousness.

'Go on.' And he leaned in a little closer. It was now or never. Maybe I was stronger than I knew. Maybe I didn't need my power. I stepped backwards and raised my fist. I had never punched someone without my power before. I pulled back and hit him in the face, which barely moved. It was like hitting a stone wall. My knuckles felt shattered. He laughed and without warning he returned the favour. My head spun round and took my body with it. Tears formed and it felt like I had been shot in the face with a brick. I fell to the floor and covered up. The man took out his phone and began recording me as he proceeded to kick me in the ribs and stand on my ankles. He laughed for the duration. I cried and called out but no one came.

'Oi!' came a cry from across the bridge and a dog came barking to my assistance. The attacker stopped recording and legged it, laughing as he went. The dog owner was old and slow. It gave me time to get to my feet and disappear. Moving required all my remaining strength. I hobbled off into the darkness and sat down against a wall to catch my breath. My ribs made breathing difficult and my ankles were painful to walk on. Worst of all was my face. Luckily for me nothing was bleeding. I just wanted to be home, in bed. I had taken a beating, someone had been mugged and the attacker had gotten away, again! Why had he recorded it? What was that about? To show his mates? For his own pleasure? I got to my feet once more and was on my way, every step painful. Never again. I was done with this. It wasn't right for me. It took an age for me to get home but I managed to sneak in undetected. I crawled upstairs and rolled into bed, defeated. With a bit of luck no one would ever find out about this.

14

I couldn't sleep. Every turn, twist and roll was met with pain. I got up and checked my face in a small mirror I keep in my room. There was some slight swelling. No visible cuts or bruising, which was lucky and so nothing I'd have to explain. My ribs, however, were in agony and they were bruised. I could barely stand up straight. There was no way I was going to school today. After checking myself in the mirror I climbed back into bed and buried myself away.

'You getting up today?' My dad shouted while knocking on my bedroom door.

'I'm not well,' I called back and he entered. I rarely take days off school. I get ill but never quite ill enough to stay home.

'What's the matter with you?' he asks with a weird mixture of intrigue and disbelief.

'It's my stomach, and I've got a blinding headache.' I wasn't even lying.

'Hmmm,' my dad said, coming to stand by me. This really wasn't his area of expertise.

'Nothing to do with Molly?' A stab in the dark. He whispered this as well, as if my mum could hear him through several doors, walls and floors. Some women do have superhuman hearing. Men have something similar, called selective hearing.

'Molly? No of course not. What's Molly got to do with me being ill?'

'All right, don't have a go. You just got back late and now you don't want to go to school. Just thought something might have happened walking her home last night.'

'I'm just not well, dad. Every now and then I get ill.'

'Oh ok, I'll let your mother know and one of us will phone the school.' Why hadn't I just been honest when I got in last night? If I'd told him I was beaten up walking home I'd surely be allowed a day or two off anyway. Part of me was embarrassed, I guess. I just wanted to forget what had happened, put it behind me. My bedroom door closed and then opened again several minutes later. It was my mum, somehow covered in paint already.

'You ok, sweetie?' she said sympathetically in the same manner adults talk to new-borns: as if they're idiots. This was more like it; mums know how to do this properly.

'No,' I said as if speaking cost energy by the letter.

'Everything ok with Molly?'

'Oh god, what is this?!'

'Okay sweetie, calm down. You just take it easy today.' She patted the duvet lightly and left. I went back to sleep.

I woke up later and checked my phone. It was mid-morning and Molly had texted me asking why I wasn't in school. I lied and then rolled onto my back, staring up at the ceiling. I was hungry. I got to my feet and put on my dressing gown. I opened my door and stood listening. The house was quiet. I made my way downstairs to find Mum had gone out for tea with an old actor friend. Artists attract artists and I assumed the actor friend she'd mentioned previously was Harold Barton. I had met him a few times. I made some toast and took it back to bed with a cup of tea.

Once in bed I reached for my laptop. I had a whole day to kill. I checked my social media pages and nearly gave myself third degree burns. News travels fast. A video had been shared several times on the newsfeed of a boy being beaten up on Bridge Street. I immediately clicked play and watched it a handful of times. My face was hidden by my hands and having my hood up helped a lot. I was relieved to find you couldn't recognise me. I followed the link to see who had uploaded it. It was an anonymous posting. The comments were a mixed bag of people calling me a wimp or cry-baby and other people saying it should be taken down or shown to the police. I guess I should have known he'd upload it; what else do you record videos for?

Even though no one could know it was me I felt like they did. Everyone in school would have seen this by the end of the day. This was certainly one way to get me to stop moonlighting. I wondered how many pupils were off today. Would anyone make the connection between me being ill and this video doing the rounds? Would Molly join the dots? I read through more of the news to find something to take my mind off it. Someone had posted another picture of their new-born baby (yawn) and a few others were talking about a party they had been to last night. Something popped up at the top of the page. Someone had shared a status.

Sally Moore shared Jack Walker's status.

"Last night I was mugged on Bridge Street. I was walking home and I was attacked. While I was being robbed a kid came out of nowhere and stood up to the mugger. He didn't have to, but he came to my aid. He took a real beating trying to help me. Whoever it was I want to thank them, even though they essentially did nothing."

The original post had three hundred and forty-seven 'likes'. It also had my undivided attention. One hundred and three comments had been posted. I scanned a few and one woman had used the word 'hero'. This raised my spirits. A few comments down from that and 'hero' was there again. Hero. Hero in the making. Hero in town. Loser. Hero. Cry-baby. Hero. Weak. Hero. Hero.

Jack Walker had commented, saying, 'We need more people like this in the world.' It's all right for him, he wasn't stuck in bed beaten black and blue. I couldn't subject myself to repeated beatings regardless of how many people thought me heroic. If only there was a way to fight crime on my terms. It's all right for Batman and Wolverine, everything is scripted for them. They know what's coming.

Somewhere in my head a light came on.

The front door opened. Mum was back. She was with someone, probably Harold. I looked in the mirror. My face was fine, just a little swollen and that was only noticeable on close inspection. My ribs were the problem. I stood as straight as my body would allow and I went downstairs, taking my plate and mug back to the kitchen. Harold spotted me first as my mum had her back to the room, making tea.

'Toby,' he said. He always seemed drunk. 'How are you, lad?'

'Not so good today, are you sweetie?' my mum answered for me. I feel 'sweetie' shouldn't be used in front of anyone who isn't an immediate member of the family. I gave a half nod, half smile.

'Well, I hope you're better soon.' He laughed a little to himself. 'Your mother and I have been a little naughty. I took my hip flask to morning tea.' He turned to Jenny, who didn't say anything. This was news to me and I wondered how often this happened, but I had other, more pressing, matters to attend to.

'How do you find work?' I said.

'Toby!' my mum snapped.

'No, I didn't mean it like that,' I said quickly, injecting the antidote before the poison could spread. 'I mean, how do actors in general find work? What's the process?' That was better. Probably went straight over his head, the pissed-up has-been.

'Are you wanting to go into the arts, Toby?' he said.

'No, just curious.'

'It's a tough business,' he began, 'lots of rejection. You have to be thick-skinned'.

Just answer the question.

'We audition.'

One of the first actors is believed to have been an ancient Greek called Thespis. He would speak to the people as if he were someone else, a separate character and from Thespis's name derives the word thespian, which as an adjective means relating to drama and the theatre and as a noun means an actor or actress. Acting requires a wide range of skills, including vocal projection, clarity of speech and a well-developed imagination. Many begin as what's called an extra or background artist and they find work through websites, casting calls, agents and, most importantly, auditions.

'So a series of candidates take it in turn to see who best fits the criteria needed?'

'In a word, yes.'

'What's all this for?' Mum asked, bewildered at my sudden interest. Thinking on my feet I went with the classic, 'I have a friend wanting to do drama so I'm just taking an interest.'

'A friend?' said Mum. She knew I was lying.

'Well, tell them to forget it!' Harold laughed. 'It's a nightmare!' He laughed again, loudly. I said I needed to lie down and left them to it. I had work to do. If I planned this right I could be a hero and never worry about taking another beating again. I just needed to find myself an actor.

15

"If you're good at something, never do it for free" - Joker

It was December 1977 when first time parents Mr and Mrs Webb welcomed their son to the world. Snow had built up by every entrance to the hospital and vehicles in the car park were quickly disappearing under a thick, white blanket. The air was bitterly cold as people hurried from A to B, but inside the hospital, tucked away in a little room, a family had been completed. In the aftermath of birth an exhausted mother held her baby for the first time, the father standing over them, and she whispered 'Simon' to her son. Mr and Mrs Webb looked down at the wonder they had made and swore to protect his desires and dreams. No one could have known in that moment that the combined characteristics of his mother's lack of humour and his father's inability to retell a story with any interest, that together they had created the world's most boring human being. The mixture of his parent's gene pools had left Simon with a rare underdevelopment within the brain. It is a trait that most people put into practice constantly throughout each day – it's called a filter.

For example, when you're at a party and you've found someone you like, you have to 'woo' them first - these are the rules. Very few people can walk up to someone attractive, invite them to bed, and get the desired result. Most of us have to sweeten the deal with witty banter or money. People like to be reassured they're not being taken home by someone that is going to shag, kill and eat them - and not necessarily in that order. A solo attack is common but people are known to have what is called a 'wingman'. The term comes from aviation, as you might expect. A wingman is a pilot who supports another pilot in a potentially dangerous flying environment. In social terms a male wingman to a male lead will be someone that lends support when approaching potential partners. They are on the inside and are used to aid in any way they can to 'big' their lead up. So you take incidents from your past, edit slightly (if needed) and test the water. When you're with someone you like, a queue forms in your mind of jokes, compliments, personal information etc. The brain gives the ok to send anything down, he's top floor and busy, the brain does minimal checking as he's management and got a lot on. So the doors open and the information travels. Once at the mouth it has a final check by bouncers, like on the door of a club. A compliment about her hair? Free to go. A satirical joke about the state of the national health service? Funny and thought provoking - enjoy your night. A short story about realising you forgot your wallet when at the till of a supermarket?

No. Go back upstairs; we'll deal with you later.

Simon didn't have this filter. Anything and everything would spill out and infect. He was raised without humour, without interest and without the basic concept of what's worth sharing and what should be locked away forever.

Simon began to notice he was different at an early age. People avoided him and he couldn't make friends. Children at school called him 'boring Simon'. They weren't very inventive but the name stuck and he learned to face the fact that he was boring. The older he got the more he tried to fight it. He would plan spontaneity and try to appear as if he was going against the grain just to seem interesting. One year he auditioned for the school play. That's as wild as a young adult can be at school. Taking pity on him and in recognition that he was clearly trying, the drama teacher decided to give him a chance to prove himself. He got the leading role, playing the husband of fellow student Catherine Hobbs. He was different to all the other boys and on that basis she fell for him quickly. One day she invited him over to practise their lines. Of course he agreed - people would talk about this, thus making him interesting - but things went downhill shortly after he arrived. She didn't really want to go over lines; she wanted to get to know him. She asked questions about himself, his home and his sudden desire to be on stage. Simon's absent filter resulted in the inevitable and Catherine Hobbs' poor mind just wasn't prepared for the avalanche of boring information that followed. An early evening dog walker was just in time to see the body of a young woman float from her bedroom window in a cloud of glass, and crack her head open on impact with the driveway. A lot of screaming ensued and Simon wasn't asked back.

He had been told he was boring but no one had told him that being boring is dangerously powerful. The school production was cancelled that year out of respect for Catherine and kids at school made up rumours she had killed herself due to Simon's bad acting. Simon refused to believe he could be boring *and* bad at acting. Out of sheer stubbornness he made a promise to himself that he would make it as an actor one day. The jokes and bullying consumed Simon and he grew to hate his contemporaries. An anger brewed deep inside, like an active volcano, waiting for the day. He channelled his pain and taught himself to control his power. He designed his own filter and his witticisms, memories and verbal tangents grew even more boring; unleashed on demand. He could manipulate minds, boring them to a point where he could get them to do things, outside of their control. A trance-like state. It took him years to perfect and he used his power to fit in. None of it was real of course but he bored people into liking him, bored teachers into giving him good marks, he even bored girls into spending time with him. He poured so much boredom into the school that they all but forgot about Catherine Hobbs. His powers were limitless. He never grew bored of his life; he was boring himself, so how could he? Years went by and Simon grew strong.

University brought new challenges but Simon was well trained. A lot of his peers had partners, serious relationships, not like secondary school where two weeks feels like nine years and the whole courting period is built around a ritual of saying hello in the morning as you pass each other in a busy hallway. Simon was jealous. Nights out were spent watching his make-believe friends 'getting off' with each other while he tried to maintain a conversation. He decided to get his own. He scouted for weeks for a suitable partner and on another night out, somewhere down the line, he was introduced to Carol Greene, a friend of a friend. She met his needs and within an hour of meticulously discussing the DVD extras of an early series of *Doctor Who*, she was his. They kissed, a scene that could have been mistaken for a mother bird feeding her young. Carol couldn't remember a thing in the morning but agreed to meet with Simon again, after being told they were caught snogging. And so Simon bored her again, on the ins and outs of whether or not *Star Wars* could be real. And there was another meet and another. He bored her into a deep sleep the first time she stayed over and he fed her information on a loop throughout her slumber...*I love Simon Webb...He is a great actor...He is anything but boring...I love Simon Webb...He is a great actor...He is anything but boring...* (tape changes sides) ...*I love Simon Webb...He is a great...*

After university Carol went into a well-paid job in the northwest and she and Simon moved into their first property, number 31 of Sullart Street, Cockermouth. This was very much against the will of Carol's parents. They didn't care for Simon and repeatedly warned her that he was no good. He couldn't support her while chasing a dream to act. Carol replied the same way each time.

'I love Simon Webb... He is a great actor... He is anything but boring...'

Carol became unrecognisable to her loved ones. Years in a entranced state had aged her. She grew distant from her family and lost touch with her friends, bored out of her mind. She would go to work and then come home to Simon. Week in, week out. Year after year. When Simon was thirty-one and Carol was twenty-nine they found out they were having a child. The sex was very Victorian - two minutes in the dark with no eye contact. The excitement was moderate and nine months later Jamie Webb was born, giving Simon more reason to stay at home. Up until that point he had worked here and there on odd jobs. He was still chasing the fame and fortune acting can bring and getting nowhere with it. No one ever called back.

At least the birth of Jamie brought with it five more years at home trying to find his breakthrough role. Carol was a robot and working every hour she could get. Debts were slowly building and the marriage became a marriage of convenience. Carol kept him afloat financially, enabling his deranged mind. Simon stayed at home and raised Jamie but he was becoming more and more expensive. They were slipping further and further into debt. Money was leaving the house in every direction. Simon was beginning to worry. He couldn't be seen to be failing at something else. He had been haunted since school about not making it into the play, an original story written by our drama teacher about a drama teacher that went on to inspire a generation. You might be wondering why Simon hadn't used his power to gain an acting role but he couldn't cheat that. He used his power to create a world that would allow him to pursue his acting. It had become something he had to prove to himself and he couldn't cut corners with it. He needed this; it was all he thought about, it had to come naturally. Everything revolved around proving his acting worth.

You could also be wondering why he hasn't used his power for personal gain, financially perhaps, but remember: he's not a criminal as such, he's just boring. He just wanted to fit in. It's one thing to bore a woman into spending the rest of her life with you but the power needed to manipulate multiple minds to successfully rob a bank and then the ongoing efforts to keep oneself out of prison is something different entirely. He was powerful but not that powerful.

Carol was at work and Jamie was sleeping in Simon's arms on the day he came across a casting call for actors. It was local, which was a plus. Very local. *Actors wanted.* Simon clicked on the link for more.

ACTORS WANTED
Local hero needs evil mastermind.
No names or address.
Part-time paid work.
Auditions Sunday 12th, Papcastle Village Hall, 4pm.
Come in costume.

This would make him an actor. Carol came home from work and was bored into sorting out Jamie and the evening meal. Simon needed this job. With each passing minute he wanted it more and more. He could flex his evil muscles ever so slightly and at the same time cross off a long overdue goal. Then, if the day came that he wasn't boring enough to avoid another school reunion he could share with everyone that he was an actor. He could finally tell everyone that, after 36 years, he had found a job. That would show them all. He wanted to impress at the audition but not go over the top. He tried outfit after outfit, all as ridiculous as the one before. In the end he decided to keep it simple. An eye mask was ordered online along with a black, pin-striped trilby. This required a lot of thought from Simon and being this creative put his brain under a lot of stress. It was all he could manage and would have to do. He hadn't thought of a name yet but that would come after having initially met with the hero. They might have some idea for the part; he was taking orders after all, not giving them, something he wasn't used to at all.

The big day came, Sunday the 12th. Simon arrived at Papcastle Village Hall at 4pm. He stepped out of the car and donned his eye mask and trilby. He took a deep breath and prayed that today would change his life forever but, as we all know, you should be careful what you wish for.

16

I was excited and nervous for today. I had placed the ad and booked the hall. All I needed now was for people to turn up, which is where the worry came in. I didn't know if people would take my ad seriously.

Would *you* take my ad seriously if you saw it?

I was expecting either no one to turn up or the criminally insane. The tragedy is that the criminally insane would make for an excellent nemesis but working with them in an employer/employment capacity just isn't practical. I needed someone fairly level-headed, someone who knew what they were doing and, more than anything, someone who could act. No one knew I was here. By that I mean my parents or Molly. To cover my back I had told my parents I was with Molly and vice versa. I had arrived at the hall in costume, all in black, hoody up and toecap on. I had a small table set out with two chairs in the middle of the room. I sat down at 4pm, facing the door, and waited. I just needed someone to make me look good. No names or addresses; that would ruin it. For safety on both parts, we should know as little about each other as possible. No names or addresses – it was a deal breaker. A man came through the door and I stood up.

'Hi, I'm Tim Dawson. Bollocks.'

'Thanks Tim,' I replied and he turned around and left.

The clock pushed on but within a few minutes someone else had arrived.

'Hello!' said a man carrying a large bag. He came in looking over his shoulder. He was nervous and twitching.

'Hello,' I said, 'Are you ok?'

'Ha ha. I've hopefully impressed you.' He looked behind him again. 'I want this job. I need it. There's no work these days. So I thought about how to stand out and I came up with something I doubt anyone else will try.' He was proud of whatever it was he had done and at the same time a sweaty, jumping mess of a man.

'Which is what?' I said.

'To impress you I thought I'd get the ball rolling.'

'Go on...'

'I've just robbed a shop!'

'What?'

'Pretty good, eh? That's what villains do isn't it? I've committed a crime. I got a gun and robbed a shoe shop.' He was smiling, assuming I was impressed. I looked down at the bag he had brought in. I was becoming increasingly aware that I was sat with an actual criminal and an armed one at that. He had jumped a few steps for me. He probably shouldn't be here.

'Did you get much?'

'No, it has been a slow week.'

'So what's in the bag?'

'Just shoes, really. And my gun.'

'So, armed robbery?'

'Yeah.'

I chose my next words carefully. 'Well, Mr.?'

'You said no names,' he remembered quickly.

'But of course. Well, I'm afraid you're overqualified.'

'What does that mean?'

'You're too good.'

'What?'

'Well, bear in mind that this job was for an actor.'

'...Yes...?' He needed a little push.

'And actors make a living from doing what?'

'They...pretend?'

'That's right! Now, did you pretend to rob a shoe shop?'

'No,' he said disheartened; he was realising his mistake.

'That's right, you didn't. You actually robbed an independent shoe shop, and a struggling one if what I know about the economy is correct. Do you see where you went wrong?'

'Yeah, all right. Well, what do I do now?'

'I suggest you take the shoes back, apologise and hope for the best.'

After a forlorn moment, he picked up his bag and slumped off. My heart calmed down. I had just talked a gunman into returning some trainers. My hands were shaking but I had to compose myself as someone else was coming in. I hadn't thought today was going to be so popular but if the quality of lunacy continued I might give up and go home. A figure stood in the doorway. He wore black and his face was hidden under a hood. Sparks of red were jotted about his clothing and he walked to me with confident strides. I'm not sure where he had been, maybe he had run here, but he was giving off some heat. No, it was a different kind of heat. It felt familiar. The heat was delightful, it soothed me and I felt like I could curl up in a ball and sleep. I knew this heat. I knew I knew it from somewhere. It clicked. Luke Cook gave off this heat in my French lessons. Was this really him? I had no idea he was an aspiring actor. I'd rather not hire someone that I know; the whole point was to not know them. No names or addresses. I couldn't let him know who I was otherwise this whole facade is over.

'I'm sorry but the position has been filled.'

'So that's it, is it?'

'I'm afraid so.'

'You don't even want to see what I can do? You don't want to hear my story?' he asked.

'I'm sorry, but the position has been filled.'

'This is your last chance...'

I had to think of something else to say, something better. 'I'm sorry but the position has been filled.' After a moment I could swear the air grew hotter.

'Fine,' he said, 'but you will regret this.' And with that he left.

Time was burning up and I only had the hall until five. That's £25 I'll never get back. I stood up and began packing the chairs and table away.

'Excuse me?'

'If you're here for salsa dancing it doesn't start until six. I'm just leaving.'

'I'm here for the acting role,' he said. I turned to see a smartly dressed man wearing a trilby and an eye mask. It was simple but he looked good. I smiled enthusiastically and introduced myself properly.

'I'm Toecap. Do you have a name?'

'I've been stuck on that for some time but I think I've come up with one.'

'Yes...?'

'The Fiddler.'

'The Fiddler?'

'Pretty good eh? What do you reckon? The Fiddler sounds good, don't you think? Evokes fear?'

'Not sure it evokes fear as such. It sounds like you shouldn't work with children.'

'I like it. Yeah, I'm sticking with the Fiddler. The Fiddler.' He couldn't get enough of it. I checked my watch. I could take my chances with the Fiddler or wait another week before trying to find someone new. I looked him up and down. What the hell.

'You're hired.'

17

"Shut up crime" – Crimson Bolt

Our first task together was to set up an easy way of communicating with each other and we decided to go with email - better than a text and quicker than a message in a bottle. We exchanged emails a lot to begin with as I briefed him on what the job was and what I needed from him. He was keen to learn and his enthusiasm was impressive. I felt like we were really onto something. This wasn't the proper way to fight crime but a superhero's best weapon is providing society with a standard of morality that is easily achievable. If we all stood up against crime it wouldn't have a chance. Superheroes are symbols, setting an example for the everyday hero to follow and learn from. As far as the public were concerned, they didn't need to know that the crime I would be fighting was an out-of-work middle-aged man I was paying below minimum wage. It was the example I was setting that was important. Not the example about the illegal, cash-in-hand, substandard salary – a lot of people have learned that lesson already and, thinking about it, I'm a little embarrassed to be one of them. But not every superhero has the Wayne fortune to call on that Batman has. I'm getting side-tracked again. Forget about the money issue.

The Fiddler was the best of a bad bunch, but we did seem to click and things were going well. We came up with the idea of performing

Public Interactions of Staged Situations (or P.I.S.S for short). We wanted to get the ball rolling fast, in at the deep end and all that. We wanted to inspire, to get people believing in each other, to get them to look out for their neighbours and to get them caring about the community as a whole.

So we began planning our first P.I.S.S. together - grow up. We never told each other personal details; we kept it strictly business as emails went back and forth. We weren't trying to be friends, we were playing two characters that fought one another and I felt rather pleased knowing I would win every encounter. He explained to me that the term 'fiddler' can informally mean a cheat, so in the end I agreed that it made sense as a name for a villain, but warned him about where and when he called himself that - know your audience. He was a fair bit older than me and he must have known I was young but we never mentioned it.

I was on track to being a superhero without any danger involved. Pretty crafty isn't it? My double life had begun and it was easy. I had found a crime that I could schedule. I kept my toecap on permanently and lived my life. I had fixed the problem with my power, I had the girl and I suppose I even had the guy when you think about it. We planned carefully and with precision. The first P.I.S.S. took some time as we wanted everything to be just right. Logically, we decided to start small. We came up with the idea of bog-standard assault. We'd do it at night and in a busy part of town so as to have witnesses that would inevitably spread the news around the water cooler the next day. The only problem was that the Fiddler would actually have to fight someone. He'd fight them and try to run and that's when I'd come in and save the day. We'd scuffle a little and then I'd come out on top. I continued to book Papcastle village hall on a regular basis so we had somewhere we could rehearse. What we were doing would have a positive effect on the community. Criminals would come to know my name. Maybe if things with the Fiddler go well I can upgrade to fighting actual crime. It would go something like... The Fiddler > school bully > one petty thug > one thief > one career thief etc.

It looks like a shopping list for an evil genius. Minus the school bully; you can't have kids working full-time in warehouses and underground lairs. In the real world Jacob could have been my nemesis. He would certainly consider me an enemy once he found out about me and Molly. Things were great between us and things were going very well with Randall and Willow. I was pleased for him and pleased that him being in a relationship meant less time spent with me, which in turn meant I could spend more time with Molly. Willow was nothing like a bike. She was very sweet and, like Randall, she saw the world in her own unique, mental kind of way. It just goes to show that there really is someone out there for everyone. Molly and I had been official for a few weeks and tonight she would be coming over and for the first time my parents would be out of the house.

Tonight was the night, if you catch my drift. I was nervous. It was a rare occasion when Molly and I had the house to ourselves. Sam and Jenny had gone on a double date and would be out late. Molly was coming over any minute now and I had 'protection'. Protection in the form of alcohol because with it I could protect Molly from remembering anything that would happen. I had a condom as well, obviously, that goes without saying, and the night would be romantic; don't get me wrong, it's just that the romance would start once I was certain Molly had enough alcohol in her bloodstream. I just didn't want her to hate it and I felt getting a little drunk would relax us both. Everything is more fun when drunk, that's common knowledge. I bet even drowning kittens would lose its sting with a bottle of mint Baileys and someone to share it with. I love cats, let me make that clear. I needed to stop worrying about tonight. I was going to see a woman naked, totally naked. I had seen naked women before but Molly is different, I care about Molly and I didn't have to keep her hidden in a box under my bed. It went some way to calm me knowing that Molly was also a virgin. It wasn't even definite it would happen tonight. We had talked about it because friends of ours had started doing it and tonight we had an empty house, which I told her four times was very rare. She also knew I had nicked a couple of condoms from my dad's supply. I don't know what's worse, finding a box of condoms in your parents' room or finding an empty box of condoms in your parents' room. A part of me thought that if my parents had sex often Sam would notice he was missing a couple, but if they didn't then he wouldn't keep track of how many he had. So far he hadn't mentioned it to me so I assumed not much was going on in that department. Unless they had stopped using them altogether. Oh god, they might be trying for another baby. Why do they need another? What's wrong with me? I can't believe they're fed up with me already.

There was a knock at the front door. It was Molly. My beautiful Molly. One day soon she will go a long way to helping my understanding of the alien life-forms known as women. A woman's mind is an impregnable fortress, guarded and...with a moat? (I don't know where that metaphor was going).

'Hello.'

'Hello,' she said, walking past me into the house. 'Mrs Malloy, you look incredible!'

I closed the front door and found my dad standing right next to me. He just stood there looking at me for a long time.

'Have a good night, son.' He knew I had taken a condom. I knew he knew. I've never seen that look before.

'Thanks,' I said awkwardly.

'We should be going,' my mum said. My dad told Molly to help herself to whatever she wanted, food and whatnot, for which she thanked him.

'Right, let's go,' Jenny cheered and after a quick goodbye they were gone.

The house was quiet. I waited by the door for my parents to come back and say it was all a joke and that they weren't really going out, they'd much rather stay in and count how many condoms they had left.

'Are you ok?' Molly asked.

'Yes, fine, why?'

'You just seem a bit weird.' At least she was honest. I snapped out of whatever mood I was in. I hugged Molly and we kissed, then I offered her a drink. Before you assume anything, I just meant 'drink' as in I was trying to be a good host, I wasn't desperate to get down to it. When people come around, you offer them a drink, that's standard practice, so I put the kettle on. I may be a teenage boy but my mind isn't entirely focused on sex, regardless of how rare it was that I got the house to myself and I think I may have mentioned that to Molly. The kettle boiled and I asked Molly if she fancied a little 'kick' in her tea. She accepted with excitement and we settled down in front of the TV. We shared a sofa together. I had my tea with a little whiskey and Molly had a large whiskey with a little tea. Shut up.

After the kettle had boiled a few more times we found everything funny. Every little man or woman that walked onto the screen became the funniest person in the world. We laughed and spilt tea and got closer and closer. Once a fourth tea had been and gone Molly asked to watch TV in my room. I liked how she took control. I was too nervous to ever make a move. If it was left to me I'd have left a note in the toilet for her to see on her next pit stop. I turned off the TV and we laughed our way upstairs and into my room. It seemed somewhat real now. A part of me didn't want to do this. Sex is a big step and, as I hadn't taken it before, I didn't know what changes come with it. All I knew is that up until this point everything had been perfect. The kissing was great, we laughed at everything and even the meals with my parents had become something I didn't completely hate. Do we need to have sex, I wondered? Can't we wait until we're married so she can't leave me if I'm rubbish at it? I hope it's something that comes naturally to me. Even if it's not, I can afford a few mistakes on my first go surely? Mistakes? What mistakes am I referring to? I know where everything goes. Why isn't Molly looking as nervous as I do? What does she know that I don't? Maybe this wasn't her first time, maybe she has lied to me. All these thoughts ran through my brain, before I told myself, almost out loud: stop being stupid and stop worrying so much.

I closed the bedroom door and joined Molly, who was now sitting on the bed. She smiled at me and I tried to smile back. She took my hand in hers and put her other hand on top.

She kissed me and told me everything was going to be ok and then, suddenly, it doesn't matter where I am or how I got here or even what comes after. All I see is Molly and for the next few minutes she leads me through a beautiful experience that we discover together. It's not awkward or forced or rushed. It just happens and if we were in the wild and David Attenborough was watching he'd be saying how natural it is and everyone at home wouldn't mind that it's being shown at 7pm on a Tuesday. Some might change channel, but no one would phone in to complain.

We lay together afterwards and I pulled the duvet up over our naked bodies. We slept for a little while and when we came round we both showered and met in the kitchen for food.

'Are you ok?' she asked.

'Yeah. You?'

'Yeah.'

The toaster popped and I spread generous amounts of butter and homemade fig jam over several slices, then we reclaimed the sofa we had in a previous life. The seats seemed different somehow and the toast tasted almost like something else. We both sat chomping away with bright lights from the TV filling the otherwise dark room. Once the plates were cleared we slid into a lying-down position, me behind her. She snuggled in tight and I put my arm around her. I look down at her body and even that seems different now. The desire had been to see her naked but now that I had been intimate with her that desire had simply been replaced with another. I wanted to protect her and help her. The new enigma lay in not knowing how to do so. I had been granted special privileges to this particular being, the rarest of tickets and now she deserved my respect and loyalty until such a time when she no longer wanted that from me. Of course before tonight I wanted to protect her, but that feeling had been magnified. Her body wasn't the fortress, her mind was and she had just lowered the drawbridge.

18

I woke up feeling different. I felt stronger somehow, like my opinions should count a little more than they did last week. I had used my penis's secondary function for the first time and it had gone well, I think. It's a fun function - not that peeing isn't, it's just that I've literally peed a thousand times so the novelty has worn a little thin. I was back at school today, a place where I couldn't have sex or be a hero. I was outgrowing school. I was having relationships and intercourse, I no longer cared for oxbow lakes and Pythagoras. I needed to take on the Fiddler and soon; I didn't want to have to wait. I also wanted to talk about Molly with someone. I couldn't talk to my parents about her. I didn't want to know about their midnight romps, and I doubt they were keen on hearing about mine. I could talk to Molly about it but I didn't want to; I needed a neutral party, someone I could embellish the story with if needed.

Randall was the first person I met in the morning.

'Molly and I had sex.' I couldn't hold it in. I hadn't even said 'morning'; how rude.

'No way!' Randall said in disbelief.

'Yes way, my friend.'

'You've had proper, full-on sex?'

'Yeah.'

'What was it like? Was she naked?'

'What? Of course she was naked. We both were.'

'You were naked as well? This is sounding serious.'

'It was amazing,' I said and that was enough. Women always say they tell each other everything but when it comes to sex men keep it brief. One will ask the other what it was like and the other will, 9 times out of 10, say it was amazing, the conversation is done, we keep the details for ourselves.

'It is, isn't it?' Randall smiled. No way.

'Have you and Willow...?'

'We have.'

'What was it like?'

'Amazing'.

Done, let's go to school. Today, I wanted to learn. I wanted to make something of myself so Molly and I could have a good life together. I wanted to see her. I needed to know if she was ok this morning, that nothing had changed. We passed in the corridor at close to 9am but we couldn't swim across the blue shirted rapids of early school movement. She waved and I copied.

After my first lesson I was bored of learning. I wanted Molly and I wanted the Fiddler. I wanted to bring the date forward for our first P.I.S.S. together. I wanted to do it this weekend. Molly was with friends and I had no plans. I'd email the Fiddler tonight. I was ready, he was ready, we were ready.

I had French before lunch and Luke was late. This was unlike him. We had been set a pronunciation task in teams of two and my allocated partner was someone I didn't know existed. Luke turned up eventually, stropped over and asked what was going on. I couldn't look him in the eye. Sitting with someone different at school is one of the worst acts of humiliation you can serve up - that poor sod has to sit with someone they don't know for almost an hour. Oh the humanity.

'Who is this?' Luke spat as if he'd come home early and walked in on the two of us in bed.

'Hi, I'm-'

'It's not what you think.'

'Why can't I be your partner?' said Luke. I couldn't think of anything good to say.

'I'm sorry but the position has been filled.'

Luke glared at me. I could feel it, his eyes burning into me like concentrated rays of the sun. The air around us could have caught fire and me and my new friend begun to cook. When it was too much I forced myself to look up but Luke was gone. *What was that about?* I made a joke out of it in front of... I didn't even know who I was sitting with - who cares? I could feel Luke watching me for the entire lesson. I was relieved when the bell rang. Luke had been late, it wasn't my fault. My new friend (still don't know his name) did ok in the pairs challenge. My French pronunciation isn't amazing, you can definitely tell I'm English, but I *am* English so there you go. I'm not learning French to pass as a spy; I'm learning it to get directions to the Louvre if I happen to be over there. We did well enough in the task but I was looking forward to getting Luke back, if he'd have me. He was finalising the divorce and dividing up our things and I wanted us to look past the break and try again. This new guy wasn't up to much. I should have waited for Luke.

Walking home I tried to think of what I had learned that day. Then I tried something a little easier and tried to remember one lesson I'd attended besides French. When that failed I tried to remember what day it was. I walked home alone, which felt odd, the long straight of Castlegate Drive. I'd hate to live on this stretch. The amount of stupid kids that walk by each and every day making noise and dropping litter and you'd always see one boy trying to push his mate over a wall into someone's garden. And as the road was straight this automatically told drivers they had to drive up and down it as fast as they could, drag-racing buses for pride. Driving didn't interest me at all. I passed the sports centre and new hospital and walked down into Market Place, heading for home.

19

"I'm the best at what I do, but what I do
best isn't very nice" – Wolverine

A young group of lads were downing pints with most of it running out
of the glass and down past their chins. They were like dogs pissing
on lampposts, marking their territory. They were young and stood
out in a pub full of seasoned drinkers. You could tell they were barely
over eighteen because they were enjoying the night. Just as empty
glasses were slammed back onto the table someone would appear
with a fresh round - this looked like a game of last man standing.
Heads bobbed to the music and laughter was in abundance as every
comment was hilarious beyond imagination. It was early and at this
pace none of them would make it to midnight. Only a couple had
filled out fully, the rest looked like Popeye pre-spinach. Girls walked
by in groups but the boys weren't interested; tonight's mission was to
get smashed, the opposite sex was an afterthought.

A leader of the group was hard to pick, they all seemed equally
pointless. In a lot of ways they were perfect. A middle-aged man stood
by himself at the bar, discreetly watching them. He had picked his
targets. The drink he had ordered was helping with his nerves. Simon
Webb had never really been in a fight. He threw back the remainder
of his drink and exited the pub with his hat in hand. Once outside he

sneaked into the darkness of a nearby alley and put on his eye mask and trilby. The boys inside would be moving on soon and then he would strike. The plan was simple. Pick the biggest of the group, walk right up to him and hit him in the face. He would have to be quick and hope Toecap would be ready. The boys would be more confident than usual with the alcohol running through them but it would also confuse their balance and depth perception, making them easier to fight. The more Simon thought about this plan the more he thought how ridiculous it was. This is an acting job, he reminded himself, a paid performance, but what was about to happen wasn't acting. He was wearing a shirt and tie with a tight waistcoat buttoned up. He gave a few jabs into the air to warm up, tilting his head from side to side, ducking and weaving. He expected to take a couple of hits, probably to the face, but so be it. He was a method actor.

A raucous commotion was bounding down the street and from his position in the darkness Simon could see his payday right there in front of him. He didn't know these boys, but that helped if anything. They wanted stories to tell on Monday and he would serve up a good one. He took a deep breath and stepped out. He tried to control his breathing as he moved in on his prey. One of the boys had spotted him, but the others were in a circle on the pavement arguing about which pub to go to next. The Fiddler pulled apart the group and squared up to the biggest. The boy looked at him confused. Without hesitation the Fiddler pulled back an arm and clobbered him in the face. He dropped - one punch. His friends became very loud and began pushing the Fiddler, swearing threats and questions. Simon kept his defence up and turned to the others, ready to lash out again. The boy on the floor wasn't moving. People outside the group watched on, unsure of what had happened. One of the boys made a sudden movement which startled Simon and he jabbed out, catching him on the cheek. Another body on the floor, followed by more screams. Time was ticking on. Where was Toecap? The crowd was getting bigger and the Fiddler was up against a growing mob.

The Fiddler had just punched a third boy to the floor when I decided to pull up my hoody over my head. I was on the other side of the street, hiding in a shop doorway waiting for the right time to shine. I was nervous but we had gone over this again and again and the Fiddler had played his part well. It was my turn to take the stage. I stepped out from the doorway when someone snatched my attention.

'Excuse me, sorry to bother you, but do you have the time?'

I checked my phone. 'It's nearly half nine.'

'Thank you.'

'No worries,' and I looked back at the Fiddler as he put down another young adult.

'Do you know when the next bus to Carlisle is?'

'No, sorry, I've got to-'

'I think I might have missed the last one.'

'Oh, right...'

'I'll be waiting for ages and then two will turn up; funny that!'

'I've really got to go.'

'Can you get a taxi round here?'

'Piss off,' I said and ran across the road as the Fiddler dodged a couple of swings. I grabbed him from behind and pulled him out into the street.

'Are you ready?' I whispered in his ear.

'Where have you been?!'

I spun him round, he fell to the floor and his hat came off. There was a cheer from everyone watching and I raised my arms in appreciation, soaking in the glory.

'Good people of Cockermouth, I am...' The Fiddler jumped up and charged at me. I slipped to the side and pretended to thump him in the stomach. He crumpled over and loudly moaned. Another cheer. I held up the Fiddler's head and simulated a right hook which sent him back down to the floor. A huge cheer came. Time for the finale. I bent down and pulled the Fiddler up onto his knees.

'Good people of Cockermouth, I am Toecap!' Phone cameras flashed and clapping rippled violently through the crowd. I pointed to the middle of the mass and bellowed, 'Tow the line!' I dragged the Fiddler to his feet and led him away in the general direction of the police station. A few drunken groupies followed us so we broke into a run up Station Street and took a left onto South Street, down past the Tithe Barn pub and back into the darkness. Once out of sight I let go of the Fiddler and we broke into nervous laughter. We had done it. It had worked. Now we had to get home as quickly as possible. We would debrief later. I wasn't far from my house but the

Fiddler didn't know that and I had no idea where he had to be. In my superhero voice (which was just a bit deeper than usual) I told him to go and I would email once I was home. We had to be quick. We turned away from each other and went our separate ways. After he had disappeared from view I took off my hoody and jogged back home, happy with tonight's promising performance.

I opened the front door and was welcomed by my parents.

'Where have you been?'

'Randall's house,' I said instinctively. I hadn't thought I'd need an alibi.

'We know that's a lie. Randall is upstairs in your room.' They were now both standing, waiting for the truth. I had to think on my feet.

'Yessss and that's why I'm back, because he wasn't there. A mix-up in communication.'

'Hmm,' they said in unison.

'You keep wearing black. You're not one of those emos, are you?' my mum asked.

'An emo? No,' I said.

'We can't be doing with you cutting yourself and moaning all the time,' my dad chipped in.

'I have nothing whatsoever to moan about, trust me.'

'Good, there is more than enough drama in the world.' He turned away from me and back to the paper he was reading.

'Go on then, he's waiting,' said Mum.

Ah yes, Randall. I shrugged off my shoes and bounded upstairs, a little sweaty and weak after an unfamiliar adrenaline surge. I opened the bedroom door and found Randall curled up on my bed with his eyes shut.

'What are you doing?'

'Oh hello. Where have you been?'

'Nowhere. What's up?'

'Just bored, that's all. Willow is with Molly, isn't she? So I had nothing to do tonight. Why are you all sweaty?'

'Just been out for a run.'

'But why?'

'It's good for you. We're not getting any younger, Randall; we need to start taking care of our bodies. Fit body, fit mind.'

'Really?'

'Well, yeah, kind of. If you're healthy it will help overall, won't it?'

'What about if I do it the other way round? If I read a lot will I get a six pack?'

'No.'

'So reading my exercise books doesn't count as getting exercise?'

'Of course not.'

'Why are they called exercise books?'

'I don't know, it's too late in the day to teach you something new.'

'It's never too late to learn.'

'You are the exception to that rule. I need a quick shower; are you all right for another five minutes?'

'I think so.'

'Good.'

My heart rate had returned to normal by the time I wrapped a towel around myself and began dabbing down. Who would have thought that heating up water and pouring it over yourself would be such a remedy? You can feel the stress running off you and circling down the drain among the hairballs and bubbles. It's good thinking time and a bath even more so, I imagine. You could drown an afternoon in a bath with nothing but your own thoughts. Magic.

I came back to my room to find Randall sat at my computer. He was mesmerised by something. I dumped my sweaty clothes on the floor and put a fresh t-shirt on, leaning over him to see what was going on. He turned in his chair and looked, open mouthed, at the black hoody and trousers bundled together by the door. His mind looked as though it was doing something it had never done before.

He had been watching a video of Toecap beating up the Fiddler. It had been uploaded already. That's the digital age: blink and you'll miss something. Through his eyes I could see his mind trying to join the dots up. He looked up at me.

'Where did you go running again?'

'Just around town.'

'You're lying. This is you in this video!' He was pointing at the screen as I gave the Fiddler a right hook. I didn't know what to say.

'What have you been up to?'

'Randall, you can't tell anyone about this. I mean it.'

'I don't get what's going on. What is this?' He was pointing at the screen. The cat was out of the bag (who bags cats?).

'I'm a superhero.'

'What, like Batman?'

'Kind of'

'Superheroes aren't real.'

'I am.'

'This isn't funny. I don't get it,' he said. I couldn't say anything. I literally didn't know what to say. Randall clicked replay on the video.

'You have a name and, and a catchphrase?!'

'Yeah, sort of.'

'Who's that guy in the mask?'

I didn't enjoy lying and lying to my best friend felt even worse but I had to lie about the Fiddler, I couldn't bear anyone knowing I was a fraud. It's one thing if Randall let out that I'm Toecap but letting out I'm Toecap and the Fiddler was an actor is far worse.

'I don't know. He was fighting some lads so I stopped it.'

'Yeah you did. That right hook was powerful.'

'Thanks.'

'Why Toecap?'

'My superpower is in my toes.'

'That sounds stupid.'

'I know it does. It's hard to explain. I sometimes get superhuman strength when I hit my toes, like an unstoppable rage. I can't control it yet though.'

'I can't believe you're a superhero!'

'And you're the only one who knows it's me, so I need you to promise you won't tell anyone. This isn't like all the other times when you've promised to keep something secret and then told everyone. I need you to promise me that this won't leave this room.'

'Hmm.'

'Randall! Promise me!'

'I promise, I promise. This is just a lot to take in.'

'I know. It's quite cool though, when you think about it.'

'It's very cool!' He was coming round to the idea. 'So with Neville and Chris, was that...?'

'Yeah it was because of that. But I wear toecaps now to stop it, hence the name.'

'Toecap.' He grimaced. 'It's not great, is it?'

'Thanks.'

'If I hadn't come round tonight would you have told me?'

'The fewer people that know the better, I'm only a beginner.'

'Yeah, that makes sense. Is there anything I can do?'

'All I ask is that you keep it a secret.'

I had to wait until Randall had left before I could email the Fiddler. Deep down I knew I could trust Randall, he was my best friend, but I would rather he hadn't found out. I had to be more careful with my movements. Coming home in my costume was a rookie mistake.

I thanked the Fiddler for his performance. Emails went to and fro as we discussed, analysed and decided our next move. We thought it best to strike while the iron was hot. So for the same time next week we had our second P.I.S.S. together planned and it was something a little more ambitious. With only a week to rehearse I immediately emailed Papcastle village hall to book it. Before I logged off for the night I checked the site Randall had watched the video one. Multiple videos were now online and photos were being shared, liked and commented on. I looked good on screen, better than the other night. We had rehearsed well, you couldn't see that it was little Toby Malloy under that hood. We had gone viral.

My phone beeped and it was Molly hoping my evening wasn't too boring.

20

So Randall knew. Big deal. At least now I had someone to talk to about all this. We met up the next day. There was me and Molly and Randall and Willow - the awesome foursome as some people referred to us as (no one called us that). We ventured into town and had coffee in a local independent bookshop that had recently expanded in order to sell hot drinks and cakes. All anyone was talking about was the mysterious Toecap. Everyone wanted to know the identity of the hooded hero and the awesome foursome was no exception.

'What do you make of it?' Molly threw into the air for any takers. I looked at Randall. Randall looked at me. I sipped my coffee, hoping someone else would answer.

'It's great,' Randall began. 'Someone to look up to. It's nice to know someone is watching out for us.' I smiled - a thank you smile.

'Yeah,' Willow agreed. That was all she had to say on the matter, apparently.

'Dangerous, though,' Molly said. 'Crime-fighting should be left to the police, to the professionals. I'm sick of people these days just wanting their fifteen minutes of fame, doing anything to get noticed. It won't be genuine; no doubt he has some sort of product he's using this to promote. We don't get completely selfless people in the real world. He will end up getting himself hurt or worse, and then what?'

Randall and I looked at each other.

'That's part of the point though, isn't it? He's risking his own safety to help other people.'

'That's what the police are for. You can't have everyone going around taking the law into their own hands, it would be chaos.'

'But the police weren't there when the boys needed them to be, he - this Toecap – was,' said Willow.

'And I don't think fame is the point,' I said, defending myself.

'He knew it would be filmed, every man and his dog has a camera phone these days. He did it so people would talk about him. What about all the people who do good every day and don't brag about it?'

'I don't think people talk about good things they've done just to show what great humans they are. I like to think they tell people about it to remind them how easy it is to make a positive change in the world.'

I didn't know what was wrong with Molly. For some reason she had taken a clear disliking to Toecap. It felt like we were ganging up on her about it as well. It was time to change the subject.

'What if Toecap was Toby?' Randall asked her. My heart jumped.

'I think I'd know if my boyfriend was living a double life!'

'But what if he was?' Randall asked again, hoping for a better answer. I kicked him discreetly under the table.

'Ow!' Willow winced, having just been kicked under the table. Molly paid her little attention and carried on arguing.

'If somehow Toby was managing to attend school and work and date me and all the while going out every night to fight crime, I'd suggest to him that one of the first three of those activities could improve exponentially if he chose to give up the fourth. I don't like the idea of Toby being in danger.'

'What if I wasn't in danger?'

'What?'

'What if I wasn't in danger? What if I could fight crime like Toecap had last night and there was no chance of me being in danger?'

'And how would that work?'

'I don't know, I'm just saying. If I could do good, you know, make a difference, and I could do it without being in harm's way, wouldn't you want me to?'

'But you can't eliminate the risk of danger. You can't control that when pursuing something like this. No hero comes out the other side untouched.'

'I fully support Toecap. We need examples set for us like this and I would help if I could.'

'Do you not hear yourselves? This isn't a fairy story. This isn't a Hollywood film with a happy ending. Toecap will end up getting hurt or getting someone else hurt. You mark my words.'

Randall and Willow had been quiet for some time. We joined them in this pursuit and the next five minutes were spent with everyone in silence, slurping now and then on our drinks. Molly had calmed a little.

'Having said that, you would look good in spandex,' she said. We all laughed.

We dragged out a long goodbye before the girls went one way and Randall and I went another. Molly apologised for being argumentative, said that she was just grumpy today, but she did leave me thinking about Toecap and what it would all come to in the end. As we walked away I could tell Randall wanted to say something.

'What?!' I eventually asked.

'I was just going to say don't listen to Molly, she's wrong.'

'She is wrong. I have all this under control. I know what I'm doing and no one will get hurt. Trust me, I promise.'

'No, I mean about the spandex. You would look awful in spandex.'

21

In the blink of an eye, Saturday was upon us. Showtime. The Fiddler
and I had spent the week meticulously going over our next P.I.S.S.
together. We had raised the stakes for our second outing but if all
went smoothly it would be quicker and more rewarding than the
first. We were the talk of the town and I hadn't appeared in public as
Toecap since our debut.

Like last week, I had switched a shift at work to free up my
evening. I had had to lie to Molly as she inevitably asked what I was
doing instead. I told her Randall was coming over, another lie which
he reluctantly agreed to be part of. This meant he had to cancel his
plans with Willow and hide out in my bedroom until I got home. He
didn't like lying to Willow and I didn't like lying to Molly but people
loved Toecap and I needed this. This was good for the town.

Our second P.I.S.S. was set to be a mugging. We had decided
to do it at the local supermarket so it would be caught on CCTV
and therefore offer more exposure. We were hoping to make the
news this time and we were quite surprised our viral video hadn't
last week. Once again, we kept the plan simple. The Fiddler would
mug an elderly lady coming out of the shop, near to closing time.
There wouldn't be many people about, but all you need is one and
they would spread the word. The Fiddler was excited for his second

showing as was I, really; we were going down well. I hoped Molly would grow to like Toecap. If only I could tell her it was me and the Fiddler was a paid actor. I had to win her round, I had to prove her wrong. We were getting closer and she was learning more about me every day; could I keep this from her forever?

Toecap was what I needed to focus on. The Fiddler had parked round the corner from the supermarket and had left his car there as he walked to the entrance of the shop. He had to pass through the car park on his way and he stopped in between two parked vehicles to tie his shoelace. His laces were fine; he was hiding from view, waiting for someone he could attack. What if no one came? What if only men came out the shop from now until it closed? Elderly women don't shop at half-seven at night do they? Mind you, they're not exactly speed freaks, we might catch one that had spent all day in there. The shop doors opened and a very large man came out carrying a bag of firewood on his shoulder. No chance. Simon had his mask and hat at the ready. As the shop door opened again he put on his eye mask. It was just a young staff member on a cigarette break. But behind her there was an elderly woman shuffling outside. Perfect. The Fiddler had his cue. He appeared from between the cars and walked over to the entrance. The young employee puffing away on her cigarette recognised the Fiddler instantly. Her eyes widened and she pointed a finger in the air at him. The Fiddler walked right up to the old woman, who was being overtaken by snails, and grabbed her bag from her. She screamed at him and then began calling for help. With ease the Fiddler liberated the bag and began jogging away at a practised and very precise speed. The smoking staff member was recording all of it on her phone, as was the security camera above them. She really captured the old woman well, crying and everything, helplessly looking down at her shopping all over the floor.

'Perhaps I can help?' Toecap said.

'Argh! Another one!' the old woman screamed.

'I'm here to help'

'She had her bag nicked!' Toecap was informed by the staff member, 'He went that way!'

'I'll be back!'

I ran after the Fiddler who was waiting around the corner by his car.

'That wasn't as scary as last week,' he said. He handed me the woman's bag and said he'd email soon. I thanked him and waved him off as he drove away. I ran back round the corner with the bag in hand and went into the shop. The elderly lady had been brought in and given somewhere to sit and gather herself. I was greeted with cheers and I held out her bag, which she took with shaking hands. Once more an attack of flashes hit me and videos were taken while people cheered and thanked me. I did the only thing left to do. I pointed at the crowd and shouted 'Tow the line!'

Smooth.

22

It was odd to see yourself in the news and scattered among the papers and yet not be allowed to talk about it. To see everyone trying to guess who Toecap was and not know that it was little old me. It was a strange feeling indeed. I wasn't sure whether I liked it or not. Initially it was fun, but after a while, because I *was* the news, I was hoping someone would talk about something else for a change. If I wasn't Toecap I probably wouldn't have been bored of it. And don't get me wrong, the idea was to get people talking about me, but I was hoping they would talk about what I was actually doing rather than just who it was doing it. They were focusing on the wrong point. The whole purpose of Toecap was that it could be anyone. Toecap was showing that anyone could make a difference. The people of Cockermouth seemed to be fixated on the real identity of Toecap rather than his purpose. Finding out who I really was would be like describing how a magic trick is done. Once you know, the magic is gone. If my identity was discovered people would lose interest. That's the beauty of a superhero: they are a symbol, they can be more than just a citizen, they can be anyone.

Toecap was beginning to mean something to the town. Posters in shop windows started appearing showing support for me. Fan sites were growing and the local news seemed to appreciate my efforts – even the police joked with the idea. I had proved Molly wrong, no one was being hurt. A couple of lads had picked up a bruise and an old lady came close to heart attack but the positives outweighed the negative. I had this under control, I was good at it. With the popularity of Toecap growing, I thought the Fiddler and I should perform more regularly. This was becoming a business and it needed to grow. In time I'd like to hire more actors and expand on some P.I.S.S. ideas I had been working on, some group P.I.S.Ses. I had permanently swapped my Saturday shift so I was free and I thought about asking Randall to start a fan site and take donations. The Fiddler was keen to perform more and my relationship with him was working out well. We still knew next to nothing about each other.

When you're on a roll you have to keep rolling. You can't stop when the going's good. The first and second P.I.S.Ses that the Fiddler and I had taken together couldn't have gone better, so I didn't wait in setting up the third. A pie and peas night was taking place in the United Reformed Church and the Fiddler would be in attendance. The plan, as always, was simple. In and out, the Fiddler a mere warm-up act before the main show. The Fiddler would go in, armed, and shake the place down. On his way out Toecap would once more save the day. Easy as pie, and peas. These kinds of nights don't drag on and they usually have an early start. With this being on short notice I didn't know much else about the event, and as far as Toecap and the Fiddler were concerned nothing about tonight was any different from the previous P.I.S.Ses, but for the fact that this time the Fiddler would be brandishing a six inch knife, which obviously wouldn't be used for anything more vulnerable than a tough crust. With no rehearsal time, the Fiddler wasn't showing his usual confidence. I had faith in him though and while this was ambitious, I firmly believe the motto nothing ventured, nothing gained.

Speaking of food, I was eating at Molly's that night for the first time. Being Toecap took up so many of my nerves that it was hard for anything else to bother me. If I wasn't planning on saving a crowd of pie-eaters later that evening I would be dreading being introduced as 'the boyfriend'. I had never done the 'meeting the parents' bit before but it had gone well when Molly had met mine, so I figured it would be much the same vice versa. I tried not to entertain thoughts like *what if they don't like me?* or *what if I make a fool of myself?* I think the more you think you'll make a mistake, the more likely you will. I wanted to be confident but I had nothing to be confident about. I was confident about Toecap but I couldn't bring that up in conversation. I wondered what Molly's parents thought about him. I wondered if they'd bring him up. I wonder when would be a good time to tell Molly I was Toecap. It wouldn't make her like Toecap any more, it would make her worry more if anything, even if I told her the Fiddler was an actor. I think even Molly, who was against Toecap, would be disappointed to know he was a fraud. I enjoy being Toecap and people were talking about him but I didn't know if it was working. I didn't know if I had directly helped to lower the local crime rate. I was increasing the number of crimes if anything, as I was paying the Fiddler to commit them.

Meeting Mr Cooper was like meeting Vito Corleone on the day of his daughter's wedding, after having first gotten drunk and touched up the bride a bit. Mrs Cooper was nice; she was the cooling fan to Mr Cooper's heat-seeking missiles.

Brandon was his name.

He was extremely protective over his daughter but we had the same ideas on that so I don't know why he was being weird about it. I don't think he disliked me specifically, I think he'd just have preferred that Molly wasn't at the age of bringing anyone of the opposite sex home. Thankfully, Molly got most of her traits from her mother, Lynne, who was nothing short of delightful.

I arrived a little earlier than I had been asked to, so I waited outside until it was time. I had hoped this would make a good impression, being punctual, but the first question Brandon asked was why I was hanging around outside for so long. I laughed nervously and then Molly introduced me and we sat down to eat.

I survived the meal in the same miraculous way that a cockroach can somehow survive nuclear bombing. It wasn't too bad really – closer to a beating than being tortured, that sort of scale. It was a test and I just answered as best I could. Just like exams at school: when I didn't know the answer I'd have a guess. I held up well over my interrogation from Brandon, and I came out feeling marginally better about being captured by the enemy in a war-torn Europe.

Brandon was just being a good dad. I shouldn't make fun of him for wanting the best for Molly. It made me want to earn his respect.

I wanted to show Brandon, and Lynne, and Molly of course, that I deserved to sit at their table and count myself an equal.

Toecap had a brief mention while Lynne was serving out roast potatoes and I was the only one in his corner. They all agreed that the idea of Toecap was good but there are plenty of reasons why superheroes aren't real. It was hard arguing his case without getting annoyed that they didn't have all the facts. I was desperate to tell them that Toecap was in no danger and that nothing could or would go wrong. This topic passed when Mrs Cooper had finished serving out food and the conversation turned back to my future, and intentions. Flustered from discussing Toecap my answers grew short and by the time the meal was over I felt silly that I had let the discussion get the better of me.

After eating I offered to help tidy up, and Molly, Lynne and I cleared the table. Brandon had moved into the living room to watch TV with a beer. I relaxed a little and when it came to say goodbye I found myself hoping we could do this more often. Molly even managed to kiss me on the cheek without Brandon forcing his beer bottle down my throat.

Tonight could have gone a lot worse. I had done ok and I was on my way to proving Brandon wrong about me. Now all I had to do was prove them wrong about Toecap.

23

"In brightest day, in blackest night, no evil shall escape
my sight. Let those who worship evil's might, beware my
power; Green Lantern's light" - Green Lantern's oath

The church car park was full and the Fiddler had a bad feeling
about tonight. Something didn't feel right. Tucked into his belt was
a kitchen knife. He hadn't needed something like this before and
tonight's performance would be pure improvisation, without any
rehearsal time. His stage directions were to enter, rob and leave. On
the face of it that sounded fine and providing no one was a real-life
hero it should go smoothly, but the knife brought a new element of
danger into the equation. The Fiddler would flaunt it and happily
wave it around the room like a scarf at a football match but he hoped
to god no one came near it.

He scanned the car park, hoping to see Toecap. He wanted one
last chance to convince him that this needed more planning, but
if Toecap was here then he was well hidden. The blade dug in and
pressed against his body, making him very aware of its presence. It
was a long walk to the church. An eye mask was applied and a trilby
perched on top. The Fiddler pulled at the heavy door and stepped
inside.

There were no signs listing tonight's events but noise could be heard coming from up the stairs and to the right, so he made his way up carefully while trying to remember his lines. He came to the room from which the noise was coming and entered tentatively. As the room slowly revealed itself he saw a man, and then another. Then he saw a woman. They were red-faced and wearing tight clothing. Something wasn't right. From behind him the Fiddler heard someone cheerfully wishing him a good evening. With a hefty pat on the back, a man, carrying a water bottle and wearing a headband, told him not to be shy. The door swung wide open and the Fiddler stumbled all the way in. People began turning their heads and then froze when they saw the knife. The man behind the Fiddler was huge, so big that he looked like he had moved into a gym and spent the last three years eating other gym members. The water bottle looked like a novelty cuff-link in his hand and his sleeveless vest must have been in agony as it tried to cover his upper half. Before the Fiddler could backtrack he had been surrounded by a really odd group of pie and peas fans. But where were the pies? Where were the peas? There wasn't a table in sight. All he saw were red faces, leg warmers and brightly coloured mats. He couldn't even *smell* pies. Everything was slowly but surely pointing towards this not being a pie and peas night.

'Tim, call the police please, mate,' the mountain of a man blocking the door said calmly.

'Whoa, whoa, why?' said the Fiddler, holding his free hand up, signalling all to stop. Tim moved to retrieve his phone from his gym bag and as he bent to the floor he revealed a big board behind him that read...

Advanced Self-Defence Class with Victor Cole

'Oh my word,' said the Fiddler. He had to think fast. 'I'm here for the class.'

'What's with the knife then?'

'Improv?' He knew it wouldn't work before he had even said it. A nod was given to Tim, who dialled the emergency services and asked for the police. As soon as the Fiddler heard the word police he panicked. He and Toecap hadn't prepared, this was supposed to be a pie and peas night attended by people over a hundred years old.

Now he was stuck in a room full of people who purposefully go out of their way to make their bodies stronger than necessary and he was stood in the middle of them, wielding a knife unconvincingly. His biggest problem was Victor Cole, who was standing by the door. The Fiddler eyed him up and down and wondered where would be best to stab him with minimum chance of killing him. Victor was fiercely intimidating and he stepped forward as Tim gave an update.

'The police are on their way.' The Fiddler was really starting to freak out. He was totally out of his depth and, as far as everyone in the room was concerned he was a madman with a knife. They would never believe him if he told them he was an actor.

'I've seen him somewhere,' a woman said.

'Yeah, weren't you the guy caught on camera mugging an old woman? You have the same hat,' said someone else.

'Oh I see,' Victor said, nodding his head in confirmation of his own thoughts. He paced back and forth a little, stretching his arms.

I'm finished, the Fiddler thought, *it's over. The police are on their way and I will not be allowed to leave this room.* He squeezed the knife tightly, his only friend.

'You're in for a treat tonight, class,' Victor boomed around the room.

'Tonight I will be showing you how to disarm an armed man,' and then his eyes shot at the Fiddler, who was frozen with fear. He had no contingency for a situation where the pie and peas night went wrong; it was an 'in and out' job, too simple to have needed a back-up plan. He was amazed at how quickly a situation could change. He couldn't do anything, utterly helpless. Victor made his move.

I had seen the Fiddler enter the church but he hadn't discovered where I was lying in wait. I began the timer on my watch. I'd give him fifteen minutes or so, that should be plenty. The pie and peas night, if busy, would take the Fiddler a little time to explain who he was and what he was doing and what he wanted. I just had to sit and wait, which didn't bother me; it was a warm evening. A timer would be fine for tonight but in the future a better signalling system might be needed. I suddenly remembered watching the 1989 *Batman* film while I was grounded and deep within my research. It starred Michael Keaton as the eponymous caped crusader and is still enjoyable to watch even now, twenty-odd years after being made. Right at the end of the film Commissioner Jim Gordon is giving a speech to the few citizens of Gotham that were bothered enough about its extinction to turn up and listen - it really should have pulled a bigger crowd. A letter from Batman is read aloud, stating that if Gotham ever needed him again (he had just vanquished the Joker, played by Jack Nicholson, a flawless performance as usual) all they had to do was use the signal, to which a reporter in the crowd obviously asks...'What's the signal?'

So Jim switches on a huge searchlight that has a bat image covering the light source that's projected into the night sky. I remember this scene now for two reasons. Reason one, and it's more than likely only me that giggles at the thought of this, is that I imagine at that moment Batman gliding into shot and asking...

'Yo, what's the problem?'

'Oh, nothing. He asked what the signal was so I just turned it on,' replies Jim Gordon.

'You couldn't have just told him about it?' says Batman, annoyed.

'Well, we were right here. I thought I'd just switch it on, only for a moment.'

'Right, it's just that it takes a long time to get into this suit, you know? I'm not even that confident flying at night, it's dangerous.'

'Yeah sorry, we just...' Jim begins, but Batman cuts him off.

'Yeah I know 'you just' but I've rushed out because I thought you needed me.'

'Sorry,' says Jim.

'Stop saying sorry. You keep saying that but it's already been done. I mean, even now, right now, a crime could be taking place and I can't stop it because you're pratting around with the bat signal, calling me out here when there's nothing wrong.'

Jim and everyone around him are now quiet and embarrassed. Batman turns to the crowd like a fed-up supply teacher.

'If you can't be serious with this,' pointing at the Bat signal, 'I'll take it back. That's strike one, all right?' and then he takes a cab home to try and save his vegetable lasagne. That's how I would have ended the film but Tim Burton went in a different direction and, fair play to the man, he knows what he's doing.

So anyway, that's reason one. Reason two is that surely you can only use the Bat signal at night? If a crime is committed mid-morning the Bat signal is going to be rubbish. A crime takes place, the Bat signal is switched on and quick as a flash - twelve hours later - Batman turns up and catches the bad guys. It's useless and it's something the criminals of Gotham never clocked onto. Whenever I watch Batman films now I just think if they had done that crime first thing in the morning they might have got away with it, that's the tragedy. The sequel to *Batman* was *Batman Returns*, which is also a good film, mainly because it has Michelle Pfeiffer playing Catwoman, which is just poetry in motion. Ever since *Star Wars* came out many men (almost universally) have talked about their ultimate fantasy being Princess Leia with the gold bikini on, but I'd much rather have Michelle Pfeiffer in a full body black cat suit with a whip. Meow.

I glanced at my watch. I was getting bored. I looked up to the church, wondering what was going on in there. I sighed. In the distance I heard a police siren and began picturing myself one day fighting real crime, a day when my toe would be fully under my control. I'd be really strong; I'd just walk down the street kicking cars about. The police siren was getting louder. Such an annoying noise, but I suppose it's supposed to be. I locked my phone and put it in my pocket. As I did, someone came running out of the church looking like they should be coming out of a gym. I stayed where I was. A police car pulled up in the entrance to the church, blocking the parked cars from getting out. What the hell was going on? Another police car pulled up behind the first and four men jumped out and jogged over to the man who had come out to greet them.

'Are you Tim?' one of the officers asked, clearly the one in charge.

'Yes, sir.'

'Take us inside, please,' the policeman said. Oh no! The Fiddler was inside robbing the pie and peas night. I could only hope the two events weren't close to each other. If the police could deal with Tim quickly, the pie and peas night might not have to be disturbed. I looked at my watch. Fifteen minutes had gone but I couldn't go in now, the police would see me. I had no way of contacting the Fiddler, we only ever relayed messages by email. I didn't have his phone number. I didn't know what to do. Eventually the Fiddler would come out with a bag of money and a knife and he would walk straight into several police officers. I wanted them to hurry up. I didn't know why they were here but whatever it was, *please* hurry up. The Fiddler would come out any moment and it would be all over. What could I do? I couldn't think straight. Three officers had entered the building and one had stayed behind, guarding the front doors. I could try to distract him but how? If the Fiddler came out the front door I could run at the police officer, but that wouldn't work because I was supposed to take the money back in. This was disastrous; I had rushed this and certainly hadn't expected the police to turn up to a different event in the same building.

What if Tim was part of the pie and peas night? He was dressed inappropriately for it but what if he was involved? What if the police were here for the Fiddler? What if something had gone wrong? If the police were here for the Fiddler then it *was* game over. I would be in serious, serious trouble. The Fiddler didn't know anything about me but he had my email address, which he could give to the police and they could track me down. Why *wouldn't* he dob me in? It wouldn't change his punishment but why would he take this alone? He didn't owe me anything, we weren't close. If the Fiddler got arrested then I was screwed. What would my parents say? What would Molly say? Knowing that I had purposefully put people in danger to look like a hero. People would definitely think I was mad. *Get a grip,* I told myself, *you don't know what's going on inside. Stay calm, no use jumping to conclusions.* The Fiddler could be fine. He wasn't though, because two police officers were leading him out of the church in handcuffs. He had been arrested.

24

'Cock-juggling thunder cunt!' I couldn't believe it. I guess there are some situations where that combination of words is acceptable. The Fiddler being pushed into a police car which then backed out of the church entrance and drove off into the night was definitely one such occasion.

Before long, all the pie and peas eaters came out and went their separate ways. On a side note, they all looked in great condition for people that eat a lot of pies. Their clothes looked like a uniform, like a club or like a team. Was pie and peas a sport? I was so confused. Maybe they looked this good because they were on some sort of pie and peas diet, consisting exclusively of pie and peas. New diets appear daily, it's hard to keep track. I had to move quickly as these particular pie-eating champions were heading to the cars I was hiding behind. I made my way along the car park wall and then ran all the way home.

Once I got back in, I ran straight upstairs to the safety of my room. I paced back and forth and then sat down on my bed. My heart was racing and I looked down at my hands. I was shaking and still in costume. In a panicked rush I changed into some old clothes, the t-shirt had a couple of small holes in it and the sweat pants had been stripped of elastic. I sat back on the bed trying to figure out the worst that could happen. The worst that *would* happen.

Ok, so the Fiddler had been arrested. He would be taken to the station and asked for his real name. Then he would be questioned, I guess, in one of those small rooms where the police play good cop bad cop. What would he tell them? He would say he was an actor on a job, which they'd ask about, and that's where I'd come in. Fucking hell, what had we done? What had *I* done? I could tell the police I had nothing to do with it but the Fiddler had all our emails to link me to it. It was his only insurance. I should have been clever about this, I should have thought it through more. I had no idea what kind of trouble I was now in. I was trying to think what it was I had actually done. I had paid a man to punch a couple of kids, mug an old woman and attempt to rob a room full of people with a kitchen knife. When you say it out loud it sounds mental. I was under eighteen though; I couldn't go to jail, could I? What would I be charged with? Extreme theatre? Should I go to the station? Would that help my case, if I cooperated? Or should I just sit tight and play it out?

There was a knock at the front door.

I'm dead, my life is over. Completely over. How could I possibly bounce back from this in a small town like Cockermouth? I felt sick. We'd have to move, start again, uproot the family. No more school, no more Molly and no more Randall. Oh Randall. What I wouldn't give to have Randall here now saying something stupid to make me feel better. What about the Fiddler? I knew nothing about him, did he have a family? Did he have a wife, children? Whoever was stood outside knocked again. It was the police, it must be. The Fiddler had told them everything; they would have seen the emails and tracked them to me. They were here to take me in. I could have cried. I could picture the look on my parents' face. My poor mum as she had to listen to the police telling her what I'd been up to. Molly would end things. She'd be long gone. I had ruined everything. Midway through a third barrage of knocks someone downstairs answered the door. Everything was quiet for an agonising moment.

'Toby?!' my mum shouted up the stairs. I jumped. I could hear it in her voice. Her voice told me everything.

'Toby!!?!'

I couldn't reply. I couldn't move. I never wanted to leave this room again. I wanted to curl up and hide forever, never see another human being for as long as I might live. I heard a mumble and then heavy footsteps on the stairs. One long, slow plod after another, getting closer, getting louder. Thud. Thud. Then nothing. There was a small knock at my door. I just sat staring at it, knowing the end of my life was waiting on the other side, waiting to introduce itself. The handle was pushed down, the door opened and Molly came in, smiling at me.

'Hey,' she said. I didn't say anything, I couldn't breathe. I tried to smile.

'Did you not hear me shouting at you?'

I just looked at her, confused and still unable to speak.

'You ran right past me just moments ago. Flew right by,' she said. I was still working on my smile.

'Are you ok? I know you've been running a lot lately but that was some run!' She was just talking to herself really, I couldn't concentrate. 'Toby?'

Still nothing left my lips. I suddenly felt very tired.

'Are you ok?' She came and sat down by my side. 'You're sweating all over!' I was just amazed at how much she had said already without an actual response from me.

'I'm ok,' I said, still listening out for the door. It would be worse now. The police would turn up and Molly would be here to see them take me away. We lay on the bed and I stopped sweating. We talked and time ticked on, minute by minute. I kept checking my watch but no one knocked on the door. The phone didn't ring. Sirens couldn't be heard charging down the street. I asked Molly to just stay next to me and before I knew it, we had both drifted off.

I woke up and had a split second of peace before I remembered everything that had happened earlier. It came back in a hot spread through my body. I checked my watch again. It was getting late and we had school in the morning. I should wake Molly and take her home. I watched her sleep, peacefully unaware of the trouble I had brewed, bottled and sold locally. Why hadn't anyone come for me yet? What had happened with the Fiddler? These questions buzzed around my head. The room was dark but I could make out Molly's face. I could see her chest rise and fall ever so slightly with the intake of breath, a beautiful display of catch and release. I wished she could stay with me that night. I placed my hand on her shoulder and rocked her gently, softly asking her to wake up. Her eyes opened and she lay there looking at me.

'It's getting late,' I said.

'Ok.'

'I love you,' I said. Her eyes pinned open and burned brightly in the dark room. Her feet touched mine and I thought about the toecap I was wearing.

'Come on, let's get you home,' I said, kissing her on the cheek. I was still nervous about leaving my room. I could picture my parents, the school headmaster, the police and the Fiddler all waiting on the landing for me to leave my safe place. Hours had passed since my accomplice had been arrested and I had heard nothing. I dressed in silence and Molly gathered her things. She opened the door and to my surprise the landing was empty. We made our way downstairs and after saying goodbye to my parents we stepped into the night and headed for Kirkgate.

Town was quiet, the Fiddler not yet news. To more than most it hadn't happened yet. It would be breakfast chat to most of Cockermouth. I was desperate to just run over to the police station and find out what was going on. In the hours that had passed since his arrest I had aged a hundred years. Molly was also quiet. Maybe she was tired, maybe she knew I was acting strange or maybe it's because I had told her that I loved her. She hadn't said it back but it didn't bother me. That's not why I had said it. I had said it because I could feel my impending doom and I hated myself for letting her down. I wanted to say it while I still had the chance. I felt awful.

Neither of us were talking, we just walked side by side. Her house came into view. I would be in bed soon, I'd fall asleep and wake up to a new day. I didn't know what tomorrow would bring but I had a feeling I wouldn't like it.

'I love you too,' Molly said, before giving me a quick hug and disappearing behind her front door.

25

"We create our own demons" - Ironman

Simon Webb had never really had nights away from home. Romantic trips, last minute getaways and wet weekends in Reigate are far too exciting to appeal to a man championing such levels of boredom. He was led out of the police car and into the station. It was warm inside and the front desk was tidy and clean. Simon looked at the officer on duty, who, in turn, faced the arresting officer and engaged him in routine conversation. When an arrest is taking place there are a very specific series of events that must be followed. Correct me if I'm wrong, but now that Simon was at the station he would be held in custody and later questioned, once everyone involved had had sufficient doughnuts, although I think that particular ritual is only practiced in America. I don't know what the British equivalent is - scones? Simon couldn't see any scones as his eyes wandered this unfamiliar place. A custody officer explained his rights to him but Simon wasn't really listening. They have to do this and your rights aren't half bad. For example, you have the right to get free legal advice or you have the right to tell someone where you are. You can even have medical help if need be – they have plasters and all sorts.

The police can hold you for up to twenty-four hours before they have to charge you with a crime. They can apply to hold you for up to thirty-six hours or even ninety-six hours if you're suspected of a serious crime. If you've been pratting around with bombs they can hold you for up to fourteen days under the Terrorism Act. I think I've got that right. In order to make an arrest the officer either has to personally observe a crime or have probable cause to believe that the person being arrested has committed a crime. Police officers have to be able to justify their arrests by showing tangible evidence - like a six-inch kitchen knife. I'm sure you've heard of the Miranda Rights, as used in America. The British caution goes something like this...

"You do not have to say anything, but it may harm your defence if you do not mention when questioned something which you later rely on in court. Anything you do say may be given in evidence."

On TV you always see arresting officers say this as they are making the arrest, but they don't have to read you your rights there and then. They do have to be read to you before any form of interrogation though and this is why officers do say it straight away, so they can crack on with doing their goddamn job. How the Miranda Rights came about is a great story; read on.

In the year 1963, a chap called Ernesto Miranda was arrested in Phoenix, Arizona, for stealing a whopping eight dollars from a bank worker. He was charged with armed robbery. Crikey, if you're going to commit armed robbery, at least make it worth your while. Ernesto already had a record for armed robbery - I dread to think what for - a can of Tizer and a Curly Wurly? He also had a juvenile record including attempted rape, assault and burglary. While he was in police custody he signed a written confession to the robbery, and also to the kidnap and rape of an 18-year-old woman. After the conviction, his lawyers appealed, on the grounds that Ernesto didn't know he was protected from self-incrimination.

The case of Miranda v Arizona made it all the way to the Supreme Court, where the conviction was overthrown. In a landmark ruling issued in 1966, the court established that the accused has the right to remain silent and that prosecutors may not use statements made by defendants while in police custody unless the police have advised them of their rights. These rights came to be known as the Miranda Rights.

The case was later re-tried; Miranda was convicted on the basis of other evidence, and served 11 years. He was paroled in 1972, and died in 1976 at the age of 34, after being stabbed in a bar fight. A suspect was arrested but chose to exercise his right to remain silent, and was released. Incredible.

Simon knew a Miranda. It's a satellite. How boring. It is a satellite of Uranus, the eleventh closest to the planet, with a diameter of three hundred and one miles. It was discovered in 1948 and it is the innermost and smallest of the five major Uranian satellites and blah blah blah. He loved information like this, but even *he* thought it best not to share this with his newfound friends. He didn't know these officers very well and none of them had given him strong reason to believe they were interested in astronomy. It can be hard making new friends. After his rights had been read to him he asked for his phone call.

Carol. She would have to know sooner or later. Simon was led to a phone and left alone to make the call. He was annoyed when no one answered. Where could she be at this time? She had been home all day; he had bored her into doing the housework as usual. Simon didn't like it that she hadn't answered the phone. He couldn't be away from her for too long, she had been living in a deep trance for years and needed daily boosts. He had no idea what would happen if the trance broke; his life had been so boring that he had never had to think this scenario through. Had the trance broken already? Was she out partying? Where was Jamie in all this? Was he partying? As he held the phone he glanced up and down the room, wondering how boring he would have to be to get out of here. But we've discussed this before; keeping Carol in a trance-like state of submission was easy as he saw her every day. At a push he could bore himself out of the station but within minutes the trance would break and they'd come after him. He saw several officers milling about, coming and going, and all of them would have different interests. You could bore one with the Miranda satellite but another might somehow find it mildly interesting. He shouldn't be here, this was Toecap's fault. This was all Toecap's fault. He slammed the phone down but held onto it. The gravity of the situation was really kicking in, as if it had been waiting in the phone receiver and had only just crawled into Simon's head. He had been arrested and he was inside a police station waiting to be charged because he had tried to rob a room full of people with a knife. On top of that, he had been caught on camera mugging an old lady and there were countless witness statements detailing how he had beaten up several local teenagers. For the local paper this was front page news. By the morning everyone would know who the Fiddler was. His wife would know - what would she make of all this trance-free? Simon knew Toecap had rushed this P.I.S.S. What was he supposed to do now? Very shortly the police would want to know who Simon was and why he had committed these crimes. Would they believe the truth?

An officer approached. "Please come with me".

Simon let go of the phone. He had been caught red-handed but he wasn't going down alone. The Fiddler was led into a room and a chair was pulled out for him. Seated across the table was yet another officer. He shuffled papers and once the officer that had brought Simon in had gone, he pressed play on the tape recorder to his left and leaned forward.

'It's getting late Mr Webb and I want to go home.'

'In my defence, I thought it was a pie and peas night.'

'How will that help your defence?' It was a rhetorical question. The officer was sleep-deprived, all baggy-eyed and prickly.

'So,' he continued, 'why did you do it?'

'It was a performance,' replied Simon. He would try his luck with the truth.

'Go on.'

'I'm an actor.'

'An actor? Have I seen you in anything?'

'No.'

'No TV or film?'

'No.'

'A West End play perhaps?'

'No.'

'How about a local production?'

'No.'

'Have you ever acted before?'

'...No.'

'Shall we dabble with the truth then?'

'I am an actor. I was hired to fight, and to rob that woman, and do this tonight. It's the truth.'

'Who hired you?'

'I don't know his name.'

'You don't know his name?'

'No.'

'Well what does he look like?'

'I don't know.'

'What do you know about him?'

'He's about sixteen, at a guess.'

'Sixteen? Mr Webb, you should start taking this more seriously.'

'I'm telling the truth.'

'I wasn't born yesterday, Mr Webb. You expect me to believe a teenager hired you to act out these crimes because you're an actor?'

'Yes. Yes please.'

A light came on in Simon's head - the emails. *Tell the officer, then.*

'This isn't going away. You will be charged with assault, robbery and armed robbery. You will go to jail. Mr Webb, your life as you know it is over and to sit here and spin this ludicrous web of lies is only making things worse...'

The Fiddler and Toecap had contacted each other by email. Simon's life was over but he'd go down swinging. The police could track Toecap through his email and bring him in. What would then happen to Toecap? He was only a child. He wouldn't meet the same fate as the Fiddler. How was that fair? If only Simon could get to Toecap before the police, then he'd get what he deserved. With retribution in mind, Simon kept quiet about the emails. In fact, he didn't say another word.

'It's late and I'm tired. We'll deal with you further in the morning.'

With this, the interview was over and Simon was taken to a cell for the night. He retreated to the back of the room. The mattress was thin, well-worn and heavily stained. He sat down slowly, easing the sharp springs into his buttocks. He had a busy night of planning ahead of him. He had thought the Fiddler would be his breakthrough role. A stepping stone to a better life. He had dreamed of attending school reunions, taking his awards along to rub in the faces of all those who had ever doubted him. That was all over now, all because of Toecap. Right now Toecap was in bed, warm and cosy, dreaming of girls and the next party worth attending. Simon spent the night fixating on this, getting more and more angry. All he cared about from this moment on was getting his hands on Toecap before anyone else did.

26

I woke up face down. Monday had arrived. I took a deep breath and slowly let it out - my breath was rank. Climbing to my feet, I reached for my dressing gown, which was sleeping over a chair. I shuffled into my slippers and headed downstairs. The smell of coffee was in the air and voices could be heard in the kitchen. It was a bit early for visitors; Mum must have the radio on. I made my way through the house, waking each room as I passed through. Opening the door into the kitchen I found two police officers seated at the table. A huge amount of food had been laid out beautifully but nothing had been touched. Both officers looked up at me. Mum was standing over the cooker, juggling frying pans overflowing with yet more eggs and bacon. My dad was at the head of the table, hidden behind a paper. My mum addressed me.

'These two officers are here to see you,' she said. I looked from her to the officers. Dad didn't move from behind his paper. I said nothing, waiting for someone else to start.

'Last night we arrested a man calling himself the Fiddler. Do you know him?'

I shook my head.

'He certainly seems to know you. Calls you Toecap?' the other said. I continued to shake my head.

'He says you've been paying him to commit crimes; is this true, sir?' said the first one.

My mum turned the heat off the cooker and my dad put down his paper, his face was painted like a clown with a big red nose and huge fake ears. Everyone was looking at me. Just at that moment Molly appeared behind me. She saw the police and asked what was going on. The morning paper dropped through the letterbox. I shook my head.

'We need to take you down to the station please, sir,' said one of the officers. I shook my head. The back door opened, which led right into the kitchen and, amazingly, Zooey Deschanel came in wishing everyone a good morning and holding out a bottle of milk in one hand. I shook my head and took a step back. The two police officers stood up and neither of them was wearing any trousers. My mum turned around from the cooker and cried out that she was out of eggs. Dad was pulling an endless handkerchief out of his sleeves, laughing to himself, and Molly began whistling show tunes. I shook my head abruptly.

I woke up.

I had beaten my alarm. I had made it through the night; no one had come for me. Yesterday had been awful. I had no idea what was going on with the Fiddler and I now had other things on my mind, like my relationship. We had said the 'l' word and I don't know if you know, but it's kind of a big deal. I tentatively made my way downstairs, wondering if there really were two police officers in the kitchen. I followed the smell of bacon, and that's when it hit me. I knew I was safe. I laughed to myself. Mum was cooking bacon. There couldn't be police officers in the kitchen - you don't cook bacon with pigs in the house.

My dad was sat reading the paper and mum was standing over the cooker. No police.

'Morning,' my dad said without looking up.

'Morning,' I said.

'You hungry?' said mum, who didn't look at me either.

'Very.' I sat down and asked if we could have the news on.

'Good to see you taking an interest in the world,' they said, almost in unison.

'Our top story today: a local man, addressing himself as the Fiddler, who has been arrested for attempting to rob an advanced self-defence class last night in Cockermouth's United Reformed Church. Simon Webb entered the church with a six-inch kitchen knife but came up against more than he'd bargained for. Simon's alter ego, 'the Fiddler', as he told the arresting officers, has since been connected to two other recent crimes, including assault and theft. There's no more information at present but we will keep you updated as and when we have more. In other news...'

Simon Webb. The Fiddler had a name. A name I could have sworn I'd seen somewhere before. With Simon under arrest there was no Toecap. What were we heading towards anyway? I was learning nothing new about my power or how to control it. We were just putting on a show. If Simon got out would he want to continue? Somehow I doubted it. Where did that leave me? I was no further forward than I'd been at the start of all this. I'd learnt nothing.

I didn't listen to any more of the news; I had what I needed from it. After breakfast I took a shower and got ready for school. Then I met Randall and we headed off to find education, personal development and detention. This morning Randall was running late.

'Morning!' he said.

'Did you oversleep?'

'I had a late one with Willow last night.'

'Oh yeah? What did you get up to?'

'We did a jigsaw.'

'Oh right,' I said.

'It was a hundred pieces. We finished it in under an hour.'

'Incredible.'

'It said five to seven years on the box.' I let this one go, life is too short.

'I'm not going to be Toecap for a while,' I said, changing the subject.

'Why not?'

'For no other reason than I've thought about it and arrived at the conclusion that it is dangerous.'

'But what about your power? Your toes or whatever it is?'

'My power isn't within my control but I can suppress it with the toecaps I wear. Maybe I'll come back to it when I'm an adult or something, but right now I'm just a teenager and I can't spend my nights dressing up and running around looking for trouble. That's a job for the police.'

'Isn't it your calling or destiny or something?'

'I knew a girl called Destiny once and she made me wait ages before I could do anything with her so my destiny can back off a little'

'Fair enough. So what now?'

'I just put it behind me. I've got school, work and most importantly I have Molly. We've both said the 'l' word, by the way.'

'The 'l' word?'

'Love.'

'Oh yes of course. That 'l' word. Congratulations.'

'Thanks.'

'How did you do it?'

'I told her as she was waking up.'

'Nice.'

'Have you and Willow...?'

'Yeah, I bought a thousand Post-It notes and while she was in the shower I stuck them all around her room with 'I love you' written on each. Then I cracked open two cartons of apple juice - her favourite - and I gave her an early edition of her favourite book that had taken me weeks to track down.'

'See, this is what I mean: without worrying about Toecap I can spend more time doing this sort of nonsense. How did she take it?'

'Very well, if you catch my meaning.' He winked.

'Really?'

'How did Molly take it after you told her?'

'She went home.'

'Oh...cool.'

I wanted to spoil Molly. I really wanted her to know just how much she meant to me. I'd never liked anyone more than her; she was my favourite thing and with Toecap on sabbatical I could focus all my efforts into our relationship. I could use what would have been the Fiddler's wages to treat Molly, take her out somewhere or buy her an early edition of her favourite book. I don't even know what her favourite book is. It's just typical that Randall is a failure in every aspect of life but somehow he totally gets women.

As always, I sat down next to Luke in French. I know what you're thinking by now: I only talk about French lessons. *What about English or Maths?*, but nothing happens in those subjects. Nothing much happens in French, apart from that business with Neville, but French is the only lesson I sit next to Luke in and I have reason to mention it today because Luke wasn't his usual self. Everyone was talking about Simon Webb, or the Fiddler as people liked to call him. Well, Luke had also taken an interest in the story.

'I saw him once, you know.'

'Who?'

'The Fiddler.'

'Really? Where?'

'At the village hall.' That's right, I thought; I had forgotten Luke had auditioned to be my nemesis.

'Really?'

'Yeah, I didn't know it at the time but I met Toecap as well, in the same place.' He paused to look at me.

'Yeah...Toecap was auditioning for a nemesis.'

'What?' I laughed, unable to improvise something better.

'Bit odd isn't it? A superhero having to hire a villain?'

'What were you doing there?' I asked.

'We all have our secrets,' he said.

'You can't be sure it was Toecap.'

'Oh I can.'

'How?'

'Because for weeks after the audition I frequently visited the hall and I saw Toecap and the Fiddler rehearsing for their live shows.'

'And?'

'Well, the odd thing is that after the Fiddler had left the hall I saw you changing out of Toecap's costume.' He was smiling now, proud of himself.

'Have you not got any mates?'

'Shut up, Toby!' he snapped.

'Shh, boys,' the teacher said, briefly raising his head.

'So, what now?' I said.

'Now you have a new nemesis - a proper one.'

'What?'

'"The position had been filled." That's what you said to me. Looks like the position is open once more, with Simon Webb banged up. I warned you then that you'd regret turning me down.'

'Shh, boys! I won't tell you again!' said the teacher unconvincingly from the front of the class. He didn't even look up this time.

'And putting all that aside, do you really think you can just sit next to someone new in class and nothing will happen? Do you think I'm going to let you get away with that? I had to sit with Ben Fowler. Ben fucking Fowler! No offence, Ben,' Luke said as the boy in front turned around, looking a little deflated.

'So, what, you're going to seek revenge on me? Beat me up or something? You going to tell the world I'm Toecap?'

'I don't need to tell the world.'

'What does that mean?'

'You'll see,' he said.

'What does that mean!!?' I snapped at him, losing myself for a moment.

'Right, Toby Malloy, get out of my class,' the teacher demanded. I stared at Luke, who sat smirking.

'Now, Toby!' the teacher barked.

I stood up, shoved my belongings into my bag and exited the room. I hadn't taken enough precautions. I hadn't thought any of this through. There is a reason we don't have superheroes in the real world. Who was I kidding that I could get this up and off the ground? I had an adult in the police station and a psycho at school threatening to tell my secret to the world. I slumped down onto a chair in the hallway. I needed time to think but I wasn't the only delinquent here. I looked up and opposite me was Jacob Pike.

'This is all I need.'

'Toby Malloy,' he said as if they were dirty words.

'What?'

'We meet at last.'

'I didn't know you wanted to.'

'You have something that belongs to me and I want it back.' I really didn't need this right now. I had Simon to worry about, as well as Luke; I couldn't sort out Jacob as well.

'Molly doesn't belong to either of us.'

'You took her from me!'

'Can we do this another day, please? I have a lot going on.'

'I will get her back.'

'No, you won't.'

'I will, I will find a way of seeing you crash and burn. Whatever it takes, I will find something on you that will end you and Molly.'

'Good luck with that.' And then I left. Fuck this, I headed down the hallway to get far away from both Luke and Jacob. There was too much going on in my head. Too many risks swirling around, my thoughts were clouding, my foresight was murky. It was bad enough that Simon was in jail, but now Luke knew who I was and Jacob was after anything to bring me down and get Molly back. What was I supposed to do? Three on one isn't fair. Luke was my biggest worry as he was the only one that knew both my identities. He had kept it a secret so far, so he must have something planned. He must be waiting for something.

I walked down some stairs and without thinking my feet carried me outside and away from the foreign language block. It was still morning but I needed to find somewhere I could think all this through. I was still on school property but I had half an hour or so before the bell for the next period sounded out. I wandered around the back of the maths block and sat down on an old bench that was nicely out of view. I put my head in my hands and closed my eyes. Simon, Luke and Jacob. Luke knew who the Fiddler was and who Toecap was. From the advert and his own research he also knew that the Fiddler didn't know who I was. Luke wanted me to suffer and so would tell Simon Webb who I was. That's information Simon would want, as it was because of me that he was locked up. That made sense.

What Simon would do to me then I couldn't predict. What could he do? He was locked up. If he had wanted to tell the police about me he would have done by now. As for Jacob, he was just an inconvenience. I didn't see him giving me much trouble, providing he didn't speak to Luke. Luke had known for a while who I was and so far hadn't told anyone, and I didn't think he'd divulge information like that to someone with Jacob's reputation. Luke was the one I had to stop. I had to find a way to get him back on my side and keep him from speaking to Simon.

I lifted my head and looked around. He had wanted an audition; I could give him that. Plus I would promise to always sit with him in

French, no matter what. He could be my new nemesis; we could do P.I.S.S.es together. I stood up. I had to find him and sort this out today, sort it out now. The bell would ring any minute, I had to get back to class. I ran all the way back, through doors, upstairs, and through people. Pupils flooded out of rooms and I spotted Luke while my contemporaries bounced off me. I could see from his face, even at a distance that he liked knowing he had control over me.

'What?' he asked as I turned and walked with him.

'We need to talk.'

'You've got two minutes before Geography.'

'What, here?'

'You're wasting time.'

'Fine, I will never sit with anyone else in French and you can be my new nemesis. Ok? Just don't tell anyone who I am.'

'No,' he said before I had finished. I grabbed his arm and we stopped walking. He glared at me like a king would if a peasant had reached out and touched him.

'You've had your fun. Now I'm going to have mine.'

'Why?! Because I sat with someone else?'

'No!' he snapped. 'I've kept it secret who I am, what I know and what I can do. And I've kept it secret because this is just a small town, it plays no bigger part. In a few years I was going to move away and start there but you've forced my hand. This town loves Toecap but you and the Fiddler are a joke, just a couple of frauds, and I hate how easily you've fooled everyone. I hate it. I hate them for being so stupid. They don't deserve a hero and they don't deserve to be saved. You all need to be taught a lesson. I'd rather this town had a true villain than a fake hero. The Fiddler must be pretty keen to find out who you are now you've landed him in jail. I may need an adult's help for what I want to achieve and no one hates you as much as I do other than him. Together, we're going to bring you down and the whole town will be watching.'

I let go of his arm and he walked off. He turned a corner and was out of sight. I fell against a wall and slumped to the ground.

'You're going to be late for class.' I looked up and saw Jacob Pike smirking at me from the end of the hallway.

'Hurry along...Toecap,' he said.

This was the worst day of my life, and I'd thought yesterday was bad. Everything was spiralling out of control. I was getting to the point where I just wanted to shut myself off from the whole world. I had started out thinking being a hero would be easy or at least fun. I had thought of the fame, the respect and the gratitude. I hadn't anticipated things going this wrong. Luke was right, I wasn't a hero. I had failed to make a real difference even when I had pure intentions. Then I had tried to fake it and it had played out worse. I had tried to take shortcuts and now it felt like everyone was against me. I woke that morning hoping to keep my identity from Simon, but it wasn't even lunch yet and two people who didn't like me knew I was Toecap. Denial is a strong emotion, a blessing and a curse. The power to not believe is as strong as the power to believe. It is also the most predictable response among the human spectra. When we hear something bad or something we don't want to hear, our first reaction is often to deny it. No way, no thanks, not today please. People deny all sorts of things in the hope that simply denying it will make it go away. It's futile, but I had decided to live in denial right now. This day couldn't get any worse. Simon Webb was in jail because of me, Luke Cook had embarked on what seemed like a lifelong vendetta and Jacob Pike had promised to do whatever he could to get Molly back. Two thirds of that boy band knew I was Toecap and there was nothing I could do to stop them shouting it from the rooftops.

So, that's why I was just pretending none of it was real. Too much had happened recently that I had failed to predict. It obviously wouldn't help in the slightest, but I decided that was something future Toby had to deal with. Present Toby was fine ignoring it while he could. I had lunch to look forward to. I could hang out with Randall; he'd take my mind off things. He was the one person I could talk to about Toecap and yet these days I saw less and less of him. Even when I did see him Molly and Willow were always present. And as great as they were, I did miss time spent with my little sunflower. Molly and Willow had switched onto packed lunches so we could all eat together. It was sweet, I know it was, but Randall and I hadn't played Shithead in ages and I missed it. I needed things like Shithead more than ever. So much had changed and so much remained to fuck up that I wanted to go back. Back before all this. Back to a normal life. I had received the toecaps before I started any of this. I should have just popped two on and forgotten about it. People never know when to stop. I just couldn't think what I should do when all this came out. I needed a miracle to make it out alive. If only some higher power could take care of Simon, Luke and Jacob for me then I'd have promised to do good things with my life. Maybe Randall would take Simon and co out? He was my oldest friend. He wouldn't want any harm to come to me. I could have asked him. But I didn't need to anyway because nothing was wrong. Life was just dandy. Lunchtime with my best mate and my girlfriend. Wonderful.

I was the last of the group to arrive. They were laughing and calling me over as soon as I entered the room. I tried to smile. It was nice to be with people who didn't want to hurt me.

'Hello!' I said. I kissed Molly on the cheek and sat down.

'Hello, mate,' Randall replied and I just wanted to lean across and hug him. No I didn't, why would I? Nothing was wrong.

'Having a productive day?' my sweet Molly asked and I just wanted to curl up in her arms and disappear. I'm joking, of course I'm joking. Nothing was wrong.

'How was French?' Willow joined in and I just wanted to run home to my mum and cry. *Obviously* that's not true because nothing was wrong.

I smiled at all of them and hoped that that was enough of a response.

I bit into my sandwich and let my brain just focus on the flavours. Enjoy the tuna mayonnaise; it might be your last. Do you get tuna mayonnaise sandwiches in prison? Do you get salt and vinegar crisps? What about bananas? I always had a banana at lunch. Would I be allowed a banana at lunch in prison? I wouldn't even go to prison because I was too young. It would be some sort of detention centre for bad lads. That's not too harrowing actually; it might turn out to be good training for my power. I still didn't want to go, though. I couldn't go to prison, I had important exams this year and we'd want a holiday come summer. I took a gulp of water and smiled at Molly. Would she visit me while I was doing time? Or would it be too much for her? Would she write to me, would she stay faithful? Or would Jacob swoop in and claim her back? This was really good tuna mayonnaise. Mum must have made it; Dad always goes a little heavy on the mayo. Mum gets it just right, like mums do. I couldn't think about either of them, it was too painful. They had no idea what's coming. Neither did I. Maybe nothing would come, and I was being serious now, no more of this denial stuff.

What if nothing happened? Simon clearly hadn't mentioned the emails to the police. Luke and Jacob knew I was Toecap but that's not to say anyone would believe them if they shared my secret. Unless Luke had proof of me and the Fiddler at the village hall then it was really just his word against mine. He said he had seen me there. If he had really wanted to frighten me he would have said he had proof. Maybe I was being too dramatic. Maybe this wasn't as bad as it seemed. The Fiddler might not even have the emails, maybe he deleted them. Maybe Luke was just all talk; maybe he just wanted to blackmail me for something. A lot of 'maybes' were being thrown around but 'maybes' do happen. Maybe everything would die down in a day or so and things would start getting back to normal. Could I risk a little hope? It felt like my only option was to wait and let things unfold. I wasn't prepared, but I had no idea what to prepare for. I washed down the remainder of my sandwich and made a start on my banana. The banana had seen better days. A simple life. Grow, be picked, be eaten. Its last act on this world would be providing me with energy, enough to see me through P.E. that afternoon. Not that I needed much energy to sit and watch.

I had barely said a word during lunch but no one had really noticed. I nodded and smiled now and then, which seemed to have the desired effect.

Being a superhero has too much responsibility. A role in which I had proved myself useless. No more Toecap for now. The last thing I needed was to antagonise Luke and Jacob further. They might team up together. Jacob could tell Luke about Molly; they could start their diabolical plans with her and turn her against me. Would she believe that I was Toecap? I'm going to say something that might come as a shock - Toecap was the worst thing that had ever happened to me. It was my biggest regret. I wished I could take it all back. I wished I could pinch myself and wake up from all of this. I pinched myself and it hurt but nothing changed.

'Did you just pinch yourself?' Molly asked.

'Who?'

'You, you weirdo.'

'Pinch myself? No, don't think so.'

'Certainly looked like it,' Willow added. All right, Willow, calm down, mate.

'Anyway, we had better go, lunch is nearly over. See you both.' And with that Molly blew a kiss and left with Willow at her side.

'I saw you pinch yourself,' Randall said once they had gone.

'I have a problem.'

'Pain *can* be addictive.'

'Not with pain, you berk! I have a problem problem.'

'Oh right. What is it?'

'Both Luke Cook and Jacob Pike know I'm Toecap.' The room was next to empty but we spoke quietly.

'That's not good.'

'No, it fucking isn't!' I snapped, but I was actually relieved to finally be able to talk to someone about this.

'What are you going to do about it?'

'I don't know what I *can* do about it without murder being involved.'

'How would you do that?'

'I was going to ask my best friend to do it for me.'

'I'm not sure you've been going out with Molly long enough to ask her that.'

'I mean you! Molly isn't my best friend, she's my girlfriend.'

'Oh, ok.'

'Wait a second. Are you assuming because she is my girlfriend that makes her my best friend?'

'I dunno,' Randall shrugged.

'Is Willow your best friend?!' We were getting off topic but this was suddenly important.

'I dunno,' he repeated.

'This day *can* get worse. Who knew?'

'I don't know how these things work. It's all very new to me.'

'Well it's something you talk to your best friend about.'

'I can't ask Willow, she's *in* the relationship.'

'I mean me!! *I'm* your best friend!'

'Oh right, yeah.'

'Give me strength.'

'My biggest worry is that she'll just go off me in time.'

'Oh my heart bleeds for you and all your worries. What about me?! My life is in ruins.'

'I'm not sure I'd be very good at killing people, mate. You should get a professional to do it.'

'I can't afford a hit man.'

'Are they expensive?'

'No, I'm sure it's a labour of love.'

'Get an amateur, they will charge less.'

'Your suggestion for having a professional job done is to get an amateur to do it?'

'Well, why don't you just pay Luke and Jacob not to say anything?'

'Because I will become a cash cow. They will just keep coming back for more.'

'They might be honourable men.'

'We're teenagers; we're *all* dick heads!'

'Fair point. I could have a word with them if you like?'

'What on earth would you say?'

'I'd sit them down and say, "look lads, this...this really isn't on..."'
I just stared at him, waiting for him to finish or for the bell to ring, whichever would kill me first.

27

"Sometimes anger can help you survive" - Storm

Simon had barely slept and the lack of sleep had spent the night colouring in the bags under his eyes and adding worry lines in unexpected places. His thoughts had spent the night bouncing off the cold cell walls like scruffy tennis balls thrown by prisoners in films. Where do they get those balls from? He thought of home, of his wife and child, but above all he thought of Toecap. Anger can manifest at an alarming rate and before dawn Simon was obsessed with the boy he hardly knew. He woke from his unsettled dozing hungry, even after a night of feeding his imagination. He had convinced himself that Toecap had done this on purpose. Toecap must have become jealous that his portrayal of the Fiddler was starting to get some recognition and people were taking notice. Toecap had set him up, he had thrown him under the bus. A metal clunk echoed around the room and his door opened.

'You're famous,' a female officer with her hair in a bun announced.
'What?'
'You're on the news, pet.'
'Already? Can they do that?'
'Why not? It's exciting; it's not often we get a genuine supervillain in our midst.'
'My life is over. I can't believe it.'

That was it then. Everyone knew. He was officially a criminal.

'Can I make a phone call please?'

'You had your phone call last night.'

'No one answered. No one knows I'm here.'

'I think they do,' she scoffed.

'It's a bit early for jokes, don't you think?'

'One phone call and then you're straight back here until further notice, do you understand?' She held the door open and Simon stiffly clambered out and plodded off towards the same phone he had used last night. He picked up the receiver and entered a long number of buttons into the machine before holding the phone to his ear. It rang for a little while.

'Hello?' said Carol.

'Hello.' There was silence for some time.

'Well...?'

'It's Simon.'

'I know it's you, Simon. What do you want?' Carol sounded different. Her voice was firm and assertive, stronger than Simon had remembered.

'I wanted to let you know where I am.'

'I know where you bloody are, the whole county does.'

'Yes, that's right, they do. Are you ok?'

'Am I ok? Is that a serious question?'

'You sound different.'

'I feel different. I woke today with a clear mind, no fuzziness. My thoughts felt free and I noticed things I haven't noticed in a long time. I felt good and then I wondered why you're not here. I had to hear you've been arrested by someone I work with; do you know what that feels like? But the odd thing is the one day you're not here and I feel better than I've felt for years. I feel like I'm in control of myself again. This isn't a coincidence. I try and think back to how I got here and do you know what?'

'What?'

'I can't remember. I haven't a clue how I got here. I don't remember when we bought this house. I don't remember our wedding day. Who the hell decorated the house?! I can hear a baby crying down the hall, has that got something to do with us? The last thing I remember in detail is my first year of university and everything since then is a blur. All the time spent with you feels like a drunken night out. And this is the hangover. I can't believe you've been arrested. What are you being charged with?'

'Armed robbery, assault...and a bit more robbery.'

'Fucking hell, Simon. You bastard. I'm so angry with you.'

'Please, Carol, you have to listen to me.'

'No, you listen, Simon!' she screamed down the phone. Simon had never heard her like this and as his eardrum reverberated he realised that he no longer had control over her.

'I never want to see you again. I mean it. Never again. I will go to my parents' house and I will be filing for divorce as soon as humanly possible.'

'Carol, you can't!' But she hung up. Simon put the phone down and made his way to reception.

'Let's get you back in your cell. They're not ready for you yet.' The female officer had a softer voice now and Simon noticed a cup of coffee in her hand. Simon led the way and every now and then he heard small slurps behind him. Once he'd stepped inside the cell Simon turned to face the officer. They both wobbled as a deep, low rumble passed through the building. The female officer looked concerned. Another rumble, louder than the first. The water sprinklers on the ceiling came on. She told Simon to stay in his cell but she was cut off as a huge explosion erupted behind her. Simon ducked down and the policewoman cowered forward into the cell, dropping her coffee as bricks shot out of the wall in every direction. She took a couple of hits to her back and one brick clipped over her head, forcing her onto her knees. Dust filled the corridor but through the fog flames could be seen, great big rugs of fire rippling in the morning air. Another couple of rumbles and furniture rattled and ceiling lights swung violently from side to side, almost cracking against each other. Simon stood up and squinted ahead through the haze. The female officer was back on her feet, rubbing her head and standing in front of Simon.

A silhouette appeared through the smoke. The officer began to address the figure but a fat spurt of fire poured over her. It ran down her to the floor. She didn't scream, she didn't make any noise; it all happened so fast. She slumped a little and raised her hands as the fire consumed her. Her skin blistered and popped, her clothes burnt away and her lips burst in the heat as she melted on the spot. Skin peeled off her, falling in big slabs, her hair blazed away and her eyeballs ran down over her cheeks. She looked like she had visited Tenerife for a fortnight, lost her passport, and had to stay sunbathing on the beach for the next fourteen thousand years. Very quickly she was just a molten lump on the floor, spreading out over the cold tiles. That is some way to go. Whoever was orchestrating this must have got their hands on a powerful flamethrower. Had they got what they wanted? Were they after the female officer? What on earth did she get up to in her private life?

'Mr Webb?' someone shouted from the other side of the smoke. They were here for Simon. He didn't want to die like that, it looked bloody awful.

'No.'

'Oh, right, sorry. Was that him I killed just now?'

'No, that was an officer, a woman.'

'Do you know which cell Mr Webb is in?'

'What's it about?'

'I'm here to rescue him in the hope he'll help me in exposing Toecap to the world.'

Simon thought for a second.

'Sorry, did you say Mr Webb?'

'Yeah.'

'I'm Mr Webb.'

'Oh hi, great to meet you. I'm Luke Cook but my alias is Luke Warm.' He came into view as two armed police officers came charging down the corridor shouting for everyone to stay calm. Luke Warm turned to face them and with each empty hand motioned throwing something. Simon was confused but Luke's hands burst into flames and two miniature suns flew through the air. They made impact with the police officers and encased them in flames. While they screamed to death, Luke and Simon continued their conversation.

'How do you suppose your plan will work?' Simon asked. It was then that he saw, over Luke's shoulder, that another man was present. They were both young, very young, not even adults yet.

'Mr Webb, I'd like you to meet Jacob Pike.'

'All right?' said Jacob sheepishly.

'Hello, Jacob' Simon replied politely. 'Is Jacob here to help?'

'We both can,' Jacob said, smiling at Simon.

'How is that?'

'Because we all want the same thing.'

28

It was nice to be showering with boys again. And I say that in the manliest way possible. I had been allowed to participate in P.E. once more and I had forgotten how much I enjoyed trying to avoid being passed to through the fear of making a mistake. Responsibility really isn't for me. I sat drying myself off while other boys did that thing with towels where they roll them up tight and whip each other. Shrieks of pure delight filled the air. The first batch to re-dress stood waiting for everyone else, all with their heads down messing about on their phones. Some people just wouldn't survive without their phones, they are like little life support machines - if you turn them off the owner dies. One lad held his phone up and started shouting about something but it was hard to hear exactly what he was going on about over the yelps of pain from the boys enduring the meeting of rather nasty towel tip and bare bottom cheek. Another boy on his phone, sat near to me, began making the same sort of noises.

'The news, check the news!'

'Why?' someone at the back asked.

'The police station has blown up!'

'Don't be a twat, Gary,' shouted someone else.

'He's not lying!' another boy called. I reach across to check my phone and I was lost for words when I began to take it in. Breaking news was that the Cockermouth police station had suffered multiple explosions and was severely damaged by fire. There had been several casualties and firefighters were still tackling the blaze. The number of casualties was unknown. Maybe a gas leak?

'I wonder if Toecap is there?' squeaked a small boy no one knew. I scattered my vision to gauge reactions.

'Tell you who *is* there: that Fiddler bloke.'

I hurriedly gathered my things. The Fiddler was in the police station. Was it too much to hope for that he'd been brutally murdered, putting an end to one of my problems? Hang on a minute. The police station hasn't had so much as a bird crap on it since it was built. And now, within the space of a week, the Fiddler is arrested, Luke and Jacob threaten to make my pubic years even hairier, and now the entire station goes up in smoke? A bit of a coincidence isn't it? Luke and Jacob couldn't have been involved in the fire because you need signed permission slips from parents if you're to leave the school premises during lunch and I knew for a fact they hadn't got them. They'd be in serious bother if they had sneaked out. Could Simon have done it? I haven't read the beginner's manual on demolitions but it can't be wise to level a building while you're still in it. I pulled my other sock up.

'Where was Toecap when the Fiddler was arrested?'

'With your mum!' someone gushed, which earned them a round of applause. This is always a classic wise-crack at school. It's quick, it's sophisticated and it's perfect for almost every type of question or argument. Remember before, when I was talking about denial being the most predictable emotion? Well 'your mum' is the most predictable comeback at school. In fact the only way to trump it is if your mum is genuinely dead. But be warned, if you say she's dead and she isn't, then that is going to be a really hard lie to maintain for the rest of your life. And if you are caught lying about having a dead parent then you deserve everything you get.

The bell rang and that was both P.E. and the school day finished with. I was to meet Molly at the lockers and I was running late but she always took a little while getting her things together. Randall and Willow usually walked with us and I had grown to like this part of the day. I liked being seen with Molly outside of school. I pulled on the door and entered the locker area to find just Randall and Willow.

'Is she in the loo?' I said, looking at Willow.

'Who?' Who did she think?

'Molly.'

'No, I don't know where she is.' That's a bit odd, they're best friends, fully synchronised as only women can be. When girls are best friends they become like twins. Twins that secretly hate each other.

I looked at Randall in the hope that he knew more, but he came up blank. It wasn't the first time.

'Didn't you have Biology together last period?'

'She wasn't there,' Willow said.

'Maybe she went home ill,' said Randall.

'She was fine at lunch and she would have texted me anyway.'

'I'll ring her now,' said Willow.

Randall and I stood waiting, sharing expressions of puzzlement and concern. School had finished a little while ago and only a few nerds and people due for a detention were hanging around. This wasn't like Molly. Had I done something to upset her? Was Willow covering for her?

'Any luck?' I said to Willow once she'd taken her phone away from her ear.

'Nothing. Her phone is off.'

'Anything could have happened, family-related or something.'

'You're right, Randall, I'm sure she's fine.'

'Can we go then?'

'Yeah, let's go.'

The walk home was long and quiet and interspersed with bouts of giggling from the happy couple. Where was my giggling buffoon to mock the world with? Too many odd things were happening in succession for them not to feel related and I had that awful feeling in the pit of my stomach. On the long stretch that is Castlegate Drive I repeatedly tried to phone Molly but it went straight to voicemail each time. It was beginning to annoy me. Willow said goodbye and crossed the road, leaving me to walk the rest of the way with Randall.

'Did you hear about the police station today?' I said.

'Oh yeah, I did! I heard the Fiddler escaped.'

'What? Really? When?'

'Just before you got to the lockers.'

'Who told you?'

'The people on the TV.'

'He's escaped? Like actually escaped?'

'Yeah.'

'So he was there one minute and then, like, by his own doing, wasn't there the next minute?'

'Yes. I heard he was helped by at least two men.'

'Who told you that?'

'The people on the TV.'

Two males. Luke and Jacob? This was sliding horribly into place. Where could they get bombs from, though, and how quickly could they muster up two forged permission slips to leave school grounds at lunch?

'Does the report say who helped him escape?'

'No, just that they were youngish and that they all left together.'

I'd have to see the footage to confirm my fears.

'We need to go home.'

'Where *were* we heading?' said Randall.

'I mean quicker than we had planned to.'

'Aw, is this to do with Toecap? I thought you were done with all that?'

'I am, but that doesn't mean everyone else is.'

As soon as the front door opened my mum was on approach and asking if we had seen the news. She couldn't believe it - explosions in Cockermouth, it was unheard of.

'What's the latest?'

'At least three officers dead and one inmate. That Simon Webb chap, you know, the Fiddler, has escaped. Police are beginning to think it was a rescue mission of sorts.' She seemed excited that our little town was entertaining such skulduggery. She spends too much time inside painting the outside world, she needs more fresh air.

'A rescue mission?' Randall pondered.

'Yes, footage shows that before the explosion two young men were seen on site and after the explosions three men left, one of which was the Fiddler,' she said, scurrying off back to her studio, flicking paint on the walls as she went.

Once upstairs, Randall did his best to stop my train of thought.

'Just leave this to the police,' he said.

'They're busy.'

'What with?'

'Seriously?'

'If the Fiddler had help escaping, he must be part of some criminal organisation or he has friends in high places.'

'I know who helped him and I know what they want. Worst of all I think they know how to get it.'

'What are you talking about?'

'I can explain better once I've seen the footage.' I was seated at my computer with Randall standing behind me. I had switched it on but it needed to update.

'Why does it always have to update when you're in a rush?'

'Seeing as we have to wait, I have a game we could play. We were playing it earlier. If you could have dinner with five guests, anyone in the world, who would you pick?'

'We don't have time for this, Randall,' I snapped. We continued to look at the screen as it slowly ticked from 0% to 1% completion. We looked at each other. He looked hurt.

'Ok, let me think.'

'I know mine.'

'Wait, I'm thinking, although this is just off the top of my head because my mind is on other things, if you can believe it.'

'Ok, ok, get on with it.'

I spun round in my chair to face him.

'Right, ok, here goes...' I gave myself a little longer to think.

'Come on. I know mine.'

'Don't hustle me! This is important.'

'Can I just tell you mine?'

'No! I would have...who would I have?'

'I wish I hadn't asked.'

The computer hit 7%.

'Steve Coogan, Rob Brydon, Stephen Fry, Hugh Laurie and Piers Morgan. There.'

'Right. Explain yourself.'

'Well, you want funny people at such an occasion, I think. A one-off meal like this I want to remember and I want to have a laugh. I've invited Coogan and Brydon for their impressions. Fry for his intelligence, stories and anecdotes. Laurie in the hope he performs a little. He doesn't have to bring a grand piano - a keyboard will suffice. And Piers Morgan so we have someone we can take the piss out of.'

'Well played. Food?'

'A classic dish. Spag bol, garlic bread.'

'To drink?'

'Erm...bring a bottle.'

'Nice.'

'That was good fun actually. What about you?'

'I'd have James Bond.'

'Ok, he's not real, but which one?'

'Doesn't matter. So I'll have James Bond and then four Bond girls.'

'Which?'

'Doesn't matter.'

'You just want to get off with a Bond girl really, don't you?'

'Yeah.'

'Why invite Bond then?'

'I didn't think the girls would come otherwise.'

'This is a hypothetical fantasy. Why is it that even in this make-believe world you've made yourself unattractive to women?'

'I just think he'd be a good wingman.'

'Wouldn't they rather just get off with him?'

'Shut up. For food we'd have curry.'

'A lot of garlic in curry. Not ideal if you're wanting to pull, is it?'

'You're having garlic bread!'

'I want to get in Coogan's head, not his pants.'

'And beer to drink.'

'You really think the Bond girls want beer?'

'Aw god! I haven't even met them yet and they're doing my head in!'

'They'd want cocktails or dry martinis like Bond.'

'I can't afford that!'

'Again, why are you putting restrictions on your own fantasy? This isn't going to happen and yet you're worrying about the bill.'

'They will drink beer and be grateful.'

'What would Willow say?'

'It's not real.'

'*Now* it's a fantasy. Right, I see...'

The computer hit 73% just as we hit a lull in the conversation. I thought about telling Randall the whole truth of my predicament but a part of me advised lying for as long as I could get away with it - it was a small but very influential part of the brain. Randall could always distract me from my worries and maybe that's why we've remained friends for so long. But the gap in conversation allowed me to once more hear the inner screams of my personal problems. Simon had escaped and although it was as yet unconfirmed, I'm pretty sure he escaped with the help of Luke and Jacob. If so, that meant Simon could well know who I was, along with everyone I held dear.

Even Randall was in danger. Who could hurt harmless Randall? He had just fallen in love. Mind you, so had I and I didn't know where my love was. My computer finished updating and then reset itself to finalise the changes. It was sooooo slow. I wanted to look for a new one but it didn't feel right shopping for a computer via my computer, bit of a slap in the face.

Finally I could log in. I clicked on the internet icon and had to wait some more.

'I'm going to die of old age.'

'Worse ways to go. The police reports say the victims of the station attack melted. Imagine that.'

'Hmm.'

I searched for local news as quickly as I could. I found a video and clicked what was needed to make it play. My fears were real. I knew those clothes from earlier in the day. It was Luke and Jacob. Camera footage from the station showed all three of them leaving together. The only three people I had wronged in this world were serious fugitives sharing a hatred for me. I didn't deserve this. Simon should be mad with me, yes, that was my fault, but Luke and Jacob were taking things a bit far, weren't they? A phone beeped and I snatched at mine in the hope of hearing Molly explain that her battery had died and she had left school in a family emergency blah blah blah. But it was Randall's phone that had made the noise. He had to go and so we said goodbye.

'Keep in touch and don't do anything too stupid,' he said before leaving.

What to do? What was I actually supposed to do? Simon would know who I was and roughly where I lived. They were coming to get me; I had to get in touch with Molly and get her to safety. With Randall gone I went downstairs and sat with my mum, who was watching the news. Firefighters had fought off the fire and police were now retrieving the bodies. The final count confirmed three deceased officers. Police also confirmed that Simon Webb escaped with local teenagers Luke Cook and Jacob Pike. My mum spat tea out onto the carpet.

'Aren't they friends of yours!?'

'Friends? No!'

'Same year, aren't you?'

'That doesn't make us friends. Are you friends with everyone the same age as you?'

'Those poor boys.'

'What?!'

'They are entering a world they can't come back from. They're just boys. They need better influences.'

'Yeah, I blame the parents.'

'No, I blame computer games,' she said.

'You can stop right there with that. I hate that argument.'

'It happens; the statistics are scary.'

'Yeah, well statistics show that if your kid is mental it will act mental. What about all the millions of kids that play violent videos game that don't go out and kill people?'

'Hmm.' She's not even listening. I can't change her mind on this. I thought my mum would be better than that. I play violent video games but I've never killed anyone. I've put innocent people in jail and hospital, sure, but never killed anyone.

My mum changed channel when Dad came in, then switched off the TV altogether.

'Hello, darling,' she said.

'Have you seen the news?' he asked excitedly.

My phone vibrated in my pocket, twice in quick succession. My dad sat down and began nattering away with my mum about the new wall he was building – the police might be asking him to knock a few new ones up soon. I pulled out my phone and saw that it was from Molly. Finally! What had taken so long? Both messages were from her and one was a picture message. I've heard about couples sending each other saucy pictures.

The picture was a shot of Molly tied up on a chair in an empty room. Her hair was messy and she was crying. I didn't get it. This wasn't sexy. I'm pretty open-minded in the bedroom, but we hadn't talked about this. It wasn't doing much for me. And who was taking the picture? I didn't get it. It was a good starting point and I quite liked the idea of being tied up, but it was the tears that spoiled it. I opened the other message. The message gave an address and a time at which I needed to be there if Molly was to be unharmed. I was told to come alone and to tell no one - Molly's life depended on it. Below all the relevant details the message was signed off with three initials. Three initials that I have come to hate. Initials that represent the vilest and most foul form of evil known to man. Three initials.

J.L.S.

29

"If you want peace, prepare for war" - The Punisher

Jacob, Luke and Simon had kidnapped Molly, while I sat here enjoying rice pudding with my parents as they talked about the faraway future and present-day financial worries. I tried to eat as quickly as I could but the rice pudding was what can only be described as hot. In between mouthfuls of the sun, I worked on a plan. After I had finished eating I would bag my Toecap outfit and tell my parents that I was heading to Randall's. I would in fact catch a bus from Main Street - not exactly Ethan Hunt, but I couldn't be fussy. I'd get off at the last stop and make the final couple of miles on foot, changing into costume once off the bus and out of sight. Then it would be a case of beating up the bad guys, saving the girl, and riding off into the sunset. Or in my case walking off into the sunset. I really do need to get my own mode of transport, buses are not ideal.

Batman has the Batmobile, which is a damn fine car. He could only use that for missions though, couldn't he? It's not like he could do a big shop with it - I don't think it has a boot, does it? My mum parks her car outside in an open space, surrounded by other cars and she is constantly wiping bird muck off it and yet the Batmobile is kept in a cave full of friggin' bats and the car is always spotless. Riddle me that. I wonder if the Batmobile has a glove compartment.

Somewhere Bruce could keep his sunglasses and a bag of Wine Gums for long journeys. I don't know anyone who uses a glove compartment for keeping gloves in.

I was wolfing my rice pudding down. Who knew what was going through Molly's mind?

'What's the hurry?' my dad said.

'I have to go to Randall's to finish an essay we're working on together.'

'What's it about?' he said, with no trust in his voice. I looked around the room.

'It is about...crime in the digital age.'

'What subject is that for?'

'History.'

'Doesn't sound old enough to be history,' said my mum.

'I thought you were studying the Native Americans?' said my dad.

'We are.'

'Doesn't make sense then,' he said.

'We're learning about how the Native Americans would cope if they took up crime in the digital age.'

'School is not what it used to be,' my dad sighed.

'So how would they cope?' asked my mum, trying her best to seem interested.

'They wouldn't.'

'And you have to make an essay out of that?'

'Yes and I'm already stressing; please don't add to it.'

'I'd like to read it when you've finished, sounds fascinating.'

I had one more spoonful of rice pudding, thanked them for the meal and then went upstairs to get ready.

I shouted bye to anyone that was listening and then hurried out the front door. I jogged down St Helen's Street and across Market Place, took a left at the end and passed over a small bridge onto Main Street. I crossed the road in front of an arts and craft shop and made my way along the street, passing takeaways and restaurants as I went. There is a takeaway in Cockermouth that sells pizzas and on the menu you can ask for the chef's special. When you ask for this the chef decides what topping the pizza gets and I suppose there is some kind of excitement in that. I had a friend - true story this - and he once bought a chef's special. He got home, put the TV on and tucked into his pizza. He was bloody loving it, piece after piece, just stuffing his face full. I kid you not, on the last piece he looked down and found a cigarette butt on it. Disgusting, I know, but I thought to myself that if this ever went to court it'd be interesting to find out if the chef would argue that, after all, the customer *had* ordered a chef's special. I crossed over High Sands Lane and came to the bus stop. I had overexerted myself shortly after a meal and I could feel the rice pudding teetering on the edge of re-entering my mouth. My costume was in my bag and I was good to go. I needed to get Molly back. Her safety was all that matters.

Moments later, a bus pulled up. Seated behind the wheel was a driver who looked at me with fury. Fury because I had somewhere to be and fury because I had real money to pay for it. He talked to me as if I'd slept with his wife and daughter in one go and almost pebble-dashed my face with my change. I took my ticket and sat near the back.

30

Once I had made it off the bus alive, I ran the last couple of miles. I reached the address I'd been given, tired and out of breath. It was dark by now and the inside looked just as bleak. I couldn't see any lights on and the place looked cold and forgotten. Plants covered the outside of the house from toe to top but they looked weathered and defeated. No one had lived here for some time. I knocked on the huge front door and I could hear the noise of my actions echo through the hallway, into the belly of the house. I pushed the door and it slowly opened. As soon as I had enough room to slip inside I did, pushing the door closed behind me. The hallway could fit a whale in it and all around me I could see doors, most of them closed. There was plenty of furniture about but all of it was covered in white cloths. It looked like a ghost massacre. The house was deadly quiet.

I didn't want to move. Had I got the right place? The air was thick with dust, kicked up by the draught created when I'd closed the front door. Light would help. I began feeling the walls for a switch. All of a sudden I could hear music far off in the distance. It was definitely there though and I recognised it. With the intro out of the way the song kicked in and drums, guitars, bass and vocals came together. It was "Club Foot" by Kasabian. That was our song, mine and Molly's. I gave up looking for a switch and headed upstairs, guided by my ears. The music stopped when I reached the top. In its place I could hear voices. It was Simon's voice that I could hear but he was the only one. I couldn't make out what he was talking about but I followed the sound and took a deep breath, ready to apologise for everything. It grew louder and louder the closer I got, until I found the room it was coming from. I gathered what wits I had remaining and entered the room.

But Simon wasn't there. Neither was Luke or Jacob. The room was practically empty. A table to one side had a cassette player plugged in and switched on. Tapes covered the floor and I followed the breadcrumbs to an old wooden chair, against which Molly was propped up, her head lolling away to one side, into the darkness. Simon's voice droned on and on about previous auditions and parts that he had almost got and famous actors that he had almost met. They weren't full anecdotes, they were half done, half cooked, half interesting. It was so boring that I started to get a headache. The pain grew quickly and I felt drowsy. My legs stopped listening to me and I stumbled over to the table, bashing into it; the player and cassettes jumped a little in shock. I fell to my knees, my eyes felt like they had knitting needles pushing through them and my head felt like a fully loaded moving van had driven over it. I reached out and pressed stop on the tape player before falling to the floor, gasping for air. My headache eased off and the moving van had driven on - wrong address. I rubbed my temples and sat up.

'Molly?'

Nothing.

'Molly, it's me. It's me, Toby.'

Still nothing.

'Molly, wake up, I'm here. Everything is all right now.'

She didn't move. I rocked onto my knees and moved over to her.

'Molly, wake up,' I said, shaking her. I cupped her chin and turned her face towards me. I was too late. Her glazed-over eyes stared back at me. I held her in my arms as I kneeled on the floor, cramp settling in.

She was dead.

How had this happened? They had killed her. They had brought her here and killed her. I couldn't believe it. Molly was dead. My Molly. That damned tape player. I lowered Molly back to the floor as carefully as I could and returned to the tape player; it had been going for hours. Molly had been in this room all afternoon; had she been forced to listen to all these tapes? Just seconds of it had brought me to my knees it was so boring to listen to. How many tapes had Molly heard? Simon had done this to her. This was not an equal retaliation for being arrested. I was so angry I didn't know what to do. Molly was dead. She had nothing to do with any of this and she had paid more than anyone. The room was thick with betrayal. When you're dying, you can only hope it's quick. She was in this room for a long time, force-fed poison that would have shut her down one cell at a time and I couldn't save her. Anger brewed within and to be honest I could have cried. You know when you just get one of those days where you wake up and everything is downhill from there onwards (or uphill depending how you look at things).

Think Toecap, think.

I could hear new movement within the house. I peeked out of the window and saw all kinds of problems. I looked back at Molly. Toby Malloy was scribbled repeatedly on her skin. The Fiddler had framed me. I wanted to scream. I was trapped. The SWAT teams were getting closer and any moment now the wooden double doors just feet away would burst open and it would be game over. I couldn't let him win like this. The doors seemed to be the only way in.

Behind me the rain fought for my attention as it continued to slap against the window panes. Perfect. The windows would take me outside, but I was on the first floor. I unlocked the hatch on the window nearest to me and opened it as far as it would go. I imbibed the night's air and I could concentrate once more. It was pitch black outside apart from the police lights scattered around the house and looking down proved useless; I couldn't see a thing but I *could* hear more police arriving and setting up a stronger perimeter. I had to act fast. I was gearing myself up to move outside and carefully scale down the building to avoid giving away my position but it seemed I was too late for that.

The SWAT team had reached me.

A team effort brought the door off its hinges and armed soldiers flooded the room, breach and clear. Molly, still lying there, was approached. Small lights scanned over her and found the name Toby Malloy in abundance. Luckily for me, my plan of slipping on the wet window ledge and plummeting to the ground in a big ball of flailing limbs had worked brilliantly. With minor injuries, and leaving a distinctly distorted-looking bush behind me, I limped away into the darkness. After walking off the pain and disappearing further into the night, I got as far away from there as possible.

31

"You either die a hero or you live long enough to
see yourself become the villain" – Two-Face

Here is a riddle for you.

Until I am measured
I am not known,
Yet how you miss me
When I have flown.

Who am I?

Time.

A large variety of devices have been invented to measure time. For
example, the Egyptians used sundials, which although handy during
the day, were ruddy useless in the dark – the clue is in the name. The
most precise timekeeping device of the ancient world was the water
clock, which came a little after the sundial. Water clocks were great
because they could be used to measure the hours even at night, but
they did require manual upkeep to replenish the flow of water. Along
with sundials and water clocks, we've had the hourglass, which uses
the flow of sand to measure the flow of time. Eventually though,

came the modern clock. The word clock came from the Dutch word *clocke* which derives from the medieval Latin word *clocca*, which in turn came from Celtic and is cognate with French, Latin and German words that mean bell. This is because the passage of time at sea, and indeed in abbeys, was marked by bells. Chronometry, or temporal measurement if you prefer, is fascinating and has long been a major subject of study in religion, philosophy and science. Time is the indefinite continued progression of existence through the past, present and future, regarded as a whole. You can have time and you can have the time. You can be in time, on time, out of time, behind time or you can simply pass the time - musicians can even keep time (because they're special). We are all up against time though. Everyone except Bernard Beasley, that is. *Bernard's Watch* was a children's drama that first aired around 1997. It had the kind of plot that only people who have drunk a bottle of absinthe and spent the night in a cave could have come up with. Here is the synopsis of *Bernard's Watch* from Wikipedia…

"Bernard was always late, until a postman gave him a magic watch which could stop time. He soon found out that the postman had magical powers, and that these watches were given to people who needed them. The rules of him keeping his watch were that he must not use it to commit crimes or hurt anyone. Every episode focused on Bernard, or someone to whom he'd lent the watch, facing a problem or simply doing day-to-day stuff and trying to sort it out, using the watch."

The synopsis doesn't give too much away and I know this is a kids' programme, but I have one or two questions. Ok, so question one… If the postman had special powers, why was he working as a postman? That is wasted talent if ever I heard of it. Also, nowadays if a grown man was seen giving a present to a small child who was no relation to him, he would be fired on the spot and I imagine a very lengthy investigation into his background would follow. Question two… Why was Bernard letting other people use his watch? If they really needed help surely the postman would have given them a watch? Finally, if he can stop time, like stop everything around him and then restart it when he felt like it, how would anyone know he's committed a crime? Some personal thoughts there and this show did have a long run so it must have been good (I've never seen it). So Bernard is the exception to the rule, he can do things we can't. A lot of people waste time but they don't generally mind; they partake in the most ridiculous of things because they have too *much* free time. But free time doesn't really exist. For some people time is to be respected, obeyed and even feared. I said before that you can't keep time, but really you can and I don't just mean musicians. You can keep time by pairing up an appointment with a specific time and by making those two components meet at the time you said they would. Sometimes it's hard to keep time, but very few excuses really cut it. I hate it when people use the excuse 'sorry I was late but there was traffic.' For me this isn't a valid excuse. You don't even need a driving licence to know that traffic can be found exclusively on the roads. If you have bought a car for driving on the roads you must have had an afterthought that maybe other people in the world had done a similar thing and that there will be the odd crossover point when you're driving at the same time on roughly the same stretch. 'There was traffic' is not a valid excuse because there is always traffic; aside from dead animals the only thing you will find on roads is traffic. You work out your destination and how long it will take to get there and then you compensate for the inevitable traffic you will encounter. If you say you're going to be somewhere at a time you have chosen then don't be late. It can be insulting, rude and disrespectful and I'm not the only one who thinks so. At least one man in the world agrees with me.

James 'JP' Pattinson was born in 1964 and raised by parents who lived life following strict daily routines. Everything was mapped out with time and before JP could read he could tell the time better than children twice his age. His parents drilled into him that only time was worthy of his faith and that the worst thing you can do with time is lie about it. If you give someone a time, stick to it, always. JP didn't have friends at school, but he didn't even notice. He had his watch, which kept him on the straight and narrow. Everything he did was timed. He grew up wanting to teach others, to help others. You have to teach at a young age for it really to sink in and stay. You don't see religions brainwashing adults so much, do you, unless they're grieving and therefore easy prey? No, they get in there early when they're young and easy to manipulate, perfect applicants for *any* cult.

JP decided to become a primary school teacher. That was the dream. He wanted to snap youngsters into shape, to organise the future. By the time JP started university in Liverpool he had become a young man angry at the world. People disrespect time *all* the time and it began pushing him into uncontrollable rages. People were constantly letting him down. They were always running late, forgetting dates or changing plans at the last minute. It angered him deeply that people couldn't keep to their word when it came to time. Parcels didn't arrive when they were supposed to and people never called back when they said they would. It was infuriating. He made it through the education system and found a full-time job at a primary school in Liverpool, a city he had grown very fond of. It was while working here that he met and fell in love with Debbie Johnson and, for a while, love distracted him. Debbie made him lose all track of time. His primary school children were rubbish at even telling the time, let alone keeping it, but he didn't care: his clock ticked only for Debbie Johnson, the exception to his rule.

Before long they had moved into their first flat together. Debbie also taught younglings and each night she and JP would swap stories of pupils they had failed to inspire. Debbie wasn't great at keeping time but new love overpowers all imperfections. Quite often the habits of a partner we find cute and endearing in the beginning are what we grow to hate about them in the end. He let all her poor timekeeping wash over him, adamant that love would see them through a life together. Everyone has a different honeymoon period. This is the initial stages of a relationship or marriage when everything is wonderful. It's called the honeymoon period because of the idea that the first month of marriage is the sweetest. A recent citation indicates that, while today honeymoon has a positive meaning, the word was originally a reference to the inevitable waning of love, like a phase of the moon. It's believed that the term dates from the Middle Ages. Mead, an alcoholic drink of fermented honey and water, was drunk in great quantities at weddings (and let's be honest, unless you're the one getting married then getting pissed is the only way to enjoy the day – so boring). After the ceremony, couples were often given a month's supply of mead. It was believed that by drinking mead for the first month of marriage the woman would give birth to a child within a year. And as it happens, honey has been shown in clinical studies to be a powerful fertility booster. I guess they knew what they were on about.

Over time the bad habits of your spouse are more than noticeable but we hope that they are insignificant when compared to how much you love them. You have no idea in the beginning how much you will come to hate your partner for those quirky idiosyncrasies. James and Debbie dated for some time and were engaged in just under two years. Another year on they were married and two years after that they were firmly into a stale routine. The sparks were going and JP went back to a former love in the hope of rekindling some passion into his life again. It was then that he really noticed how often Debbie was late or flippant with time. Incident by incident, her tardiness really began to annoy JP. He tried to go back to ignoring it but it was too late. He found her running late each day, a minute here, ten minutes there, it all added up and he grew to hate her for it. Work was no better: each class that passed through cared neither for time nor how to read it. Out in the world buses and trains were never on time and it made him want to scream. Five years of marriage and JP found himself wanting to leave his wife more and more.

Enough was enough, he needed out. He had prepared a speech and picked a time and place, only for Debbie to tell him that very day that she was pregnant. For a short period of time new life was injected into them both. JP thought of all the children he had taught and how stupid they were, but believed his own would be different because he would be with them from day one, mentoring. A new challenge was on the horizon. He would teach them in the same manner his parents had taught him. His son or daughter would grow up sharing the same love of time as he did. He was excited to become a dad.

Nine months came and went with little drama and a date was given. It was to be a girl and JP had spent the pregnancy preparing a room for their daughter Felicity. Day one was coming and JP was more than ready. Felicity was expected on the 5th and everything was set, everything was planned and prepared. JP was sick to his bones of being insulted and being disrespected. His daughter would be different; she would follow in his footsteps. It was his last chance.

The 5th came.

And so did the 6th.

The 7th, 8th and 9th came next and then the 10th.

Still no baby.

On the 15th, baby Felicity was born healthy and weighing in at just over seven pounds. Debbie was in tears of joy as she met her daughter for the first time. JP sat outside in the corridor overwhelmed with anger. Felicity was ten days late and he couldn't even look at her. He had never felt so insulted. She had shown a complete lack of respect for her father and JP knew then that his marriage was over. He couldn't believe the arrogance of his daughter to turn up ten days after she was supposed to. He could never love her and his dreams of raising her properly were over. He left the hospital and headed home to pack. JP disappeared from society, cutting himself off completely. He didn't even leave a note. His wife knew he wasn't happy but she had hoped Felicity would bring them back together. She spent the next few days in limbo, trying to reach him, fearing the worst had happened. Eventually she was released from hospital and her parents took her home to find an empty house. There wasn't a trace of JP; it was as if he had never been a part of their lives. Debbie was destroyed and her parents took her to live with them. For the next few weeks Debbie tried relentlessly to find her husband, waking each morning with hope topped up from a night's dreaming. Weeks turned to months and months eased into years. Given enough time, Debbie and Felicity accepted he wasn't coming back and they moved on.

Almost twenty years have passed and JP is close to turning fifty years old. To this day he has never met his daughter.

32

A small morning fire crackled as it settled into a high temperature, happy with the task at hand. The embers burned brightly and danced under the dry logs. The wood had long awaited the day to leave the stockpile and be put to use. Before long the cosy log cabin was warm and the day could formally begin. All promising days start with coffee and JP got some on the go, collecting the necessary ingredients and taking on the challenge of mug to mouth. The mere aroma of the coffee beans awoke JP's senses one by one as if in a fast-moving queue. He poured it slowly and sat by the fire. A morning ritual perfected by complete solitude. He sipped his brew to the end while listening to the fire talk.

The cabin door creaked open and JP emerged dressed well enough for a winter hike. He scanned the woodland that surrounded him, as he did every morning, and breathed in the crisp, early air. No one was there. His whereabouts was a bigger secret than D-Day. In the past twenty years no one had found his hideaway. Once a month he ventured into a nearby town to sell hides (do people still buy those?). The money he made was used to purchase essentials such as matches, soap, medical supplies and Bill Bryson books. These infrequent trips were JP's only interaction with people and it was more than enough for him. People had proved to be useless. They were constant disappointments and he enjoyed most days without their input. He passed the time learning to hunt and build, living off the land as best he could. Each day would start with a walk, a chance to stretch his legs and organise his mind.

He closed the cabin door behind him and headed off into the woods, guided by the first flurry of birdsong. JP was in no hurry on these walks. He slept when he was tired and ate when he was hungry. Everything in between happened on the basis of "as and when he wanted". It made him so angry thinking of all the times people had let him down, but over time he had learned to control it. In the early days these thoughts had filled him with such rage that he had lost control on occasions and found instant relief only in breaking something. At first it was the nearest thing to him, things like cups, plates, vases, shelves, people's legs, windows etc. It had soon got out of hand, but he spent time on his anger. He learned where it came from and why it was present in him. He remembered exactly how it felt and how to recognise it. From that, over time, he learned how to summon fury on demand, by reminding himself of past incidents. With precision training he grew strong, stronger than most men. Blind rage is untapped potential. He surrendered to his darker side and it became almost an out-of-body experience. He taught himself how to contain it and concentrate it to his will. His rage was malleable and he squeezed, rolled and kneaded it until it became a tiny little switch which he could flick on and off at will. But without people and time he had no need for rage. He grew older in peace and quiet. He often thought of his daughter while out walking. He pictured her being late for school and always had to remind himself that by now she would be a young woman. She would be at university or have a job and maybe even her own place. She might have a boyfriend or even a husband by now. She would be young yet might even have her own children. He would think of Debbie and wonder how she had aged. It had been twenty years, in which time she could have remarried and Felicity might even have a little brother or sister. He couldn't think about his family for too long, just a snippet here and there.

His walk seldom changed but he enjoyed the path he took; every day he saw something different and today was no exception. His cabin was back in sight and he stopped walking to watch a young figure, dressed all in black, knock on his cabin door and then let himself in. JP walked a little quicker back to the cabin, getting angry on the way.

33

"I'm necessary evil" - Bane

I knocked on the cabin door and then just let myself in. I didn't
have the energy to wait; I had been walking all night, I was dizzy
and I was dehydrated. I hadn't a clue where I was and I didn't care,
somewhere off the map was just fine. Right now I needed liquid. The
cabin was small and warm and a tiny stream of smoke was ascending
from a dead fire. Someone obviously still lived here but, again, I was
too tired to care. I stumbled across the room to a table and found a
couple of mugs, each with mouthfuls of something in them. I picked
up both and drank. I then began searching the table for food. The
table was covered with used plates but all I could see left on them were
bones. Some looked relatively fresh so I picked one up and sucked it.

The door opened and I looked up to see an old man standing
there with his fists clenched. I thought about opening with a joke but
he'd caught me in his house sucking on his bones and to be honest
I didn't really know any jokes.

'Who are you?' he asked.

I took the bone out of my mouth but said nothing. He took a step
towards me. He was old but he looked strong.

'Well?'

I was too tired to lie.

'Toby' I said.

'I'm JP. Toby what?'

'Malloy.'

'And what are you doing all the way out here?'

'I ran away from home.'

'Why?'

'It's a long story.'

'I've nowhere to be.'

'Do you have any water?'

'Start talking,' JP said as he moved across the room and pulled out a bottle of water from a cupboard. He handed it to me, and I all but snatched it from his hand before flicking off the lid and chugging down almost half of its contents. I wiped my chin and coughed.

'You wouldn't believe me.'

'Try me,' JP said and I studied him for a moment.

Then I told him everything. I told him about my power and the incidents. I told him about Molly and Jacob and working at the Old Grey Goat Inn. I talked about Randall and the toecaps. I explained about the trial runs and being beaten up and how I came to hire the Fiddler. I told JP about the P.I.S.S.es and how they eventually went wrong. I don't know what he made of all this but he listened well and didn't interrupt. I told him about the Fiddler being arrested and how Luke and Jacob blew up the prison to rescue Simon Webb. JP nodded as I explained how all three men were after me and how they had killed Molly to get at me.

'She's dead because of me.'

'You have a power?'

'That's what you want to ask about? Out of everything I've told you - murder and all that - you want to ask about my power?'

'Yes. You said you had a power?'

'Yes.'

'Show me.'

'I can't.'

'Why?'

'Because I don't know how. I can't control it.'

'Tell me about it.'

'I'm strong. I mean, really strong, but it's in my toes.'

'Your toes?'

'Yeah, my toes. When my toes are hit unexpectedly I become strong but it doesn't last long.'

'And it happens in your toes?'

'Yes! My toes.'

'Just a bit weird, that's all'

'Well, pardon me!' I said.

'And you call yourself Toecap?'

'Yes, it's my superhero name.'

'But I've yet to hear of something you've done that's heroic'

'Were you not listening about the Fiddler?'

'Yeah, but that wasn't real, was it? You were paying him.'

'But the town didn't know that.'

'You sold them a lie.'

'I really don't need another critic today.'

'How long did it take you to make this story up?'

'What?'

'You must think me an idiot.'

JP laughed. Then he raised his leg and slammed his weight down on my unaware foot. His heavy boot clipped the end of my big toe and I changed. I kicked out one of the front legs on his chair, sending him tipping towards me. I clenched my right fist and swung at his face, catapulting him back the way he came and he rolled backwards out of his chair, landing with a thud on the floor.

He looked pissed.

I got to my feet and kicked his broken chair at him, which he jumped over, and it skidded into the fireplace, sending a cloud of ash up into the room. JP moved in and began swinging fists. I ducked one, blocked another and caught the third on my chin, which knocked me back against the table. Plates rattled and my bottle of water rolled onto the floor, emptying itself along the way. I sat on the edge of the table, gripping it with a hand either side of me and I used both feet to push him back. He stumbled out of reach and while I maintained eye contact my hands frantically searched for a weapon behind me. JP composed himself and with my left hand I flung a plate at him, which cracked off the bridge of his nose and broke into several pieces. He gathered himself again and looked bigger than ever. Blood ran down the side of his face and I reloaded another plate. He moved at me and I took a shot. He blocked the plate and with both hands lifted me off the ground. I hit his face repeatedly but it was useless, my power had gone, dried up. He carried me over to the front door and with one hand he opened it. I hit and hit but I couldn't hurt him. He put me down and pulled me into position by my hair. My strength had gone; I was out but he showed no signs of tiring. Still holding my head in one hand he placed it against the door frame. I was panicking, my arms were heavy, I couldn't do anything. I looked up at him helplessly.

Then he shut the door on my head.

It slapped against my ear and I all but lost consciousness. JP let go of me and I fell in a heap, hitting my teeth on the wooden floor. My gums began to bleed and my ear joined in. It was over. JP picked me up and brought me back inside. He went back to the front door and scanned the woodland immediately outside.

Then he relaxed and calmly shut the door.

34

My head was still ringing when I came round. A piercing ringing like I'd been standing near a grenade when it had gone off. I was on my back staring up at a ceiling. I looked around but even my eyes seemed to ache. I was still in JP's hut. My head was pounding and my teeth hurt. I began wondering how long I'd been unconscious but I couldn't see a clock anywhere in the room and my phone battery had died long ago. I sat up, cradling my head. I could taste blood and I picked a dry line of it from my ear. It was sore to touch and my hearing had been affected. I couldn't hear anything. How hard had he hit me? It was like he had what I had. I'd only ever seen that kind of strength in one person before and that was me. It was a different kind of rage though. It moved with him, not against. He had complete control over himself. He had found a way of controlling it, of slipping into it when he desired and without effort, like putting on a slipper. This man might have the very answers I have been looking for. Damn, what a shame we've got off to such a bad start. I stood up and the floorboards beneath me creaked. I stopped moving, waiting for a reaction from somewhere. My hearing was coming back in waves. I yawned and pain rushed to my chin. I don't think I did too badly though. I vaguely remember getting a good shot off with a plate. I wondered why I was still here. I shuffled to the door and it clicked open. The heat of a small fire greeted me first and its warmth felt safe so I progressed. The old man was sat by the fire, on the chair I had broken. An obvious repair job had been applied but it was back in working use. He watched me enter.

'Sit with me.' He spoke softly and so I obeyed, easing myself carefully into another chair. We looked at each other for some time before he spoke again.

'I believe you.'

'You needed to fight me to believe me?'

'Sometimes that's the only way.'

'So, what now?'

'Start from the beginning and go slow.'

'From the very beginning?'

'Yes.'

So I did. I told him everything I already had but in more detail and I was grateful to finish my sorry tale and not be met with such poor reviews this time. In response, he said nothing, he just looked at me. I changed the subject to him while he made his mind up about me.

'You certainly keep in shape out here on your own.'

'I'm out here on my own because I'm a bit like you. We seem to share certain talents.'

'I knew it. I could tell while we were fighting. I saw the same power in you as I feel in me.'

'That's right. You're strong but you have no control over it.'

'How do you do it? You have control, perfect control, it listens to you; it *wants* to listen.'

'I have spent years perfecting my rage. Decades of dedicating time to my ability. Through persistence and will, I have learned to control it.'

'I'm just to persevere?'

'You need to remember how the anger feels. Memorise it, every aspect. You need to focus.'

'It's easier said than done.'

'You will get there in time.'

'I don't have time.'

'No, I don't suppose you do, do you?'

'You've perfected yours, will you teach me how?'

'Teach you? Me?' JP thought for a moment. He was a teacher after all. It had been many years but that was his profession. And he was happy on his own. People only brought with them disappointment and failure. Toby would be no different. No. JP couldn't do this. Man hasn't changed in twenty years. Toecap was saying anything he could now but he would slip up and JP would be left feeling disappointed yet again.

'No,' he said after some time.

'No? Just like that? What about the Fiddler? What about Cockermouth? What about Molly? She's dead because of me.'

'And that's just it, isn't it?'

'What is?'

'She's dead because of you. Not me. I didn't let her down. I didn't fail her. I didn't let her die.'

JP could see me getting angry. The mere mention of Molly and I wanted to scream.

'You ok?' JP asked, knowing fine well he had pushed a button.

'How about we make it interesting?' I said.

'What are you suggesting?'

'If I beat you in a fight, you teach me.'

'Have you forgotten what happened earlier?'

'Fighting is all I have left.'

'How about a real game?' he suggested, looking at his trashed hut and broken plates.

'Like what?'

'Cards?' JP replied.

'Cards?!'

'Yeah, cards. I used to love to play. One game. If you win I'll train you. If I win, I get to kill you.'

'Kill me?!'

'I'm just joking. If I win you have to clean my cabin. All of it. And then piss off.' He smiled. The stakes were high. 'I'll even let you pick the game.'

I froze as a thought bubble burst. JP looked cocky but I still had an ace up my sleeve (which was relevant).

'A game of my choice?'

'Any game you like.' He smiled, pulling a worn out deck from his coat.

'You're on.' I smiled back, raising my hand for him to shake and seal the deal. It was a firm shake.

'So what are we playing?' he asked.

'Shithead,' I replied.

I won and after much complaining about the rules he put the cards away and honoured his agreement of training me in the dark art of rage. We tidied up and cleared things away, we whittled for a bit (because that's what you do in the woods) and then cooked a meal. I was told to get a good night's sleep as we would be up very early.

35

"Some men just wanna watch the world burn" - Alfred Pennyworth

Training is not what I thought it would be. I hadn't slept well because I was thinking about Molly. I still couldn't believe she was dead. How can you sleep after that? Although, training with JP was so dull I felt I could fall asleep at any moment. I just didn't get how housework would help me become a better superhero. Every banal task he set me was so dull it actually made me angry. Hand-washing his clothes annoyed me. Dusting his cabin wound me up. Beating his rugs with sticks outside pissed me right off. I didn't let it show though; he was in charge, I couldn't mess this opportunity up. Who was I to question him?

By lunchtime I was raging, just below the skin. I was looking forward to lunch and having a break but I had to prepare the meal, which he then only moaned about. I couldn't believe how ungrateful he was being. I was so angry but I didn't want to say anything in case I upset him and then he'd stop teaching me. I concentrated all my efforts on not letting my rage spill out. I got used to how it felt and I kept it just below the surface. The longer I felt angry the more I became used to its presence. I was so mad at JP for wasting my time with all this bullshit. I wanted the real training to begin. He was just using this situation to benefit himself. I was so angry I wanted to lash out and smash the place up but I couldn't. I had to endure. I had to hold the rage in.

After lunch I was cleaning his boots and stripping his bed down. I began picturing different ways of killing him. I was covered from head to toe in anger. Every part of me was ready to inflict pain but I held it in. My rage lasted all day, through every degrading job JP set me. I had cleaned his cabin thoroughly, which was the forfeit he had set had he won our game of Shithead. I had won that game and somehow I had still ended up doing it. I wanted to scream the hut down. I wanted to force-feed him broken glass. He had tricked me. Maybe he had never planned to train me, he'd just wanted some free labour. I had learned nothing today. I had spent my entire time awake just being angry. I decided I was going to confront him, that he wasn't going to get away with this. I was outside in the cold but I couldn't feel it; I was almost giving off steam I was that mad at him. I needed to let it out. I found JP and he looked like he had been waiting for me.

'Congratulations. That's day one done. A good start,' he said, pleased.

'Sorry, had we started? I hadn't realised. I thought I had just been doing all your housework for you.' I spoke through gritted teeth.

'Do you doubt my methods?'

'Yeah, I do. I think you don't know what you're talking about.'

'Why did you lose yesterday?'

'Because you're a freak?'

'No. You are just as strong, if not stronger. Why did you lose?'

'Because you got lucky?'

'No. You're not thinking, you're not concentrating. Why did you lose?'

'I don't know why!'

'You lost because you have no stamina.'

'So?'

'How have you felt all day?'

'Angry.'

'That's right. I've kept you angry all day. You can maintain rage if you concentrate on it; you just needed to get used to how it feels.'

'Ok...'

'When you stub your toe it makes you angry, but the physical pain of the toe is walked off very quickly. Your rage comes and goes and doesn't last long. But you have believed that it's only accessible through your toes. You have become so fixated on your toes that you haven't realised you can access your rage any time you want to. The physical trauma of hurting your toes is fine at the time of infliction, but as a memory it's not strong enough to allow you to use it when you like.'

'Right…' It made sense so far.

'Think about today. You have spent all day angry because you think I have tricked you. That's emotional pain. It's far more powerful than physical pain. Go ahead, think about what I've asked of you today. How does it make you feel?'

'Angry, really angry. I want to hurt someone. I want to hurt you.'

JP laughed. 'That's good, that's very good. Hold onto that. Remember how it feels and concentrate.'

I was feeling it. Strength was rising in me like bread in an oven. I was angry. I felt strong. That anger wasn't forcing me around or reaching out for the nearest object. It was listening to me, waiting for orders. I held out my hands and looked down at them. They were shaking, trembling with power. I looked back up at JP, who was standing much closer to me now.

'You have a lot of potential, Toby. Look how angry you are after one day of housework for me. I tricked you and you look ready to fight a lion. Think what you could do with real emotional damage.' He was right. 'Dare I say it, but think what you could do if I mentioned -'

I held a hand up to his face and he cut his thought short. I knew what he was going to say but I didn't think I was ready for that.

'One step at a time,' I said. I stopped feeling angry and I was exhausted. I collapsed forward into JP's arms and we went inside. We had done enough for one day.

* * *

Late into the night I woke suddenly to a mouth wracked once again with pain, but it was fresh pain. I reeled with it for a minute or two, surprised and confused. It was still dark, but I could hear noises in the other room. I got up and moved into the main room of the cabin. JP was standing there fully clothed.

'Did you just hit me in the face?' I said, massaging my chin.

'You can't always be ready for an attack.'

'It hurts.'

'Good, now get outside.'

'What time is it?'

'Who cares? Crime doesn't work nine to five. Get outside.'

'Let me get dressed then first.'

'No, I've hidden your clothes. Enemies won't wait until you're dressed. Outside, now!'

'I'm definitely using the loo before we start anything.'

'NO! Get outside now or I'll drag you out!'

He meant it. Training had escalated quickly. I shuffled outside in my bare feet and found the ground wet and the air cold. This made me need a pee even more and I stood there with my arms folded, wearing just a T-shirt and my boxer shorts. I was tired and hungry. I just wanted to sleep. JP walked past me, after locking the door, wearing a heavy coat and clean boots. He looked very warm. In his left hand he showed me a key, tied to some string, which he then put around his neck and tucked in under his coat.

'This is the key to the cabin. Inside, you'll find your clothes, hot food and your bed. All you have to do to get back inside is get the key off me.'

'Are you insane?!'

'Come and get it. Remember your training.'

'This is stupid! Let me back inside.'

'This key is the only way you're getting back in there,' said JP as he jumped from foot to foot. He laughed a little, egging me on. I couldn't be bothered. I really couldn't be bothered. I was too tired to be angry and my mind was focusing on not wetting myself.

'Come on! Yesterday I was making you angry. Today you have to make yourself angry.'

'I'm too tired for any of this,' I said.

'Let me wake you up at least, I can do that.'

'No.' I was hugging myself for warmth. JP looked down at his side, sweeping his eyes from side to side until he saw what he was looking for. He bent down to pick up something.

'What are you doing?' I said.

'Fetch!' he called. He arched his right arm back and hurled a stick in my vague direction. The throw was without power or any real aim and it bounced off the cabin, landing among the grass. It did little to deter me.

'Is that the best -' Another stick hit the cabin behind me but even further away from me than the first. JP flicked his switch and the muscles in his arms burned to twice their size.

'If that's how you're going to throw, I'll stand here all day' and with that JP threw once more but this time with a little more zest. The stick flew past my face, missing it by inches, and shattered upon contact with the door. I turned to look at it in shock and then faced JP again.

'That was close!'

'You woken up then?'

'I can't do this, it's too hard.'

'No wonder Molly died.'

A tiny surge of heat burned from my core, it rippled and woke my bones a little. I glared at JP with my mouth open. He started chuckling to himself, as if what he had just said held no weight or responsibility to it at all, a throwaway comment in an unread article.

'Come on, it's cold, what have you got?'

But I couldn't think about yesterday's training. I couldn't hone in on my feelings of anger towards JP for the previous day's activities. All I could think about was Molly. I remembered her first shift with me and how embarrassed she was at tipping a prawn cocktail into the lap of an elderly gentleman. I remembered when she gave me her coat to walk home with and how I had pretty much slept in it every night until I'd had to surrender it back. I remembered spending hours in class just staring at the back of her head and trying to guess what she was thinking. I could picture the night we first had sex and how she had told me that she loved me. And then I could see her lying alone in a dusty, unused room with my name scrawled all over her skin. I would never get to see her again. I would never get to talk to her, to hear her laugh, to hold her close. Simon Webb had taken her away from me forever. I felt sick knowing he had hurt her, knowing he had touched her. He had made her suffer and I felt an anger inside me that I had never come close to before. The world around me vanished in a red blaze. My core exploded with heat and my inner body burned blue. My muscles flexed and expanded like the change in shape as a bird unfolds its wings. The ground was red, the trees were red and mockingbird JP was red as he continued to jump from foot to foot. I could see him laughing but I could hear nothing. Everything had slowed down. I turned to the cabin door and ripped out the globe-shaped door knob. I threw it up in the air once, letting it fall back into my palm, quickly learning its weight. I looked up at JP jumping from one foot to the other, talking away silently to no one. I pulled back on the door knob and fired it at JP like a cannonball. It shot through the air and hit him just above his ribs. It landed in the grass but not before knocking him off his feet. He rocked from side to side, clutching at air with his fingers and his lungs, while I stood focusing on my body's signals. Molly was awake in my thoughts, she kept my actions simple. I felt like a machine. I began to move. I could see the grass was wet but I couldn't feel it under my feet. This power was incredible. I had no idea I had this strength inside me all along. My toes were a trigger but they were not the source. I looked around me and noticed how different the world was when I felt like this. JP struggled up onto his knees, acting for all the world as if he'd caught a bullet in the chest. His mouth was moving but I couldn't hear a single word.

* * *

'Turn it off!' JP screamed, gasping for air. 'Turn it off!' He flicked on his switch but it was pathetic in comparison. He clambered to his feet as Toecap made his way over.

* * *

I could crush this man. I once feared him but the tables had truly turned. He had found a monster in me, fed it and unlocked the cage. I felt ten feet tall and I looked down at JP as if he were an ant and I a boot. He was still shouting at me but his efforts were pointless. I took a swing at him with my right fist but he saw it all the way and rolled down to my left. He headed for the cabin. *Concentrate on Molly*, I told myself, *that's how to stay strong*. I turned to face the cabin and saw JP kick the door in. He went inside, out of view. I began walking back to the house and JP re-emerged with a broom. He lifted it slightly off the ground and kicked off the broom head, leaving him with a makeshift staff. He couldn't beat me barehanded. I smiled at him and continued to advance. JP prepared to take a swing, but I felt he couldn't hurt me. He clipped the broom round the side of my head. No matter how angry I felt, that did actually hurt. The stick had struck me right across my damaged ear and while my concentration was distracted my hearing temporarily returned.

'Turn it off, goddamn it! JP shouted, 'Turn it off!'

He was petrified, I could hear it in his voice. What was I doing? JP prepared another swing but I stepped back. I looked at him. It was JP, an old, lonely man living in the woods. He was trying to help. The red mist dispersed and my anger receded. I began to calm down and he could see it. JP dropped the broom and fell to his knees, exhausted. His chest was causing him considerable pain. The cold air grabbed my skin and I remembered where I was.

'You're a quick learner,' JP said, breathing heavily and rubbing his chest. 'We'll try again later to make sure you've got it.'

'Ok,' I said, processing everything that had just happened.

'Oh, by the way...' he added.

'What?'

'You've wet yourself.'

36

I hadn't been home in two days. Two days since I had seen my parents and two days since Molly had died. JP had no phone, TV or internet so I had no idea what the situation was in Cockermouth. I had left a burning police station, mad criminals on the run and a mountain of homework that was mostly overdue. What should I do now? The police had found Molly's body with my name all over her. They would have spoken to my parents and told Molly's parents the news. What must everyone think of me? I needed to find out what was going on.

After JP had recovered from our second round we had had lunch and gone over what had happened. We headed back out in the afternoon and worked through some of his exercises, getting used to controlling my rage until I could summon it on demand. The hard part then was turning it off when I needed to. By the end of the day I was more than ready to sleep. What should I do tomorrow? Would I continue to travel and try to scrape together a new life? I didn't tell JP how I felt, but I really didn't want to end up like him. He frequently talked to himself and I'm pretty sure he had personified most of his furniture. Cockermouth would know about Molly's death by now and be begging for my blood. I guessed that clearing my name had to be my next move. I had to find Simon Webb and bring him to justice. Simon, Luke and Jacob were just three men; they were no match for me now. I needed to know what the latest was in Cockermouth. Sleep was my first port of call, and then I would speak to JP.

'I need to know what's going on at home,' I said after breakfast.

'I knew this would come.'

'They think I had something to do with Molly's death. I need to fix this.'

'I know. I know you have to go home but I can't help you.'

'Why? Don't you know where we are?'

'Sorry, that wasn't clear. I mean I can't help you fix this. I know where we are.'

'Which is where?'

'Setmurthy Woods,' he said, which I couldn't believe.

'Is that a joke?' I said. Setmurthy is a small wood that is right on the outskirts of Cockermouth.

'Are you telling me that when I thought I had been fleeing the county, running far away from Molly's body, I had in truth been running back towards town?'

'Yes.'

'Why didn't you tell me?!'

'You didn't need to know until now.'

'I can't believe it.'

'We are quite safe here. No one has found me for twenty years. Every once in a while I make a trip into town for supplies, but that's it. I used to live in Cockermouth, before I moved to Liverpool. I studied here at the school, a long time ago. I have fond memories of the place.'

'I'll never catch Simon. He must be miles away by now.'

'He will get what's coming to him.'

'But I want to be the one that gives it to him. You said you make trips now and then into town for supplies?'

'Yes...?'

'When did you last go?'

'A little over a month ago. Why?'

'I need you to go into town and find out what you can about all of this.'

'I try to avoid people. I said I couldn't help you with this.'

'I can't go! I'm a wanted man. You must help me with this, please.'

JP looked up, then down and then around the room. He was thinking.

'There are a few things I need to replace. Plates, for example.'

'So you'll go?'

'I will but I won't stay for long and if I don't find out anything then that's the end of it, no more from me. You've already disturbed me enough.'

'Thank you.'

'I'll go this afternoon and while I'm out you can clean up.'

'I can do that.'

I spent the morning outside, a short distance from the cabin, training myself to switch my rage on and off. I had picked out selected memories of Molly, ones that really meant a lot to me, probably more so now that she was dead. Added to the mix was how angry I felt at Simon Webb, Jacob Pike and Luke Cook. I thought about Luke telling Simon who I really was and how Jacob wanted to destroy me. That's a point - I wonder how Jacob was feeling now Molly was dead. His whole reasoning for standing up against me was wanting Molly back.

I had a lot of anger to work with. On and off. On and off. I spent hours doing this. I wanted full control. The day drained away and JP called me for lunch. I cleared away lunch while JP prepared for heading into town. Once he had left I couldn't concentrate and neither could I keep track of the time, because JP forbade all time-keeping devices. I finished the dishes and left them to air-dry. I had swept the porch, cut some wood, cleaned out the fire and even picked some flowers for a vase on the table. Time plodded on untracked and I sat by the window waiting for his return. I dozed off eventually and when I awoke JP was making a fire and a mess.

'Well, what happened?'

'I'm not sure where to start,' he said.

'Why? What's happened? Are my parents ok?'

'Cockermouth is under new ruling.'

'What? What does that mean?'

'Come sit by the fire. Are you ready for this?'

'Yes, yes, yes; come on!'

'Simon Webb never left Cockermouth.'

'What about Luke and Jacob?'

'They are also there.'

'Great! So they've all been caught?'

'I didn't say that.'

'So they're hiding out in Cockermouth?'

'Not hiding.'

'I don't understand, what do you mean?'

'Mr Webb is at the school.'

'The school?'

'That's where he is running the town from.'

'Running the town from?!'

'Stop repeating everything I say.'

'Sorry, I'm confused.'

'I was heading into town, but I take the road that leads to Castlegate Drive. That's my way into the centre and taking this route means I pass the secondary school. From the school, all the pavements are covered in wires and extension cables and every fifty feet or so there sits a heavy-duty speaker. The Fiddler has a public address system set up that is controlled from the school, guarded by a group of teenage boys. I sneaked past the guards and into the school. The odd thing is that the guards were really easy to get by because they are all wearing ear plugs. It must be so they can't hear what's on the PA system. Once in the school I saw two men talking and one of them addressed the other as Simon. His whole operation is being run from there. But I couldn't hear what the operation was so I sneaked out and ventured further into town and... I've never seen anything like it.'

'What was it?'

'The whole town are like robots. They don't do anything; they just plod from place to place. They don't smile, they don't even look up at you and the ones that speak talk in a monotone. It's hard to describe, but it's as if everyone has become, well, they've become really, really boring.'

'Boring?'

'Yeah. It's the craziest thing I've seen. Whatever it is coming out of that PA system is somehow putting a spell over the town.'

'In the room where I found Molly there was a tape player on with the Fiddler talking about past auditions.'

'That's mental.'

'I know.'

'Who still uses tapes?!'

'How come you weren't affected?'

'I've been on my own for twenty years; I found it quite interesting.'

'Molly died because of those tapes. The whole town is in serious danger. Why has the rest of the country not picked up on this?'

'Cockermouth is an ancient market town tucked away in the north west of England. Most Brits think that Manchester is the north of England. It could be years before anyone finds us.'

'I'm going to stop him.'

'What are you thinking?'

'Simple. Take out the guards. Take out the PA. Take out the Fiddler.'

37

"A wise king never seeks out war, but he
must always be ready for it" - Odin

Once it grew dark I transformed into Toecap with the simple act
of putting my clean black hoody on. That was it, I was good to go. I
didn't know how many guards were stationed at the school but they
must be friends of Jacob's gang so there couldn't be that many – trash-
talking already, he'll be gutted. JP had never seen Jacob before so he
couldn't tell me if he was present at the school. Luke would be there
for sure, guarding the Fiddler closely.

JP and I left the cabin and headed towards town. When the school
came into view I took several deep breaths. We stopped not too far
away, hidden by the night. JP told me he would keep an eye on the
proceedings, helping where he could - this affected him too, whether
he liked it or not. I walked away from him and Simon's voice on the PA
system came into range. JP didn't need ear plugs for protection and I
was relying on my anger to block the effects. I had my game face on.

The guards were spread out but essentially useless without their
hearing. They could only rely on sight and as it was dark they were
sitting ducks. Whose idea was this? The Fiddler clearly hadn't done
this before, because not only were the guards now deaf but they
were patrolling as single units rather than taking safety in pairs.

Henchmen always work in pairs; anyone with a TV knows that. They carried weapons, but only P.E. equipment from the sports hall cupboards: armed to the teeth with cheap tennis rackets, cricket stumps and hockey sticks. This would be a walk in the park.

Down to the left, before the entrance to the school, there is a car park. A guard was slipping in and out between the cars and stopping now and then to look about aimlessly. He was clueless. I ran over to a car near him and dropped down behind an old red Volvo. It's ridiculous how much noise I was making that went unnoticed. I moved around the Volvo and walked up behind the guard. I put my left hand around his face, covering his mouth. His hands shot up, dropping his hockey stick in the process, as he tried to fight me off. With my right hand I took hold of the back of his head and slammed it as hard as I could down into the boot of the nearest car. Any more force and his nose would have been pushed up into his brain. The car was left with a sizeable dent and the kid was out cold. I let go of the body and it fell awkwardly to the floor. It felt good. I felt like a pro; a British spy on her Majesty's Secret Service. It was like I was James Bond, deep behind enemy lines, drunk on the job and itchy from unprotected sex with strangers, not a character reference in sight. In the distance I could see another guard coming round the building from the direction of the P.E. changing rooms. I had to think fast. I ducked down next to the wheel of the car. The hubcap glistened in the moonlight, begging to be picked like a substitute on the side lines, desperate to play. I pulled the hubcap off the wheel and stood back up. The second guard hadn't moved far. I took the hubcap in my right hand and launched it through the air. It spun ferociously and made a sharp wisp as it pierced the sky, curling all the way. It clipped the stationary guard, almost scalping him. He collapsed and the hubcap rolled to a stop. I moved in a little closer and spotted a third guard by the entrance to the school. If I could take him out I could at least get inside without being detected. He was alone and carrying two cricket stumps. I walked over and he turned to face me in shock. I snatched a cricket stump from him and slapped it off the top of his head before cracking it against his temple. He fell to the floor. I was in.

Reception was unmanned and messy. To my left was the headmaster's office. The door was ajar and the lights were off. Ahead of me were three corridors. I could take the left, which leads to the sixth form area, the right would take me to a staircase leading to the second floor and in front of me there were double doors that took me further into the school, past an IT room on my left and the canteen on my right. I had no idea where to go. I was after the source of the public address system. I stood still for a moment and tried to think. The power generator must be big if it was powering a public address system all over town. It would need a big room. The canteen hall was close; it could be in there or in the old sports hall next door to it. There was a second sports hall in the middle of school next to the library, that's where I'd put it if it was up to me. I walked straight ahead and through the double doors that led me past the canteen. Since I was here I might as well tick the canteen off my list. I peered in through a porthole in a door and came face to face with another guard. We made each other jump but I reacted quicker. I pushed hard on the door, which opened into him and he stumbled backwards. I lunged forward and with both hands I forced him further into the dining hall. The tables were stacked away, folded up in their middles like giant playing cards, all pushed up against one wall, leaving the floor empty. We made our way across the room and all the while he made futile attempts to loosen my grip. In the middle of the room I stopped pushing him. I still had hold of him, but with my left foot I put my weight onto his right foot. He winced as I pressed down hard. While standing on his foot, with all my might I pushed his chest away with both hands and he snapped to the floor, hard. His right foot hadn't moved. He let loose a terrible cry of pain, which echoed off the walls. I looked down at him as several doors around me swung open and guards came flooding in. They circled me and closed in, each armed with outdated P.E. equipment. I slowly spun full circle, making sure to mark each one. Five on one. These guards didn't have ear plugs in and they looked hungry for a fight. Nobody moved for some time, before at last the bravest of the bunch stepped forward and jabbed his hockey stick at me. I slipped to the right and received a cricket stump to the side of my head from someone else. I held up my arm too late to block it and took a step backwards. They were laughing and a wave of fresh confidence washed over them. The brave one stepped forward again and swung his stick as if it were a broadsword. I ducked in time and popped up during his follow-through. One of the others stepped forward and, using a flag pole, tried to lance me in the chest, but I knocked it away.

The circle was broken and I walked backwards until I bumped into the raised stage. The five of them lined up and moved cautiously towards me. In one swift movement I turned and pulled myself up onto the stage, quickly rolling out of range of their weapons. I got to my feet and disappeared behind the black curtain at the back that stretched across the full width. The five boys looked at each other and then began clambering onto the stage after me. I was backstage and surrounded by props. I scanned the room to find something I could use to better defend myself. The stage stretched fifteen feet from front to back and after the boys had realigned and covered a little ground I came out from behind the curtain to re-join them. But I was empty handed. There was nothing backstage that I could use. The boys grinned in unison. I clenched my fists and held them up.

'This really isn't fair, is it Toby? Or should I say Toecap?' Jacob was walking across the hall towards the school's latest production. What was he still doing here? He had wanted Molly back and she was dead. Why was he still involved? I couldn't speak.

'You four back off; let's make this a little more interesting.'

Four of my assailants jumped down from the stage, leaving just myself and one other. We had an audience.

'Well…get on with it!' Jacob demanded.

The boy on stage with me moved a step closer. With my fists still clenched and upright I stepped towards him. Jacob had no idea what I was now capable of. I grinned at the armed teenager in front of me, who now seemed far less pleased with himself. I took another step and he backed off. I did this again and he repeated. His feet were close to the edge and I stepped forward yet again. With hockey stick gripped in two hands he drew it high above his head and I made my final move. I stood on his right foot with all my weight and using both hands I pushed his chest hard. Just like before the body toppled but his right foot stayed planted on the stage. He dropped backwards and the first thing to hit the floor was his head. It sunk into the wood panelling and caused his teeth to clatter together. He didn't even cry out. I released his foot. His body slackened to the floor and lay motionless in a heap. I looked down at the rest of them and Jacob angrily commanded the next contestant.

This boy was more cautious and his confidence was ephemeral. He shakily climbed the steps and lifted his rounders bat, ready to attack. I stayed where I was. He shuffled closer and closer and finally swung at me. He was so scared that I barely had to block. The rounders bat suddenly weighed too much for him, it was like he was holding a tree trunk. With my free hand I grabbed the bat. It was soft and purple in colour. With one yank I had taken it from him. I held the bat correctly in my hands and before I could continue the boy had jumped off the stage and ran away. Once more I looked at Jacob. He was frothing with anger and ordered the other three to end this. One stepped forward and I let the rounders bat fly at him. It spun round twice in the air before kissing his jaw, taking it out of socket and disrupting the order of his teeth. The force of the throw and the instantaneous introduction of pain caused a blackout and he dropped with very little grace. The other boys also scarpered and only Jacob and I were left. He hadn't been armed from the start and his helplessness dawned on him visibly. I dropped off the stage and Jacob began to gibber.

'Please don't hurt me.'

'How could you?' I said. I had switched off my rage and now it was just two school boys alone in a hall.

'What?'

'How could you get involved in this?'

'In what?'

'In this! In all of this!! What have you done?'

'I didn't know any of this would happen. One minute we were planning to expose you and before I knew it Luke was blowing up a police station. He is mental.'

'You went against me to get Molly back and look what happened! I hope it was worth it.'

'That? Oh yeah, that was totally worth it,' he said.

'So what was it? Like, a kind of "if I can't have her no one can" deal? Is that it, you sick fuck?'

'I was a bit annoyed you were with her but it's all been sorted now.'

'Can you even hear what you're saying?! She's dead because of you idiots!'

'Dead? What are you talking about?'

'What?' I stared at Jacob, who looked a little lost.

'Jacob, do you not know? Have they not told you? How have you not heard?'

'I'm feeling a little out of the loop,' he said. 'What's going on?'

'Molly's dead. The Fiddler killed her in an abandoned house days ago.'

'She's dead? Oh my god!' He fell to his knees and held a hand up to his mouth.

'I'm sorry,' I offered.

'She's dead?'

'Yes,' I said.

'Wait a second,' he said, pointing a curious finger and getting back to his feet. 'Did you say she died in an abandoned house days ago?'

'Yes, he must have bored her to death or something; *how* she died doesn't matter.'

'But I saw her this morning.'

'You are mistaken.'

'No, I'm not, we had breakfast together and then we walked into town. That was just today.'

'It's a trick, Jacob, it's another one of the Fiddler's tricks. I don't know how he has done it but -'

'Are you sure you're not wrong?'

'I - I saw her body, she was dead...' My mind was breaking away, overlapping and missing bits - everything was moving too fast to piece together. My head hurt, things weren't making sense. Jacob got to his feet and approached me with newfound confidence.

He whispered in my ear,

'Guess you'll have to see the Fiddler if you want to know more,' and then he struck me as hard as he could across the face and stepped back. He was waiting for something. A moment went by.

'What are you doing?' he asked.

'What do you mean?' I said.

'That should have knocked you out.'

'You've watched too many films.'

'This isn't right.'

'It's not my fault you didn't hit me hard enough.'

'Shut up!' he shouted. He raised his hand again but I had flicked my switch just before my fist made contact with his cheekbone, his face receiving the very first taste of a new batch of rage.

He was out cold.

I needed to find the Fiddler.

38

I left the hall the same way I had come in and turned right, heading down a long corridor. I then had the option to turn left, which I did, and I made my way deeper into the school. I slowed down and noticed on my left the entrance to a room only a handful of students had ever used: the library. I peered in for a second - just to see what it actually looked like inside - and then continued on through yet another set of double doors. I kept going straight on, through more and more doors until the second sports hall appeared on my left. The doors to the hall were held ajar by thick wires that were leading in and out of the room. An enormous heat was emanating from whatever was in there and lights flickered around it like a shit mobile disco. I pulled open the door and saw, in the middle of the room, a magnificent beast of a machine, whirling away and buzzing continuously. It was the generator that was powering the public address system the Fiddler was using to manipulate the town. It towered over me and happily continued its work as if it hadn't noticed I was there. Lights danced across its surface and beeps sounded off one by one every now and then. Cables and wires poured out of it and leaked over the floor, looking like a snake pit. These cables fed nearby computers, some working hard and some sleeping on the job. The air in here was hot and heavy, hard to swallow.

I had no idea where to start, but picked up a handful of cables and pulled them out of their sockets. They came away easily enough but nothing changed; the machine surged on. I switched on my rage and I pulled out more and more cables, ripping them free, but still the machine lived. I pulled and pulled, but nothing I did made a difference. I moved to a different part of the machine and tried again but with the same result. I shut down computers and smashed a couple of screens but it was all useless. I thumped the generator and the room was filled with silence, but only briefly.

'This explains the bodies in the canteen,' said a voice.

'Who goes there?' I looked around the room but I couldn't see anyone, I had sweat in my eyes and I couldn't make anyone out among all the lights.

'Who else is with you? How did you get past everyone?'

'Is that you, Simon?! Show yourself!'

'Sorry to disappoint you,' said Luke, stepping into view.

'You.'

'Me.' He smiled.

'What do you want?'

'I want to stop you.'

'Stop me? Luke, it's you that needs to be stopped!'

'The Fiddler and I can't be stopped.'

'I've stopped Jacob and his henchmen; I can stop a failed actor and his lapdog.'

'Jacob has proved himself useless but I was always going to ditch him; he didn't share my goal. He and his men are quite expendable. All he wanted was that damned girl. He gave us information on you and we gave him the girl. Simple.'

'Gave him the girl?'

'Yes, she's quite safe.'

'But she died. You killed her!'

'Killed her? Oh no, no, no. We did nothing of the sort.'

'I don't understand.'

'Allow me to help you.' He walked a little closer to me, looking me up and down. 'Just look at you. Why are you so desperate to play hero? You cheated the world by paying the Fiddler to lose, making you look good. You're pathetic.'

Luke held out his hand and outstretched his fingertips. Searing fire gushed from his open palm and brightened the room further. He gazed at his hand and watched it blaze away unharmed. 'You're not a hero, Toby, you're a joke. I actually *have* super powers. *I'm* supposed to be the hero. I was keeping my head down, biding my time, waiting for the right moment and then I was going to shine. I was at least going to get my education out of the way! I was going to make this town proud, but you snuck in and fooled them. They loved you and you weren't even real. They couldn't see you for what you are and their stupidity ruined me. You needed to be punished. And so did they.'

The fire burned in his hand and intermittently spurted out in unpredictable directions, melting cables and cracking computer screens.

'I watched you and the Fiddler practising routines in that hall and I couldn't bear it.'

A ball of fire formed in his palm and he threw it over my head. I flinched and heard behind me the explosion. It spread, guzzling up anything that dared to make contact.

'And then it all went wrong for you, didn't it? You got the Fiddler arrested. Your game was over. I waited for the truth to come out, for the Fiddler to expose you, but nothing happened. You had fooled the town, ruined the Fiddler and still you weren't held accountable. I couldn't take it any more. I had to step in. The world had to know that you're a liar!'

'It doesn't matter what I've done. All that matters now is stopping you!'

'We've already beaten you, don't you see? The town is ours! I could have sorted you out on my own, but where is the fun in that? I just wanted you, but Simon had a far better plan that worked out for everyone.' The room was now cooking and the machines were collapsing in the inferno. Even the generator was feeling the heat and the buzzes and beeps started to sound different, panicked.

'Simon wanted the town but knew that it would take time getting enough power together to control it and we were already on the run. We needed a distraction. This is where you and Molly came in. Thanks to Jacob we learned of your relationship. You weren't a threat, but setting you up with Molly far away would keep the remaining police officers busy while we got organised here. We kidnapped

Molly and lured you out of town and then Simon phoned the police, telling them that he had taken her hostage after leaving the station. With the police and you gone, we had all the time we needed to get our generator up and running. Simon didn't kill Molly; he merely bored her out of her mind with old audition tapes. With your name all over her and police on the way we assumed you'd run, given that you are nothing more than a coward. Which you did. But even if you had been caught you would have been brought back here with her for questioning and together you and the officers would join the rest of the town under Simon's control. With everyone under his spell Simon had the town, Jacob had Molly and I had bested you!'

He began throwing small tufts of fire in my direction.

'So Molly isn't dead?' I asked, once he had stopped.

'No, she is at home like everybody else.'

'But only because of this machine and you're burning it right now.'

'I don't care about Simon or Jacob any more. Everything I want is in this room. I have you here all to myself and I'm going to watch you burn!' He clasped his hands together and screamed as a jet of fire shot out at me. I dived to one side, narrowly avoiding the flames, and began crawling over the wires, making my way around the generator and out of sight. Once there, I got to my feet. I could hear Luke laughing loudly and the fire that was engulfing the room just kept growing. I stretched out an arm and cleared a table of machinery. My rage was back with me and I picked up the table and held it as an all-body shield. Molly was alive but she wasn't safe. I continued moving around the generator and came back to the side Luke was on. He held out his hands and fire shot out, hitting the centre of the table. It was burning in seconds, fire dripping over the edge and down onto the underside which faced me. I held on tight and charged at him. On impact he fell backwards to the floor. I set the table on all fours and positioned one of its legs over Luke's open left hand, pinning it down and rendering it useless. With all the rage I could summon I slammed my fist down on that table corner and the leg bluntly punctured his palm. He shouted out in pain, barely audible above the sound of the fire as it licked the walls and climbed higher still. He aimed his other hand at me and fire squirted out. I rolled over the table, avoiding the heat and Luke yelped again as my weight added to his injury. Off the table, I dropped to my knees, grabbed his head and snapped his neck. He was gone. I had to get going.

The generator was beginning to spark and mini-explosions were replacing the standard beeps and buzzes. I looked at the double doors I had come in through and the fire racing towards them. I ran for the exit. Computers blew up near me and the fire was swallowing everything. Just before I reached the doors I tripped on some cables and became airborne, crashing into one of the doors and barrelling into the wall the other side. I was out. The fire raged on, consuming everything within the sports hall, Luke's dead body among it. I coughed my way along the corridor, gasping for air when finally the generator exploded. The whole school shook and I was thrown to the floor. Several more explosions followed and the fire spread out into the corridor. My ears were ringing but I hauled myself up and made my way to reception. I had stopped Jacob, Luke and the PA, but the Fiddler was nowhere to be seen. Smoke filled the corridors and the very foundations of the school were beginning to fail. I ran along the walls and made my way through several doorways. At reception I looked back, but still there was no sign of Simon Webb. I headed outside and right in front of me, on his knees and blood running from his nose, was the Fiddler. Standing next to him was JP, holding a cricket stump.

'What was the explosion?' said JP.

'A madman's reign coming to an end,' I said, looking at the Fiddler.

'I'm still standing,' he spat.

'You're not, actually.'

'I don't care what happens to me now. I have nothing to lose. I will tell the police everything…from the beginning. I will take you down with me; we've already connected you to all this. And you,' he said to JP, 'you'll go down as well.'

If the police believed him this wouldn't be over for some time. They might not listen to a word he said, but could I afford that risk?

'*I* can't allow that,' said JP. With his lip curled in disgust, he thrust the cricket stump into Simon's neck. The Fiddler's eyes bulged in momentary pain and surprise and, as JP let go, with a single cough the Fiddler fell.

Sirens could be heard in the distance as the town began to find itself again.

'I should go,' said JP.

'I can't thank you enough.'

'You saved the town, remember that. You are a hero.'

'Will I see you again?'

'I shouldn't think so.' The sirens were getting louder.

'Goodbye, Toecap,' he said.

'Goodbye, JP.'

Police cars came hurtling into the car park, screeching to a halt as the school burned down before them. I turned to JP, but he was gone. The police officers shouted at me to stay where I was. Finally I could relax. It was over.

39

"Sharing the world has never been humanity's
defining attribute" - Charles Xavier

It took a long time for life in Cockermouth to get back to normal.
In the weeks that followed the Fiddler's death I spent most of my
spare time at the police station going through everything that had
happened. I told my story over and over, leaving out the fact that
Simon was a monster I had made, and eventually the police took it
as the truth - I was the only credible witness. I told them Simon had
taken over the town and I had stopped him - simple. I left out that
Luke had super powers; I said he just started the fire. I didn't want to
go into a lot of details as this story really wasn't about him. Although
the entire town was in the same trance, it affected people differently.
Most people couldn't remember what had happened. Simon Webb
was a nobody to them and Toecap was no different - distant memories
that barely anyone could reach. The story covered the front page of
the papers for some time, describing how it was all connected - the
attack on the police station and the destruction of the school. Most
people didn't care though, they weren't interested. They just wanted
to get on with their lives and that was fine by me. I was overwhelmed
when I was finally reunited with my parents and even more so when

I saw Molly, having believed she was dead. I was done with Toecap; I never wanted to hear that name again.

The school was closed for the foreseeable future while what remained of the building was deemed structurally safe and repairs were planned - which every child in town has yet to thank me for.

Luke's parents held a funeral for their son and that's the last we heard of them. They moved away shortly after.

Jacob and his friends are serving literally millions of hours of community service.

JP was never mentioned, not once. I made sure of that.

And as far as I was concerned, for everything that had happened, I was given a pass. After all, I had saved the day. All I wanted now was to get back to being a regular teenager. I wanted to forget and who better to help than my dear friend Randall?

Two months after the school had gone up in flames, Randall and I sat in the park waiting for Molly and Willow to turn up. The sun was shining as we occupied a bench, watching the world go by.

'So you've actually killed someone?'

'Yeah.'

'It's so crazy to think that.'

'Yeah, I guess it is.'

'You've ended someone's life.'

'Yeah, you should remember that when you're next making one of your weird kill lists.'

'We're mates; you wouldn't kill me.'

'You've wanted me dead before.'

'I remembered why that was, by the way. You want to know?'

'Of course.'

'You kept laughing at me about Mrs Tuck.'

'That's how I made it onto the list?'

'You earned it.'

'Seriously, you wanted me dead for that?'

'You wouldn't take me seriously and you kept banging on about it.'

'Of course I didn't take it seriously!'

'Let's not get into this,' he said as Mrs Tuck came into view, a small bag of shopping held in hand.

'Look, here she is, just ask her out.'

'What?'

'Just ask her out!'

'Nah, I don't feel like it.'

'This is why I take the piss.'

'Shut up.'

'Imagine if she said yes; what would you say to Willow?'

'I have loved Mrs Tuck since forever. Willow will understand.'

'Saying things like you love her is exactly why I can't take it seriously.'

'I might make a new list.'

'Ask her out.'

'Maybe I will.'

'Maybe you should!'

Mrs Tuck was walking our way. She had spotted us.

'Don't rush me!'

'Just do it! You're such a chicken.'

'I'm not a chicken!'

'Massive chicken.'

'Fine! I'll do it. I'm going to do it!'

'Really?'

'Really!'

'Good man.'

Mrs Tuck was within spitting distance, although that wasn't an approach likely to endear her to her teenage suitor. Randall smiled at her and I copied him. She smiled back and walked past us.

'Such a chicken,' I said.

'Mrs Tuck?' he called after her.

'Yes?' she replied. She stopped walking and turned to face him.

I held my breath.

'Nothing,' said Randall.

Books from Sid Wright

The Contemplations of a Nobody

The Further Contemplations of a Nobody

Fancy Dress Tips for Bald Men

The Escapades of Biff Digglett

Languishing in Lyrics

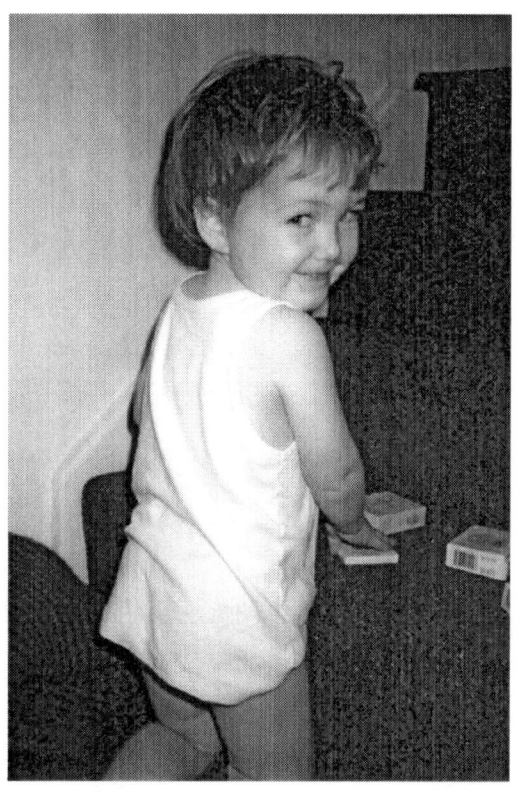

Artist. Singer. Songwriter. Musician. RGT Guitar and Ukulele Tutor. Author. Cartoonist. Illustrator. Photographer.

- www.sidwright.co.uk -

Toecap and the Fiddler was proofread by Anthony Hewson
- www.ahcopy.co.uk -